ROBERT J. HARRIS was born in Dundee and studied at the University of St Andrews where he graduated with a first class honours degree in Latin. He is the designer of the bestselling fantasy board game Talisman and has written numerous books including *Leonardo and the Death Machine*, *Will Shakespeare and the Pirate's Fire*, and more recently *The Artie Conan Doyle Mysteries*, a series featuring the youthful adventures of the creator of Sherlock Holmes. His first Richard Hannay novel, *The Thirty-One Kings* (Polygon) was acclaimed by critics and readers alike and was listed by *The Scotsman* as one of the fifty best books of 2017. He followed this with the equally successful *Castle Macnab*. He lives in St Andrews with his wife Debby.

A STUDY IN CRIMSON

A STUDY IN CRIMSON

Sherlock Holmes 1942

Robert J. Harris

First published in Great Britain in 2020 by Polygon, an imprint of
Birlinn Ltd. This paperback edition published in 2022 by Polygon.

Birlinn Ltd
West Newington House
10 Newington Road
Edinburgh
EH9 1QS

www.polygonbooks.co.uk

1

ISBN 978 1 84697 596 7
eBook ISBN 978 1 78885 280 7

Design and typesetting by Studio Monachino

To Christine and Toby, who should be
out solving their own mysteries.

CONTENTS

PART THREE: JUSTICE

PREFACE

In 1939 20th Century Fox released *The Hound of the Baskervilles*, a film based upon the novel by Sir Arthur Conan Doyle, which was to prove hugely successful. They followed this with *The Adventures of Sherlock Holmes*, adapted from the William Gillette play of that name. Although Fox did not continue the series, these films firmly established Basil Rathbone as Sherlock Holmes with Nigel Bruce as his faithful companion Dr Watson. Their identification with the characters in the public mind was further strengthened by a long-running Sherlock Holmes radio series featuring the two actors. When Universal Pictures stepped in to negotiate a fresh cinema deal with the Doyle estate, they decided, with the agreement of Doyle's family, to refresh the characters by transplanting them to the modern day, to the wartime London of 1942. As well as Rathbone and Bruce, other series regulars were Dennis Hoey, who portrayed a big, bluff Inspector Lestrade, and Scottish actress Mary Gordon as Mrs Hudson. Beginning with *Sherlock Holmes and the Voice of Terror*, which pitted Holmes against Nazi saboteurs, the series ran for a total of twelve films, which together created one of the most popular incarnations of the character. Many still regard Basil Rathbone as the definitive Sherlock Holmes against which all other representations must be measured. Inspired by that classic series, this novel further explores the world and adventures of its particular version of the great detective, confronting him with a deadly and cunning adversary. It is September 1942 and, in the blacked-out streets of London, the game is once more afoot.

PART ONE

DEDUCTION

Sherlock Holmes, the immortal character of fiction created by Sir Arthur Conan Doyle, is ageless, invincible and unchanging. In solving significant problems of the present day he remains – as ever – the supreme master of deductive reasoning.

INTRODUCTION TO
Sherlock Holmes and the Voice of Terror
Universal Pictures (1942)

1

THE DISAPPEARANCE OF
DR MacREADY

Sherlock Holmes and I were on our way to Scotland while events were unfolding back in London that would draw my friend into the one of the darkest mysteries of his career. It was on the seventh of September 1942, the third year of the war, that we received an urgent summons from the War Office, calling on us to report at once to the airfield at Croydon. A car was waiting outside our Baker Street lodgings and within the hour, accompanied by a pair of hastily packed suitcases, we were aboard a Lancaster bomber, bound for the RAF base at Kinloss on the Moray Firth.

Sitting shoulder to shoulder with Holmes on a fold-down bench in the cargo bay, both of us huddled in our overcoats, I pondered the many changes that had overtaken us since Hitler's invasion of Poland. Food and fuel were now rationed, barrage balloons dotted the skies over our coastal cities, and a nightly blackout was in force across the country. All major industrial resources had been diverted to the war effort and human resources had likewise been harnessed. I had given up my private medical practice to volunteer for the Emergency Hospital Service and much of my time was now taken up with my duties at St Thomas's Hospital. Similarly, my friend Sherlock Holmes's time was occupied less and less with private cases and increasingly with urgent calls from our beleaguered government. Holmes scarcely spoke a word following take-off. His aquiline features bore the shuttered look that told me he was exceptionally disgruntled, not simply on account of the inevitable discomfort, but at being drawn away from his flat at 221B Baker Street. I had observed of late that only among those familiar surroundings did he seem to be at his ease.

We had both played our two very different roles in the Great War, and I wonder if we would have made it through that experience if we had known that another, perhaps more dreadful war lay waiting in our future. For Holmes, this new onslaught of hostilities represented a breakdown of reason itself. The world which he had bent all the powers of his intellect to bring to order had sunk once more into an unspeakable chaos that showed no sign of abating.

I could readily understand that he should choose to retreat into his comfortable lair, surrounded by those mementos of past triumphs from which he drew strength. It was to his credit that he would leave that familiar refuge without hesitation in order to serve the interests of his country. Nevertheless, it seemed to me that some deep matter was preying on his mind about which I could only speculate. I raised my voice above the drone of the engines in an effort to draw him out of himself.

'It is a remarkable case, Holmes,' I noted. 'A castle occupied by some of the country's leading scientists and one of them – a Dr MacReady – suddenly vanished into thin air, evidently the victim of a kidnapping. What do you suppose they can be working on?'

'Doubtless some new instrument of death,' Holmes murmured without looking up. 'Our brief, of course, made no reference to its nature. These government departments are obsessed with secrecy. It lends them an exaggerated sense of their own importance.'

'Well, this certainly is important,' I persisted. 'Clearly the government are concerned that the missing scientist might have fallen into enemy hands. And surely a mystery so extraordinary will prove worthy of your deductive efforts.'

Holmes stifled a snort. 'Watson, how often must I remind you that it is the extraordinary crime that invariably proves to be simple of solution? Unusual circumstances mean that only a limited number of explanations are possible. It is the small, prosaic crime that challenges: a purloined bicycle, a missing will. Such often lead to an intricacy of motive and method.'

'And those crimes of a bizarre nature?'

'In the end what lies behind them is frequently banal.'

Before I could pursue the point, the radio operator emerged from the cockpit brandishing a large thermos flask and two tin cups. 'Fancy a spot of beef tea?' he inquired.

Holmes accepted the drink but declined the further offer of a cheese roll. As we had been hurried out of Baker Street without the opportunity for breakfast, I was heartily glad of both, and not disposed to complain that the roll was slightly stale and the cheese savoured of engine oil. By the time I finished, Holmes had retreated back into his shell, so I contented myself with gazing out of the window.

Once north of the Scottish border, the landscape became increasingly rugged until we reached the formid-able ramparts of the Cairngorms. Our passage over the mountains was anything but smooth as the flight crew battled the crosswinds swirling about the peaks. The trial, however, was short-lived, and soon we landed safely at Kinloss.

A sleek black Daimler was parked alongside the runway. As we left the plane, a stolid-looking soldier in uniform climbed out and came to meet us.

'Ah'm Corporal Paterson,' he informed us. 'Ah've been sent doon frae the castle to collect you.'

The burr in his voice told us he was a Scot, a fact underscored by the stag's head insignia on his cap which proclaimed him a member of the Seaforth Highlanders.

Paterson stowed our bags away in the boot before taking the wheel. Within minutes we were heading west along a narrow road with the sun-silvered waters of the Moray Firth glistening on our right. Sinking back in his seat, Holmes fished a briar pipe from his pocket and took to chewing the stem in silence. I decided to strike up a conversation with our driver in order to gain some advance information concerning our destination.

'Well, corporal,' I ventured, 'I suppose it's quite a privilege to be assigned to a prestigious project like this, given the importance the government obviously attach to it.'

'Privilege?' the soldier responded gruffly. 'Ah'd not call it that, sur. Nursemaiding a gaggle o' peely-wally eggheads in lab coats isnae what I jined the army for. It's that boring, I sometimes wish the Jerries would parachute in to relieve the tedium.'

I could not help glancing involuntarily at the sky. 'There surely must be some less hazardous forms of distraction. Golf perhaps?'

The corporal, it appeared, was not a fan of the great game. Instead, he spent considerable time acquainting me with the spectacular progress his local football team, Albion Rovers, had been making in the Scottish League before the war intervened and the army poached most of their best players.

Eventually I managed to redirect our conversation back to the subject of Castle Dunfillan. 'I suppose the scientific community here are so absorbed in their work, they need no other entertainment. And how do you get on with them?'

'We dinna exactly mix, ye ken,' Paterson responded dourly. 'The professor in charge – Smithers – he's a right Lord Snooty, and the rest are nearly as bad – wouldna even lower themselves to a game o' darts. Well, except for—'

Abruptly he interrupted himself to brake before a barrier guarded by two armed soldiers of the same regiment who were stationed by the stone gate lodge. They scrutinised our papers before admitting us to the grounds of the castle, which were surrounded as far as the eye could see by a barbed wire fence eight feet high.

We drove along a gravelled track through plantations of pine and sycamore. Off to our right I spotted a pool – a miniature loch, if I might so style it – its margins fringed with reeds. After a quarter of a mile the trees gave way to a luxuriant lawn bordered with flower beds that had been replanted with vegetables to serve a more utilitarian purpose. Nothing about our surroundings suggested the cutting edge of modern science, nor did Castle Dunfillan itself when it came into view.

It looked to be about five hundred years old, with battlements and towers that spoke of a time when rival clans launched regular raids against their neighbours and a laird's home was also his fortress. The stout grey walls and barred windows gave one the impression of a prison rather than a laboratory and only the aerials protruding from the roof and the vehicles parked to the right of the driveway reassured us that we were still in the twentieth century.

I observed some soldiers armed with rifles patrolling the grounds, who straightened their posture and quickened their gait at the sight of visitors. In the distance one or two outbuildings were visible – a small woodshed and what must once have been a stable but was now in a state of considerable disrepair.

Corporal Paterson pulled up at the entrance and jumped out smartly to open the rear doors for us. As we climbed out, the castle's large front doors opened and a slight, scholarly figure in a grey suit and bow tie came out to greet us. Dwarfed by the structure behind him, he actually seemed to shrink as he picked his way down the worn stone steps, blinking in the sunshine and raising a hand to shield his bespectacled eyes. He gave the impression that the outdoors was an alien environment into which he ventured only with the greatest reluctance.

'Thank goodness, you're here,' he greeted us. 'I'm Professor Smithers, the chief scientific officer for this establishment. Which one of you is Sherlock Holmes?'

Holmes, I could tell, was slightly put out at not being recognised. 'That would be me,' he responded brusquely. 'And this is my associate, Dr Watson.'

Once we had exchanged handshakes, Smithers addressed himself to our driver. 'Peterson—'

'That's Paterson, sur,' the corporal corrected him.

'Yes, yes, well, take the car round the back then fetch these gentlemen's bags inside. The housekeeper will tell you where to put them. Oh, and tell Sergeant Ross the detectives are here.'

Without acknowledging the order, Paterson climbed back into the car and drove round to the rear of the building.

'Come along, come along,' urged the professor, leading the way up the well-worn stairs to the entrance. 'We really must have this matter sorted out as soon as possible.'

The cavernous entrance hall echoed to our footsteps on the marble floor. The oak-panelled walls were hung with wooden shields and basket-handled swords as well as a handful of paintings of pipers and wild beasts. At the rear of the hall, Smithers ushered us into a large, well-furnished library. Here a group of four men gathered around us with the eager enthusiasm of schoolboys welcoming a visiting scout master.

'Sherlock Holmes – my, my, who would have thought it?'

'I recognise you, Mr Holmes, from your photograph in the newspapers. You appear taller in person.'

'And this must be Dr Watson, Mr Holmes's biographer.'

'Hardly that,' I demurred. 'I occasionally put pen to paper to share with the world some of the cases my friend has been reluctant to discuss with the press.'

Smithers silenced his colleagues with a cold glare and introduced them to us in order of seniority. Dr Westercote was a grey, lanky figure in tweeds. Dr Bloomhurst was younger with blue eyes protruding behind his thick spectacles. Dr Hatcher was dark and sallow and affected a neatly trimmed black beard. Amberson, the youngest of those present, had a round face surmounted by a cowlick of brown hair.

Holmes cast a keen eye over the gathering. 'I am very pleased to meet you, gentlemen. So tell me, how far has your work on the new aerial torpedo advanced?'

Professor Smithers' jaw dropped in such horrified astonishment you would have thought Holmes had sprouted a pair of horns and a forked tail.

'Mr Holmes, how . . . how?' he sputtered. 'Has our security been breached?'

'Not at all,' Holmes assured the flustered scientist. A flicker of amusement touched his lips as he explained. 'Dr Westercote here has spent many years initiating advances in submarine warfare, in particular the range-adjusted settings on the Navy's latest torpedo. Dr Bloomhurst is an explosives expert, Dr Hatcher specialises in gyroscopic stabilisation, Dr Amberson is a leading authority on aero-dynamics, while you, Dr Smithers, specialise in magnetic guidance systems.'

He took a moment to view the obvious pleasure the scientists took in his acquaintance with their work, then added, 'It takes no great mental leap to imagine what sort of secret project all of you might be engaged on. I confess that I am not privy to Dr MacReady's area of study but I assume, by process of elimination, that it is the development of a new fuel for the weapon.'

'Why, yes,' Westercote confirmed. 'She is an expert in petrochemicals and accelerants. The ministry have clearly sent the right man, Mr Holmes.'

'You said *she*,' I noted. 'Do you mean that Dr MacReady is a woman?'

'Exactly so, Dr Watson – Dr Elspeth MacReady.' Smithers scowled and rubbed his stomach as though plagued with a sudden attack of dyspepsia. 'How I pleaded with the ministry not to send a woman here. She was bound to be a disruptive influence.'

'In what way do you mean disruptive?' asked Holmes in a carefully neutral tone.

Smithers gave a disapproving sniff. 'She was given to wearing perfume and singing to herself as she worked. Of an evening she would insist we gather round the piano to enjoy the songs of Robert Burns, and on one occasion she even tried to enlist us all in a whist tournament. All most irrational and most distracting.'

He directed a minatory glare at his colleagues, all of whom now bore the hangdog appearance of men guilty of having colluded with the enemy.

'My friend Dr Watson is better acquainted with the vagaries of the female nature than I,' said Holmes, 'yet I do not see how even the most extreme high spirits could cause a human being to vanish into thin air.'

Bloomhurst, his eyes bulging behind his spectacles, leaned towards us with a finger touching his lower lip, as though to guard his words from prying ears. 'Professor Smithers confided to me once that she might be a spy inserted by the enemy to delay and frustrate our efforts.'

'Hush, Bloomhurst!' Smithers rebuked his colleague. 'That was merely a jest, and spoken in confidence to boot.'

Westercote inserted his lanky frame between the two men. 'Perhaps Mr Holmes would like us to acquaint him with the details of the crime itself?'

'Yes, by all means let's get on with it,' said Smithers.

He turned to my friend and lowered his voice ominously. 'Mr Holmes, there is a word which, as a scientist, I hesitate to use, but this whole affair is – on the surface of it – quite *impossible*.'

2

THE EMPTY ROOM

Holmes was clearly intrigued. 'I would be obliged, professor, if you would describe to me the exact circumstances of Dr MacReady's disappearance.'

Smithers briefly closed his eyes to marshal his recollections. 'It was precisely eleven o'clock,' he began, 'the time at which I habitually retire. I was making my way from my laboratory on the ground floor to my bedroom on the third when I encountered Dr MacReady on the second floor landing, also retiring for the night. Unexpectedly, she attempted to engage me in conversation, asserting that it would be beneficial to the morale of our group if we were to organise an excursion.'

'What sort of excursion?' Holmes inquired.

Smithers looked pained. 'If you can believe it, a day trip to Loch Ness. She suggested we go boating on the lake and make a search for the so-called monster. I ask you – what nonsense! Such empty-headed fiddle-faddle!'

With a dismissive shake of the head, he resumed his narrative. 'We reached the third floor passage she and I share with Professor Amberson, who had retired much earlier. Dr MacReady's room was the first door on our right, with Amberson's next and my own at the end of the passage. I disengaged myself as politely as I could and wished her good night as she entered her bedroom. I heard her lock the door after her.'

'Is it common practice for you to lock your bedroom doors?' asked Holmes.

'We sometimes keep confidential papers in our private

quarters, Mr Holmes, so we make it a rule to keep doors locked at all times. Each room is fitted with a lock and key as well as a sliding bolt.'

Holmes took in this information and gestured to the scientist to continue.

'I had no sooner grasped the handle of my own door than I was startled by a scream from Dr MacReady's room. I rushed there at once, tapped upon the door and called out, asking if she was in distress. When there was no answer, I tried to open it and found it locked, as I expected. After rapping again to no avail, I knocked loudly on Amberson's door and shouted at him to wake up.'

'I rushed out in my pyjamas,' Amberson chipped in. 'The professor told me what had happened and sent me to fetch Sergeant Ross.'

'I take it that is standard procedure in an emergency of this nature,' said Holmes.

'Yes, Ross is in charge of security,' said Smithers. 'Now I ask you to bear in mind, Mr Holmes, that throughout all this time I continued knocking and calling and at no point was the door out of my sight.'

Holmes nodded slowly and I could tell that his mind was already at work.

'Within a few minutes Amberson returned with Sergeant Ross and four or five of his men. I briefly apprised Ross of the situation and he bade me stand clear. He is a large man, and threw his shoulder at the door with great force. After three or four blows the wood splintered and the door gave way. Inside we found—'

Holmes raised a hand to forestall him. 'If you please, professor, I should like to make my own inspection of the room.'

'Very well,' said Smithers, 'I shall take you up. Bloomhurst, have Sergeant Ross join us upstairs. Amberson, you may accompany us to confirm the facts. The rest of you can return to your work.'

The professor led us back out to the hall and up a broad stairway which ascended in a series of wide curves. As we reached the first turning, I was taken aback by the sight of a savage Highlander, armed to the teeth, leering down at us from above. At second glance I realised it was only a large painting hanging on the wall.

'Good heavens! What a ferocious looking fellow!' I exclaimed.

'That is a portrait of Black Dougal, the seventh laird,' said Amberson. He added with relish, 'He was a bloodthirsty character who, according to legend, beheaded anyone who entered his castle without being invited. In fact, it is even rumoured—'

'That he haunts the place to this day,' Holmes interrupted disparagingly. 'Yes, yes, yes. What would a Scottish castle be without its resident ghost?'

I could tell the young scientist was miffed at being robbed of the opportunity to indulge himself in a blood-curdling tale of the supernatural.

'Really, Amberson,' snapped Smithers, 'you should know better than to entertain such superstitious rot.'

'At any event,' said Holmes, 'we are seeking a flesh and blood intruder. Ghosts need not apply.'

When we reached the third floor, the professor beckoned us to the first room on the right. The door hung somewhat crookedly on its hinges and the splintered wood of the door frame was clear evidence of how it had been forced. Entering ahead of us, the professor switched on an overhead light to reveal a spacious, well-appointed room.

Directly facing us was a window, covered by a black-out curtain. A single bed, neatly made up with a tartan spread, occupied the far left corner while against that wall stood a wardrobe. A bookcase and a reading desk were positioned to the right of the window. Some items of women's clothing lay scattered on the floor outside the open door of an en suite bathroom.

Holmes arched an eyebrow. 'I take it these are Dr MacReady's clothes?'

'When we entered the room, we found them lying just as you see them,' Smithers confirmed.

Holmes bent down and, taking a pen from his pocket, used it to lift each item of clothing for examination. 'One white silk blouse, one skirt of Harris tweed,' I heard him inventory under his breath, 'one cardigan in matching shade of green, and a pair of low-heeled brown shoes, size eight. Interesting.'

'When we entered,' said Smithers, 'we immediately noticed Dr MacReady's outer garments strewn across the floor. Through the open bathroom door we could hear the sound of water running. Thinking for a moment that Dr MacReady might have slipped in the bath and knocked herself unconscious, I entered the bathroom with my eyes averted and called her name. When there was no response I looked up. The bath was unoccupied.'

'How extraordinary,' I murmured.

'Both taps were running,' Smithers continued, 'so I bent down to turn them off. When I looked round, Ross was looming in the doorway behind me. Seeing that Dr MacReady was missing, he immediately dispatched his men with orders to search the house and grounds. He and I made a thorough examination of the room, opening the wardrobe and checking under the bed, to assure ourselves there was no possible place of concealment.'

Holmes stepped over the discarded clothing into the

bathroom. Switching on the light, he examined the bath, the sink, and the medicine cabinet. 'The water was running, you say?'

'Mr Holmes, my scientific training has not gone for nothing,' Smithers declared stiffly as Holmes emerged from the bathroom. 'I have made my own deductions and I believe I can outline the sequence of events.'

'Do proceed,' Holmes invited him. 'I'm sure it will prove enlightening.'

'After we parted, Dr MacReady fastened both locks and placed the blackout curtain over the window,' said the professor. 'She then began running a bath and started to remove her clothes. It was at this point that the intruder emerged from his hiding place in the wardrobe and seized her. She screamed. I ran to the door, and the rest is as I told you.'

'Leaving one vital question unanswered,' I said. 'What has become of Dr MacReady and her abductor?'

Holmes walked over to the window and drew the blackout curtain aside to examine the steel bars fixed there. They seemed quite immovable. He turned back to Smithers.

'The wardrobe, professor – was it open or shut when you entered?'

'It was closed as you see it now. Nothing has been interfered with.'

Holmes opened the wardrobe and scrutinised the contents. Blouses, jackets, skirts and other items were hanging neatly. On the floor to one side lay a pile of assorted shoes.

Holmes closed the wardrobe door. 'And the bath – it was overflowing?'

'No, the plug had been removed.'

'Did you examine the plug to determine if it was wet?'

'No, I did not think that necessary.'

'Quite so, quite so,' Holmes mused. He moved methodically around the room, minutely examining the walls and the furniture.

I sidled over to the desk and noted that the adjoining bookcase contained volumes of chemistry, books on rock climbing and a selection of novels by Scott, Dickens and others. A copy of Stevenson's famous tale *Kidnapped* had been taken from the shelf and lay unopened on the desk. I pointed this out to my friend.

'What do you think, Holmes? Is this a challenge left by the kidnapper or an appeal for help by the victim?'

Holmes barely glanced at the book before kneeling down to examine the wainscot through his magnifying glass.

'You will appreciate, Mr Holmes, that this puts me in a most dreadful situation,' said Smithers, thrusting his hands into his pockets and shaking his head in agitation. 'As director of this facility, such a breach of security reflects badly on my abilities and my reputation stands to suffer most grievously.'

Holmes stood up straight, pulled out his pipe and began filling it.

'Yes, professor, I quite understand that it is you who are the victim in this affair. I shall not allow my concern for Dr MacReady's welfare to blind me to that fact.'

'Mr Holmes, I am afraid I do not allow smoking inside the building,' Professor Smithers declared sternly.

'Really?' Holmes struck a match. 'How fortunate for me then that I am not operating under your authority. Ah, this must be Sergeant Ross.'

Taking his first puff, he stepped out into the passage to meet the burly, uniformed figure who had appeared there. The sergeant was a good six feet two inches with bright red hair and a broad craggy face.

'That's right, sir,' he confirmed. 'And you'll be Mr Sherlock Holmes and Dr Watson. Who'd hae thocht oor wee problem would bring ane o' the country's greatest detectives a' the way up frae London!'

'One of them?' Holmes queried sharply, his vanity piqued.

'You mean *the* greatest, of course,' I prompted the sergeant before my friend could take further offence.

'Oh, aye, just as ye like, sir,' Ross responded with a smile. 'To be frank, I've aye been a great reader o' Sexton Blake mysel'. I grew up on his adventures.'

'Sexton Blake is a fictional character,' I reminded him pointedly.

'Aye, that's true, I suppose,' the sergeant conceded, adding with some enthusiasm, 'but he is a braw, two-fisted sort o' a chap.'

'Well, in the absence of Mr Blake,' said Holmes caustically, 'I shall attempt to solve this mystery without crashing an aeroplane or dodging a hail of bullets. I hope that will not prove a disappointment.'

The sergeant gave a deep-chested chuckle. 'Nae offence meant, sir. Shall we get doon tae business?'

We returned to Dr MacReady's room, where, under Holmes's questioning, Ross confirmed the professor's account of the previous night's events without indulging in any speculations. Satisfied that all the relevant information had been laid out, Smithers prepared to leave.

'Amberson and I have been away from our researches long enough,' he declared. 'Ross, you will see that Mr Holmes and Dr Watson are served with an adequate supper and shown to their rooms, won't you?'

'Aye, professor, I'll see tae it personally,' Ross responded. Smithers made a show of waving Holmes's pipe smoke out of his face and led Amberson off down the passage towards the stairs. I saw the sergeant regard the departing scientists with wry displeasure as they disappeared.

'Sergeant Ross,' said Holmes, as the soldier led us downstairs, 'as chief of security, you must have some thoughts regarding this unusual business.'

Ross rubbed his large jaw and narrowed his twinkling eyes. 'No' tae cast any aspersions, Mr Holmes, but I only hae Professor Smithers' word for it that Dr MacReady was ever in the room at a'. No' that I question his judgement, but he has been awfy fashed o' late.'

'And why is that?'

'Well, we've been warned by the intelligence Johnnies tae look oot for the enemy seekin' tae infiltrate ane o' their agents into the project. It's made the professor as jumpy as a moose in a hoose full o' cats.'

More than this he refused to say. At the bottom of the stairs he opened a door and waved us through into a spacious kitchen redolent with the warm smell of cooking.

The presiding genius was Mrs Sienkowski, a Polish émigrée, who served us a hearty supper of mutton stew accompanied by crusty bread and mugs of tea. As we ate Holmes asked her many questions about the castle's daily routine and the layout of the rooms. When he touched on the personalities of the principals, Mrs Sienkowski grumbled in her thick accent.

'Dr MacReady we like. She is true woman, and only proper soul out of all of them. And yet big professor, he want rid of her. Not good, not good.'

The rooms we were allocated had a connecting door between them. Leaving it open while we unpacked, I took the opportunity to air my thoughts in Holmes's hearing.

'Professor Smithers was alone outside Dr MacReady's

door for at least a couple of minutes,' I pointed out. 'Is it possible that, given his antagonism towards her, he took the opportunity to do away with her?'

'And then dispose of the body so completely that it cannot be found?' Holmes shook his head emphatically. 'I ask you, Watson, does he strike you as a man capable of such bold action?'

'No,' I confessed, 'he does not. So what do you make of his reconstruction of the events?'

Holmes indulged in a short laugh. 'The professor is like a blind man who tries to identify an elephant.'

'I know the fable. You mean he has grasped the trunk and so assumes the animal to be some sort of snake.'

'Yes. Consider the assumption that Dr MacReady was assaulted by an intruder who was waiting in the room. For Professor Smithers to have heard her scream before entering his own bedroom, the scream must have come no more than ten seconds after she closed and locked her door. Is that really enough time to put up the blackout curtain, set the bath water running and partially disrobe? I think not.'

'Then what are we to make of it all?'

'I have not reached a definite conclusion as yet, but the evidence is very suggestive.'

'Evidence? What evidence?'

'The fact that the clothes hanging in the wardrobe were well ordered but the shoes below them were piled up in a heap, that the bath taps were running but the plug had been removed. Then there is Dr MacReady's blouse, on which a button had been pulled loose.'

'Surely as the result of a struggle,' I said.

Holmes shook his head. 'A struggle which resulted in the blouse being stripped from her body would have involved considerably more damage than one loose button. And then there is the rubbery mark on the wainscot to the left of the door.'

'None of that tells me anything at all,' I protested.

Holmes stepped into the open doorway and sighed. 'Evidently it does not. But you have surely noted the most significant fact about Dr MacReady?'

'You mean that she is a woman?'

'I mean,' said Holmes with emphasis, 'that she is Scottish.'

'Scottish? What on earth has that to do with anything?'

'It has everything to do with it. Don't fret yourself – all will be clear in the morning.'

Not for the first time I was provoked by my friend's habitual reticence. 'You wouldn't care to elucidate now?'

'My dear fellow,' he said, closing the door, 'I already have.'

3

THE TRAIL OF BREAD CRUMBS

I was woken at the earliest hour of morning by an energetic rapping at the connecting door. As I struggled upright on my pillows, the door was flung open and Sherlock Holmes strode imperiously into the room. He was fully dressed, and at close quarters smelled of soap and hair oil.

'Come along, Watson,' he exhorted me briskly, 'this is no time to be a slugabed. My nostrils are twitching with the scent of a breakfast being cooked.'

Even through the blackout curtain, I could tell it was still dark outside. 'Holmes,' I grumbled, 'it's surely too early for breakfast.'

'Too early for us, but not for certain others. Come along, man. Get dressed quickly and meet me outside.'

With that he was gone. Clambering out of bed, I pulled on my clothes, ran a comb through my hair, and stumbled downstairs. Holmes was pacing up and down outside the front door in a fever of impatience.

When he spotted me, he pressed a finger to his lips. 'Quiet now and keep to the shadows,' he instructed, and beckoned me to follow.

We made our way round the north wing of the castle to the rear where we crouched behind a rain barrel. From this vantage point I could see Holmes's gaze was fixed firmly on an open door in the basement level. From the scents wafting through the air I had no doubt that this was the back entrance to the kitchen. Why we should be spying on Mrs Sienkowski's efforts was beyond me, while the smell of cooked breakfast stirred a sharp hunger in the depths of my stomach.

Holmes abruptly yanked me down deeper into hiding as a uniformed figure emerged from the doorway and made its way steadily up the small set of steps to the ground level. I recognised at once the burly outline of Sergeant Ross. He was carrying a tray which held an assortment of covered dishes. As we watched, he set off into the surrounding woods.

Holmes turned to me with a gleam in his eyes. 'Come along, Watson, and go cannily. Sergeant Ross is our trail of bread crumbs.'

Crouching low and darting from one patch of shrubbery to the next, we followed the sergeant into the trees. There was no difficulty about keeping him in sight even at a safe distance, as he was making no effort at concealment. He clearly did not expect anyone else to be abroad at this hour and strolled casually along a narrow, winding path.

'Holmes, where on earth can he be going?' I murmured.

'Can you not guess?' Holmes sounded genuinely surprised.

In a flash it occurred to me that Ross must surely be taking this breakfast tray to the vanished Dr MacReady.

I said breathlessly, 'Are you suggesting that the sergeant is actually an enemy agent? That he spirited Dr MacReady away and is holding her captive somewhere in these very grounds?'

Holmes clucked his tongue reprovingly. 'I'm suggesting nothing of the sort. Surely I explained it all last night.'

'You did everything but explain,' I retorted with some warmth. 'Perhaps you might begin with the loose button on the discarded blouse to which you attach such importance.'

'It was pulled loose because the blouse was removed in haste,' said Holmes. 'The fact that the shoes were kicked off willy-nilly and the skirt was only partially unzipped before being pulled off tells the same story.'

'Are you saying that Dr MacReady was in a hurry to take a bath?'

'If she had intended to take a bath, she surely would have put the plug in before turning on the taps. No, no, the clothes in the doorway and the running water were intentional distractions. Then there were the spaces on the bathroom shelf from which a few essential toiletries had obviously been removed. On the other side of the room was the telling evidence of the wardrobe.'

The path forked ahead of us and Ross turned off to the left. As we followed, Holmes continued to discourse.

'You saw the disordered shoes in the otherwise tidy wardrobe. They had been thrust aside to make room for a bundle. Then, of course, the clothes hanging there, and the shoes themselves, clearly indicated that Dr MacReady is quite a tall woman.'

I felt myself bewildered but pressed on. 'And the mark on the wainscot?'

'Made by the thick rubber sole of a boot. Someone was pressed tightly behind the door out of sight. Of course, none of this was possible without the aid of Sergeant Ross and some of his men.'

'But why on earth would Ross connive at the doctor's disappearance?'

'From his choice of reading matter,' said Holmes with a grimace of distaste, 'which he was so annoyingly eager to share with us, we know he has a taste for adventure. It may be why he joined the army in the first place, only to find himself incarcerated here with a party of dry, bookish intellectuals. Few things incline a man towards mischief more surely than boredom.'

Still following the sergeant, we came within sight of the loch I had observed upon our arrival. Nestled among a stand of willows on the shore was a wooden building in a poor state of repair, that must once have served as a boat house. Ross ducked under a low door and disappeared from view.

'Last night you told me that the most significant thing about Dr MacReady is that she is a Scotswoman,' I reminded Holmes. 'What did you mean by that?'

'Come, Watson,' said Holmes, leading the way to the boat house. 'You surely noticed that her colleagues are all English and are held in various degrees of contempt by the Scotsmen who guard them. She alone has a spark of life, she alone is happy to mix socially with the soldiers and, like them, she has taken a considerable dislike to the officious Professor Smithers, particularly so as he disdains her purely on the basis of her sex.'

The full realisation of the plot now dawned upon me. 'So when you told Professor Smithers that he was the victim in this affair, you were not simply being ironic.'

'Indeed not,' said Holmes, bowing his head to step indoors.

Following him inside, I saw, seated on a pair of wooden stools, Sergeant Ross and a tall, handsome woman, her russet hair tied in a tight bun.

She was dressed in a plaid shirt and hiking trousers with a tweed jacket over her shoulders. I guessed at once that this must be the elusive Dr Elspeth MacReady. Between them on a packing case was the tray with its bowls of porridge and plate of oatcakes uncovered. A kettle of tea was brewing on a nearby Primus stove.

They both started up at our entrance, but Holmes waved them to keep their seats.

'Don't be alarmed – we come as friends,' he announced genially. 'Dr MacReady – you are safe and well, I take it?'

Ross chuckled and Dr MacReady gave a broad smile. 'Mr Holmes,' she said, 'I suppose it was only a matter of time before the world's most famous detective tracked me to my lair. I hope you understand that it was never my aim to put you to all this trouble.'

'Indeed. You have gone to considerable effort for the sake of a jape.'

Dr MacReady looked slightly abashed. 'Yes, I apologise. I only meant to put Smithers through the wringer to squeeze some of the vinegar out of him. It was never meant to go this far.'

'Following only a brief acquaintance with that gentleman,' said Holmes feelingly, 'I find myself in complete sympathy with your desire to take him down a peg.'

'You seem tae have got the truth o' it gey quick, Mr Holmes,' said the sergeant, pouring himself and the doctor each a mug of tea.

'All that was required,' said Holmes, 'was the easy assumption that Dr MacReady had contrived her own abduction and all the details fell neatly into place.'

'Details, Mr Holmes?' The doctor pouted in mock disappointment. 'I'm afraid I was foolish enough to think I had covered my tracks rather well.'

'Well enough for the officious Professor Smithers to rush to the intended conclusion that you had been abducted, when a moment's actual thought would have exposed that conjecture as nonsense. In fact, as soon as you had locked yourself in, you began hurriedly to remove your outer clothes so that you could change into the soldier's uniform, complete with army boots, that you had thrust in a bundle into the bottom of your wardrobe earlier in the day.'

'It sounds as though you had it worked out very quickly,' Dr MacReady complimented Holmes.

'My first indication of how it was done came when Professor Smithers told me that Sergeant Ross was accompanied by four or five of his men. When a man so fussily precise as the professor is inexact about a small number of men, it indicates an unconscious confusion.'

Ross gave a chuckle. 'We were counting on the fact that Professor Smithers pays as little attention tae the men that guard him as he does tae the furniture.'

'Please go on, Mr Holmes,' Dr MacReady invited.

'You timed your scream so that the professor would hear it and hurry back,' said Holmes, 'rapping futilely at the door while you continued your preparations. Once you were fully dressed in your disguise, you put the blackout curtain in place and started the bath water running. When Sergeant Ross arrived and forced the door, the professor's attention was immediately drawn to the clothes strewn by the open bathroom door and the sound of running water. He investigated that at once, leaving you free to emerge from hiding behind the door.'

'Are you really saying, Holmes, that no one noticed Dr MacReady at all?' I objected.

'Professor Smithers was in the bathroom with his back turned. Dr Amberson was out in the passage, being kept at a safe distance by one of the soldiers. The sergeant had picked a few men he could trust to be in on the scheme. In uniform and beret, and with her rifle held strategically to obscure her features, Dr MacReady is tall enough to pass for a man just long enough to mingle with the other guards. Sergeant Ross was quick to send them all off on a bogus search, allowing Dr MacReady to disappear, apparently into thin air. It was all quite neat.'

Dr MacReady clapped pleasantly. 'Well done, Mr Holmes. I hadn't intended to remain in hiding quite this long, but when I heard you had arrived, I feared subjecting myself to your interrogation. I suppose you're going to expose the whole caper now.'

'I feel no such obligation,' said Holmes, a familiar impish gleam in his eye. 'I am happy to return you to the anxious Smithers as though by magic without giving a word of explanation. The rest I leave to you. Whatever story you choose to spin to further baffle the professor is entirely up to you.'

The scientist took a bite of oatcake and chewed it thoughtfully. 'I'm torn between saying I just slipped out to visit my mother and telling him I was abducted by fairies.' She grinned broadly. 'It's going to drive him daft for weeks.'

'As for us, Watson,' said Holmes, 'once we have delivered the good doctor back into the bosom of the scientific community, I shall have the football-loving Corporal Paterson drive us to Inverness. There we shall catch the first train south and avail ourselves of the pleasures of the dining car. I do not intend to entrust myself again to the hospitality of the RAF and their unappetising cheese rolls.'

4

CONCERNING MR SHERLOCK HOLMES

A few hours later Holmes and I were settled in a first class carriage on our way back to London. We had each purchased a newspaper before boarding to find the war looming large in the headlines. Once I had absorbed the news, I set about tackling the crossword. Holmes, having quickly digested any matters of interest, cast his paper aside in an untidy heap. His fingers were curled around an empty pipe as he regarded the passing landscape with an expression of the deepest meditation.

'Reflecting on another triumph of deductive reasoning?' I wondered aloud.

'Hardly that,' Holmes responded with a hint of weariness. 'Dr MacReady would have reappeared without any interference from us once she was satisfied that she had given Smithers a sufficient fright.'

'She certainly succeeded in that aim.'

'She is indeed a remarkable woman,' Holmes commented unexpectedly, 'both intelligent and resourceful.'

I was more than surprised to hear the pleased approval in his voice. It was rare for him to express such admiration for a woman. Generally he seemed to keep his distance from them as though they might be hot to the touch and he knew what it was to be burned. But this was merely an impression on my part with no facts to back it up. Whatever romantic affairs lurked in his past – if any – were shrouded in a fog of secrecy it was beyond my powers of perception to penetrate.

I could not help suggesting playfully, 'Perhaps she has, in some manner, made the journey worthwhile for you?'

'No, no,' Holmes countered brusquely. 'While so many are fighting and dying, we have merely passed the time in an empty frolic.'

'You exaggerate its triviality, Holmes,' I said. 'You demonstrated that your gifts are as sharp as ever.'

'But to what end?' His eyes drifted to the newspaper headlines that spoke of the latest turn in the battle against Field Marshall Rommel in North Africa and the ongoing struggle over the Russian city of Stalingrad. 'War is crime writ large, Watson. It uses the same weapons of violence, terror and subterfuge and good men must oppose it as best they can.'

'We both saw our share of action in the last war, Holmes,' I reminded him in hope of banishing his sense of futility. 'Given the hazards we faced then, and the perilous adventures that have befallen us since, we are fortunate to have survived into our fifties in sufficient health to still be of service to our country.'

'Service?' Holmes echoed in a melancholy tone. 'Yes, back then we more than played our part, and that at great cost.'

'Now you play a different role,' I said, 'guarding the home front against our enemies, while I offer what assistance I can to the sick and wounded who fill our hospitals. Why, if not for you, Vosperian's spy ring would still be carrying on its acts of sabotage all across the country.'

'Perhaps so,' Holmes mused, sinking back into his own thoughts. 'I may yet have some work to do.'

Over the years I had grown used to my friend's abrupt changes of mood, the bursts of frantic activity often followed by a period of listless melancholy. When we first met at Bart's after the Great War, his energy and intelligence were immediately apparent to me, and the suggestion that we share digs together had obvious attractions, both in terms of economy and stimulating company.

How stimulating I could not immediately have guessed, for at first I took Holmes to be merely a scientific researcher specialising in certain abstruse areas of investigation. Only over the course of the first few weeks at 221B Baker Street did I begin to discern that crime was his primary interest, and before long I found myself drawn into a series of extraordinary adventures at his side.

Some of these had international ramifications, such as the mystery of the Six Sundered Threads and our perilous encounter with the Society of the Blasted Tree. Others were of less matter but dramatically demonstrated my friend's remarkable powers of observation and deduction, such as the affair of the Unstable Stable Boy and the case of the Purloined Spectacles.

When it became clear that Scotland Yard, eager to preserve its own reputation for competence, was reluctant to give due credit to my friend's efforts on their behalf, I decided to write up some of his exploits for publication in a popular magazine. These tales both enhanced his reputation and spread his fame all across Europe and beyond. I believe they also flattered his vanity, even though he never referred to my literary accomplishments other than to chide me for some romantic exaggeration which he claimed obscured the most telling points in his solution.

Such reserve was typical of him and was indeed one of the hallmarks of his remarkable character. In all the years I knew him I gleaned little of his background. He had let it drop that one of his distant relatives, General Theophilus T. Holmes, fought for the South in the American Civil War, while another Holmes served in Lincoln's White House. There had been at least one artist of note in the family while an uncle had become Lord Mayor of Liverpool. A distant cousin had struck gold in the Klondike and a certain maiden aunt gained some renown as an archaeologist.

Holmes's own father devoted himself to the world of business, primarily shipping and insurance. After suffering an unforeseen financial collapse, he fell ill and died, to be followed shortly by his wife. Holmes's only close relative now was an elder brother, of whom we shall speak later.

In his youth, Holmes, by his own choice, attended Repton School, one of the most renowned public schools in all of England. Here he learned the high value placed on Stoicism, particularly on the sports field, where one was expected to face defeat without any show of emotion. From here he went on to Cambridge where he studied science and languages with equal enthusiasm.

It was during this time that he was first approached by our intelligence services. As well as excelling at scientific studies he was also a sportsman, an expert boxer and fencer. In addition, his linguistic proficiency in both French and German and his leading role in the college's amateur dramatics club made him singularly qualified as a potential undercover agent who could infiltrate the ranks of the enemy both at home and abroad.

During the Great War, using the code name Altamont, he performed an invaluable and hazardous service under an assumed identity deep inside the territory of the enemy. One careless word would have exposed his true identity and placed him before a firing squad, which was the immediate fate of anyone captured as a spy. It was under these extreme circumstances that he acquired that cold reserve and emotional distance which so marked him for the rest of his life. The strain they placed upon his nerves can only be imagined, and yet he left me in no doubt that the information he and others thus acquired was vital to the eventual victory of the allied nations and therefore worth the high price that was paid in lives and personal sacrifice.

I myself, as soon as I had completed my medical training at the University of London, joined the Army Medical Corps. Only a few weeks before the armistice, while attempting to rescue one of our wounded soldiers from no-man's-land, I was shot in both legs by a German machine-gunner. I was shipped home to recuperate and it was many months beyond the end of the war before I was to make a full recovery. I retain the scars to this day and in cold or damp weather I still exhibit a residual limp.

After the war, Holmes with his many intellectual gifts might have become a leading figure in the law or one of the sciences. He might even – if he could have tolerated the empty cant that forms such a part of it – have risen to high political office. Instead he chose a solitary pursuit, a profession which he himself had invented, that of the consulting detective. This allowed him to operate as an independent agent with no company or institution miring him in its grip.

Even I, who shared rooms with him for so many years, rarely penetrated beyond the surface of his chosen solitude. When I married my beloved Mary, whom I had met in the course of one of our many investigations, Holmes was left alone in his bachelor apartments. He still recruited me as an assistant from time to time, but I perceived that he was becoming increasingly reclusive in his habits and exhibiting the signs of some great personal strain pressing upon him.

This came to a head in 1935 when Holmes abandoned Baker Street and to all intents and purposes vanished from the face of the earth for a period of some two years. Rumours spread of his death at the hands of his enemies and

I would have made the same tragic assumption except for the sporadic postcards I received from several exotic parts of the globe, all signed with a different name while being scrawled in the distinctive spidery hand of Sherlock Holmes.

Upon his return, which set the whole country abuzz with excitement, he told me he had been pursuing important business overseas and that the matter was now concluded. I could no more have prised the truth from him then than I could have mined diamonds from the depth of the ocean.

With Mary's death the following year I found myself engulfed in a terrible loneliness, relieved by evenings spent in my old lodgings with my friend, sharing a late supper and discussing his latest investigation. Though I continued living in my marital home, surrounded by keepsakes of those happy years, I was now more pleased than ever to hear that rap on my door summoning me off on another colourful escapade.

This was the period of such notable adventures as the case of the Poisoned Wishing Well and the mystery of the Indigent Cavalier, as well as the time when Holmes refused the unwanted notoriety of a knighthood. As war grew dreadfully closer, the government offered him leadership of their elite code-breaking unit at a classified location. Holmes declined on the grounds that he could only think clearly in the familiar surroundings of Baker Street.

Late in 1940, when my home was obliterated by a German bomb, Holmes willingly threw open the door of our old Baker Street apartments. Mrs Hudson greeted my return with such unbridled joy I felt that it was only the strictures of rationing that prevented her from serving up a fatted calf for the first supper of my renewed residence.

'I can't tell you how happy I am to see you back, Dr Watson,' she confided in me. 'I've been worried about him, more so than at any time since he returned from that secret sojourn of his. He's become more reclusive than ever, spending more time with his pipes and test tubes than with his fellow human beings.'

So it was that we became comrades in arms, sharing again our old barracks. Now as I sat watching his hawkish profile gazing upon the passing landscape, his head nodding slightly with the rhythm of the carriage, I reflected that, for all the cases solved in the course of his illustrious career, the greatest mystery of all remained Sherlock Holmes himself.

Such were my thoughts as the train bore us rapidly south. Awaiting us in London was a horror which not even the background of a world-wide war could in any way diminish. It appeared to me at the time that the most bloodthirsty spectre of our gas-lit Victorian past had returned to haunt us in our darkest hour.

5

THE INSPECTOR CALLS

We arrived home late to a city living in darkness. With the horrors of the Blitz still vivid in everyone's mind, the blackout was rigidly enforced. Though the bombers no longer came night after night, the threat of a raid was constant and every effort was made to conceal the great target that London had become. Streetlights and neon signs were extinguished, windows covered in blackout curtains, and air raid wardens patrolled the streets with their harsh cry of 'Put that light out!'

After a day spent in the stuffy confines of a railway carriage, we were happy to walk the modest distance from King's Cross Station to Baker Street for the sake of some fresh air. From a nearby club came the sound of a frenzied jazz band and revels undampened by the weight of war. Indeed, with death liable to strike from the skies at any moment, many people took to their pleasures with a new, feverish energy, all too aware that the next few hours might prove their last.

From the direction of Westminster I heard Big Ben strike ten o'clock. Though the famous clock tower was shrouded in darkness, the great bell tolled out the hours as regularly as ever. It was like a strong heartbeat, telling me that this city, which had taken such awful damage, still survived and would live on.

We made our way carefully through the gloom, our eyes adjusting gradually to the dark. Without street lights it was all too easy to collide with a pillar box, a dust bin or another pedestrian. Sometimes it felt as if the whole city was engaged in a humourless game of blind man's buff.

When we arrived at last at Baker Street, there was a palpable sense of relief about Holmes, now that he was back among the familiar surroundings of our sitting room: the leather sofa and armchairs, the Persian carpet, the shelves crammed with vintage books and meticulously updated crime files, the gramophone with its small but scrupulous selection of classical records. Even the scimitar hanging on the wall had the comforting appearance of an old friend.

Mrs Hudson – forewarned by telegram of our return – had prepared a light supper and would not let us off to bed until we had consumed every morsel while being obliged at her insistence to extol at length the beauties of her native Scotland. When at last I was permitted to retire, I experienced a curiously dreamless sleep, curious because if ever an occasion called for a premonitory nightmare, it was the morning that followed.

I was once again roused before my accustomed hour, this time by an insistent pounding on the front door downstairs. Such an early morning summons to action had formed so regular a part of my years with Holmes that I was instantly awake and sliding out of bed.

I heard Mrs Hudson call out to the visitor to be patient as she shuffled to the door in her slippers and peered through the peep-hole before admitting him. There followed a familiar heavy tread, ascending the stairs to our rooms, seventeen steps in all, as Holmes had pointed out to me many years ago in an early demonstration of those almost unconscious powers of observation which years of self-training had made second nature to him.

Pausing only to note that my pocket watch read five thirty-four a.m., I threw a robe about myself and entered the spacious sitting room where Holmes had already preceded me. His own dressing gown was tied at the waist and he sat casually cross-legged in his favourite leather chair, as though he had been expecting a caller at precisely this hour.

Inspector Lestrade entered, clad in his customary mackintosh and bowler hat. There was none of the reluctance of the early years of our acquaintance when he displayed a disgruntled embarrassment at being compelled to consult a mere amateur and discuss with him a troubling piece of police business. Now his already flushed face radiated sheer relief at the sight of Holmes carelessly lighting a cigarette.

'Thank goodness you're here, Mr Holmes. I was told you'd gone to Scotland.'

'A short fishing trip, Lestrade.' Holmes waved a dismissive hand. 'The salmon weren't biting so we came back. Please take a seat.'

'I won't if you don't mind.' Lestrade's usual stolid manner had given way to a nervous agitation that prompted him to remove his bowler hat and rub his balding head, as though to relieve some pressure on his brain.

'The matter is urgent, I take it,' I offered.

'More than urgent, doctor,' Lestrade confirmed. He appeared grateful that I had spoken the words for him.

'I can think of only two crises which would bring you to my door at such an unholy hour and in such a state of alarm,' said Holmes. 'One is the kidnapping of the Prime Minister and the other is a dead body discovered in the most striking circumstances.'

'It's the second, Mr Holmes,' Lestrade responded solemnly 'and very striking it is. I'd appreciate it if the two of you could get dressed and come with me directly to the murder scene. I'd like you to look it over before the press gets wind of any of this.'

Holmes took a long draw on his cigarette and a hard gleam came into his eye as he regarded Lestrade. That the doughty policeman had received a severe shock was evident to both of us.

'Come, Watson,' Holmes declared, leaping to his feet, 'we must not keep the inspector waiting.'

On previous visits from the denizens of Scotland Yard I had seen Holmes refuse to budge as much as an inch before every detail of the case in question had been laid before him. On this occasion, however, Lestrade's obviously heightened nerves appeared to galvanise him. Within minutes we were fully dressed and accompanying the inspector downstairs to where a black police car awaited. We slipped into the back while Lestrade bundled himself into the passenger seat and ordered his driver to a location in Seven Dials.

'Can you give us any idea of the nature of the crime?' I asked, addressing the back of the inspector's head and broad shoulders.

'I'd sooner let you and Mr Holmes look it over for yourself,' Lestrade responded grimly. 'I don't want to fog your judgement with any half-baked ideas of my own.'

After so many experiences of seeing my friend unravel conundrums which had baffled the finest minds in Scotland Yard, Lestrade was concerned, in a matter that clearly was of oppressive importance, to do nothing that might in any way hinder Holmes's process of deduction. So much had his respect grown over the years.

When we pulled up at our destination, the sun had risen barely enough to silhouette the great dome of St Paul's and cast a sullen red glow over the tethered barrage balloons that floated above the city. There were four policemen guarding a small courtyard at the rear of a vegetable storehouse and they were more than enough to see off those few civilians abroad at this hour and keep them from intruding on the scene of the crime.

With Lestrade in the lead we were admitted to the dingy courtyard where the smell of stale cabbage clung cloyingly to the air. We were surrounded by grey walls with dripping pipes and gutters. A few broken packing cases stood stacked against the farthest wall and scraps of paper littered the bare paving.

My eyes were drawn at once to where police surgeon Marchbanks was kneeling beside a woman's body. He looked up at me, his face so blanched at the horror of it that it was obvious he had arrived only minutes before us. He stood and wiped the back of his hand across his mouth before addressing us.

'Dr Watson, Mr Holmes, it's a nasty one. I'm more than happy to turn it over to you.'

'We'll work on this together, Marchbanks,' Lestrade corrected him. 'Though, like you, I am very glad Mr Holmes and the good doctor were available.'

As we stepped closer, I saw the victim was a woman in her twenties, though the bloom of her youth had been violently disfigured. I noted the bulging eyes, the swollen tongue and the deep cut to her pale throat. I forced my gaze downward to where her fawn overcoat lay open, revealing a blood-soaked white blouse and grey skirt, both of which had been ripped asunder to expose the abdomen. Here a long, deep incision had been made to produce the most ghastly sight of all. The lower intestine had been removed and placed above the girl's outstretched left hand.

'From the limited spread of the blood,' I commented with a dry mouth, 'we can guess that the organ was removed post mortem – thank God!'

Marchbanks and I exchanged unhappy glances. Even for medical men who had seen our share of death and mutilation, the sheer savagery of this attack was still enough to make our spirits pall. This was the true face of crime, not ingenious or fascinating, but brutish and repellent.

Only a slight twitch at the corner of his mouth betrayed Holmes's outrage at the sight. Otherwise he appeared quite unmoved as he carefully circled the body and applied his analytic powers to the macabre scene. Dropping to one knee he peered closely at the face and neck.

'Away from the cut one can still discern ligature marks round the neck,' he observed, so matter-of-factly you might have thought he was delivering a lecture. 'These show a definite upward movement, scraping the skin raw. This indicates that she was dragged into the shadows while being garrotted, which is confirmed by the fact that one shoe has fallen off while the other bears scuff marks on the heel.'

He pointed to the lost shoe, which lay a few yards from the body.

'It's a savage attack to be sure,' Lestrade commented gloomily. 'I don't turn a hair when it's some tough bloke that meets a sticky end, but a young girl like this – well, it makes even a hardened copper like me sick to my stomach.'

'The savagery is merely on the surface,' Holmes countered. 'This is a cool, calculated killing.'

'How can you say that, looking at . . . at . . . ?' I gestured helplessly at the dead girl.

'The victim was taken from behind and garrotted. Whatever her struggles she would have been dead within a minute. The body was then laid out here quite neatly before the throat was cut. Then a single, deep incision was made in the abdomen. Only one organ was removed and laid beside the dead woman before the killer departed the scene. There is nothing frenzied about this.'

'We don't know for sure about the organs, Mr Holmes,' said Marchbanks. 'It's possible an autopsy will reveal other missing parts.'

'Taken as souvenirs?' said Holmes with a shake of his head. 'In that case the lacerations of the flesh would be more extreme. No, our killer has removed his single trophy and left it here for us to find.'

'The work of a madman, surely,' I said.

'Perhaps,' said Holmes. 'We shall see.' A narrowing of his eyes told me that a further thought had occurred to him. 'It is a dreadful crime, Lestrade, but that in itself would not have propelled you to my door in such haste.'

Lestrade rolled his wide shoulders, as if trying to shake off some oppressive weight. 'You're right, Mr Holmes. The fact is that this is the second such killing.'

'You mean there has been another,' I asked, 'with the same degree of mutilation?' I was surprised that we had heard nothing of it.

'It was a few weeks ago, doctor,' Lestrade shuffled his big feet uncomfortably, 'and at that time we hoped it might be a single incident.'

'The victim?' Holmes prompted.

'A woman,' said Lestrade, 'in her forties. A working girl, if you take my meaning.'

'A prostitute,' Holmes mused grimly. 'The sheer impoverishment of their lives drives them on to the street where their very occupation brands them as victims. No one is so in need of the law's protection and yet so far removed from it.'

'They do take the risk upon themselves, Mr Holmes,' said Lestrade defensively, 'even though the blackout makes the whole city doubly dangerous.'

'This young woman appears quite respectable,' I observed, gazing piteously upon the victim. 'Are you quite sure it is the same killer?'

Lestrade nodded soberly. 'As well as the similarity of method, doctor, he left a signature.'

'A signature?' Holmes raised an intrigued eyebrow.

Lestrade pulled a torch from his pocket and flicked it on. 'An identical name to this was found at the other murder scene.'

He directed the beam at the west wall of the courtyard. Crudely scrawled across the brickwork in bright red chalk were two words.

CRIMSON JACK

6

A SHADOW OF THE PAST

'Crimson Jack,' I heard myself murmur in sheer disbelief that anyone could be so barbaric as to sign his name to such a horror.

'The same name was left at the other crime scene, in the same hand?' Holmes inquired, closely scrutinising the chalked letters.

'Yes, Mr Holmes,' said Lestrade, holding his light steady to aid Holmes's examination.

'And was it also in this vicinity?'

'No, it was across the river in Bermondsey. I can show you the photographs back at the Yard. Ah, here comes Simmons now.'

Simmons, the sandy-haired police photographer, entered the square with his bulky camera dangling from his neck. 'What, again?' he exclaimed when he caught sight of the name on the wall.

'Snap your pictures of the body first,' Lestrade instructed the photographer as he adjusted his flash. 'Then get some shots of this writing here before we wipe it off.'

'Isn't that destroying evidence, Lestrade?' I queried.

'Best we keep this to ourselves, doctor,' Lestrade informed me grimly. 'If this name was to leak out, we'd pretty quickly find it scrawled all over town by some tearaways that think it's a lark. And if it's fame this maniac is after, I'm not serving it up to him on a plate.'

'You did not think to consult me on the first murder, Lestrade,' asked Holmes, 'in spite of this ominous signature?'

'Well, back then we couldn't say for sure the name on the

wall had anything to do with the body,' Lestrade explained. 'It might be the mark of some gang or a sick joke by persons unknown.'

Holmes nodded his understanding. 'Now we know the worst.'

We turned at the sound of the mortuary van arriving and Lestrade switched off his torch. 'You appreciate the importance of keeping a lid on these details?' he inquired of us.

Holmes and I acknowledged this. If word got out of a colourfully named killer stalking the blacked-out streets of London, the press would sensationalise the matter into a carnival of fear, making the job of the police even more difficult.

'Fortunately,' said Holmes, 'we can rely on the war to keep these crimes off the front pages. Tell me, Lestrade, what was the date of the first killing?'

'Let me see,' said the inspector, casting his mind back. 'It was early on a Monday morning they found the body, so that would have been eight days ago – August the thirty-first.' He paused to signal the mortuary men to keep clear until Simmons had completed his work, then turned back to us.

'I tell you frankly, Mr Holmes, this strikes me as one of those fiend killings. There's none of your usual motives behind it, not money or love or revenge, just some twisted maniac who does it because he likes it.'

Holmes nodded grimly. 'Rare as they are, there have been murders motivated solely by bloodlust. It is too early to say if this is such a crime.'

Lestrade's eyebrows shot up. 'Too early? Do you mean to say you expect more killings?'

'Don't you?' With a wave of his hand Holmes took in

the ominous scene that surrounded us. 'Everything about these murders indicates that this is only the beginning. The manner of death, the signature, and above all the dates.'

Lestrade's brow wrinkled and I shared his confusion.

'The dates?' I prompted.

Holmes cast a final eye over the scene as we prepared to depart. 'August the thirty-first and today – September the ninth. Those are the dates Jack the Ripper's first two victims were discovered in 1888.'

At those words I felt myself possessed by a sudden chill, as though a door had been opened to admit a cloud of icy fog wafting out of London's most notorious past.

At Scotland Yard we settled into Lestrade's office where we were provided with a meagre breakfast of strong tea and charred toast. Holmes had had the presence of mind to bring along one of his pipes which he puffed on while reviewing the file on the body discovered on August the thirty-first. Lacking his foresight, I resorted to accepting a cigarette from Lestrade.

I pondered the striking coincidence of dates my friend had pointed out while he reviewed the file on that earlier killing. Lestrade also gave every indication of being disturbed by this new aspect of the case.

'Mr Holmes,' the inspector ventured at last, 'you're surely not telling me we have a new Jack the Ripper on our hands, are you?'

'Certain aspects of this case are suggestive,' said Holmes, looking up from the file. 'The dates, the similarity of the wounds, the removal of organs, and, of course, the adoption of the alias Jack.'

He cast an eye over the scanty report on the first victim then summarised it aloud.

'Margaret Jane Hopkin, known to her friends as Mags, was forty-six years old. Born in Liverpool where she married Walter Brough, a shipyard worker. She herself worked in a textile factory. Ten years ago she left him and moved to London, supposedly in search of a better life.'

'She certainly didn't find one,' I noted soberly.

'She quickly found that she could make a living by picking up men in the street and that became her primary occupation, though she occasionally supplemented her income with short stints as a waitress or a barmaid. She lived in a small bedsit in Andover Street but also had the use of a flat belonging to a friend when she had a client she did not want to learn her true address.'

Holmes laid the case photographs out on the desk and I glanced them over sufficiently to assure myself that the injuries and mutilation were the same, right down to the intestine laid beside the corpse. And there – no less unsettling in stark black and white – was the chalk-scrawled name of Crimson Jack.

'The body was found in a narrow alleyway behind a warehouse in Copeland Street by a blackout warden on patrol,' Holmes continued. 'The chalk signature was a few yards away, scrawled above some dustbins.'

'Did you turn up any leads, Lestrade?' I inquired, pushing away the blackened remains of my toast.

'Nothing to speak of.' Lestrade shrugged resignedly. 'We spoke to a few of her friends, tracked down some regular clients. We even asked the boys in Liverpool to have a nose about for that husband of hers.'

'And?' Holmes prompted.

'They couldn't find him. Moved on to pastures new, he had. But you know how it is with this sort of woman – often as not they come to a sticky end at the hands of a nasty client or a pimp who thinks she's holding out on him.'

'Was she then in the employ of such a man?' I asked.

'No, she was what you might call an independent operator. But that doesn't mean some local villain wasn't trying to force her into his employ. Some of them are happy to slap the working girls around to mark out their patch.'

'According to this file,' said Holmes, tapping it with his finger, 'the case was closed quite quickly.'

'It wasn't the sort of thing we could spend much time on,' Lestrade responded, 'not with the resources we've got.'

'But surely everyone has the same right to justice under the law,' I said.

'That's a very pretty sentiment, doctor,' said Lestrade, 'but that's not how it works, see – specially not now. We're stretched pretty thin since the military nabbed some of our best. Jenkins – you remember him? A promising young chap – he's in the RAF now. And Polingshaw, him as helped break up the Broad Street Gang, he's joined the Navy along with his brother.'

'Yes, I understand the impulse to be on the front line,' said Holmes, 'no matter what important work there is to be done on the home front.'

'And on top of that, there's the lads we lost in the bombing,' Lestrade added. 'So here we are with our numbers down, carrying a heavier load than ever.'

'You mean the extra duties required by the war?' I suggested.

'I mean, doctor,' said Lestrade ruefully, 'that these are booming times for crime. Oh, I know the public face of things is that we're all pulling together, everybody doing their bit for Britain. And right enough, I've seen plenty of that spirit – folks lending a hand to them that's been bombed out of their homes, or volunteering to help out in the kitchens and the hospitals. But there's another side.'

'Yes, the shortages and deprivation lead to a thriving black market in all manner of goods,' said Holmes, 'and with the blackout criminals can move virtually unseen.'

'Added to that there's the jackals that move in to loot bombed-out buildings before anybody can stop them.' Lestrade rubbed his lantern jaw unhappily. 'Crooks aren't scared off by bombs and blackouts, and it takes more than a few patriotic speeches to keep their hands out of their neighbours' pockets.'

'If your notion of this man imitating the historic Ripper is correct, Holmes,' I said, 'then he will be preying exclusively on prostitutes. And yet that girl this morning didn't look like one to me.'

'They come in all shapes and sizes these days, doctor,' Lestrade informed me in a wearied tone. 'There's plenty of married women out there looking for business. With their husbands away at war, they're left to fend for themselves, sometimes without even a proper job. So some of them take to the streets for a spot of passion with some money on the side.'

'Do we have any information on this second victim?' asked Holmes.

'We got a name and address from her papers,' Lestrade answered, flipping open his notebook. 'Clara Bentley, 31 Clerkenwell Gardens. I have Froggat looking into her background now. We should have more by this afternoon.'

'And the medical examination?' I inquired.

'Old Len King is on that. I've sent word that we'll be round to see him at two.'

We were provided with a driver to take us back to Baker Street, this being WPC Laurel Summers. Catching sight of her chestnut hair and bright hazel eyes as she opened the rear door of the Morris saloon for us, I could not help but be reminded of a more innocent age and a happier England, both of which might now be lost for ever.

'I've been put at your complete disposal, sir,' she informed Holmes with a smile when we disembarked at our destination. 'Just let me know when you'll require me.'

'In that case, Constable Summers,' my friend instructed, we'll need you to collect us for a meeting at Bow Street mortuary at two.'

'Right you are, sir,' the pretty young woman responded.

As she drove off, I could not help but wonder if she had been forced to gaze upon horrors such as that we had witnessed this morning. Given the many awful deaths at the height of the Blitz, I could not doubt that this was the case. And yet she retained the sunny, hopeful air of youth.

Once Mrs Hudson had served us our luncheon of Dover sole and boiled potatoes I waited until she returned to her own rooms downstairs before broaching the subject of our current case.

'If my memory serves me correctly, the Ripper claimed five victims, did he not?'

Holmes nodded as he swallowed a small morsel of fish. 'Over a period from August the thirty-first to November the ninth, 1888. All of their throats were cut and each of the bodies subjected to varying degrees of mutilation.'

It did not surprise me that my friend was well acquainted with the details of Jack the Ripper's victims. The history of crime was not merely a hobby with him but a vital element of his method. Many was the time he cracked a mystery by recognising parallels with an earlier case, often an obscure incident in some far-off country. There was nothing obscure, of course, about the Ripper killings. His was the most notorious series of murders in the annals of crime, and that all too apt name was as famous as his true identity was unknown.

'If our new killer holds to the pattern of his predecessor,' Holmes continued, 'then we have only three weeks to track him down before he strikes again on September the thirtieth.'

I shuddered at so ghastly a prospect. 'It's dreadful, Holmes, to think that a sentence of death is already hanging over some unsuspecting woman.'

'It is worse even than that,' said Holmes grimly. 'On September the thirtieth the Ripper claimed two victims in a single night, excelling even his earlier brutality.'

I set down my cutlery and wiped my napkin across my lips. In an instant my appetite had quite disappeared.

'We must find him before then, Holmes. We *must*.'

7

KING OF THE DEAD

We arrived at the Bow Street mortuary promptly at two and found Lestrade waiting for us in company with the lavishly mustachioed Sergeant Arthur Froggat. We entered the examination room with its metal tables, sinks, instrument cases and bottles of disinfectant, the walls decorated with anatomical charts and posters exhorting the utmost cleanliness. Here we found chief pathologist Dr Leonard King writing up a few last notes. Behind him on a raised table lay the body of Clara Bentley, respectfully shrouded over now that King had completed his work.

He looked up at us, his round, grey face imbued with an expression of utter sadness, which could hardly have been more extreme if the girl were his own daughter. Like myself, he had been a medical officer in the Great War, so I knew he had seen more than his fair share of disfigured bodies even before taking up his current position.

Many in his line of work – detectives, police surgeons, medical examiners – who were faced with such horrors armoured themselves by using gallows humour that would sound distasteful to an outsider, but was merely a defence against nightmares. Others cultivated a studied indifference that made them appear cold and dispassionate, when in fact they were simply suppressing their finer feelings in order to carry on with their job.

Leonard King not only had to confront the ugliest crimes of man, but had to perform his own surgical intrusion into the bodies of victims one might in all decency judge to have been sufficiently violated already. Unlike so many others, he appeared to have no defence. He merely absorbed the pain and the sadness into himself, stifling it as best he could, but I could see in his eyes a deep melancholy that only increased with every gruesome autopsy.

'What have you got for us, Len?' Lestrade inquired.

'Nothing good, George,' the pathologist responded solemnly. 'But then it never is, is it?'

He half turned back to the body and made his report from memory. 'The victim is a woman of twenty-five who appears to have enjoyed good health. The obvious wounds were not the cause of death. The girl was strangled first and was quite dead before a sharp blade, possibly a medical instrument, was brought to bear.'

Holmes gave a barely perceptible nod as his own observations were confirmed by this closer examination.

'The throat was cut in one stroke with an upward slant to the right indicating that the killer was right-handed. A deep cut was then made to the abdomen in order to open it up so that the small intestine could be removed.'

He gestured towards a steel bowl in which the severed innards had been placed. 'The incisions were made post mortem, so there would no blood spurt to stain the killer's clothing. Those cuts also indicate that the knife was held in the right hand.

'No organs were removed other than those found beside the body. She had not recently had intercourse and there is no evidence that she was sexually assaulted either pre or post mortem. Stomach contents show that she had not eaten in the five hours preceding her death, which I place at somewhere between eleven p.m. and twelve thirty a.m.'

He concluded with a sigh and laid down his written report. 'It's all in here. Hope you catch the bastard.'

'Let's hear what you've come up with, Froggat,' Lestrade instructed.

The police sergeant flipped open his notebook and cleared his throat. 'Clara Bentley was twenty-five years old, having celebrated her most recent birthday only last week. She lived at 31 Clerkenwell Gardens with her aunt and uncle, Beryl and Charles Bentley. The uncle works as a foreman in a broom factory.

'After leaving Queen Anne High School, Miss Bentley studied at Whittingley Secretarial College while supporting herself with a part-time job as an usherette at the Rialto cinema on Theobald's Road. She so impressed her employers that she was taken on as an assistant manageress. On the night in question the film being shown was *Fingers at the Window* starring Mr Basil Radford as a mesmerist who masterminds a series of murders in Chicago.'

The sergeant looked up from his notes. 'Sort of ironic, don't you think?'

'Never mind the irony, Froggat,' Lestrade remonstrated sternly. 'Stick to the facts.'

'Sorry, sir.' Froggat cleared his throat again and continued. 'She was last seen alive by the projectionist Rupert Jameson when they locked the place up for the night. They went off in separate directions and he recalls that she was headed east up the road. As far as he knew she was headed directly home for a good night's sleep.'

Holmes touched a finger to his chin and I knew he was consulting the detailed map of the city which was stored in his memory. 'And yet, the spot where the body was discovered lies in the opposite direction to her address,' he remarked. 'In fact, she appeared to be headed towards Covent Garden and Leicester Square, perhaps in search of a late supper.'

'At any rate,' said Lestrade, 'there's nothing to indicate she was out to pick up a man.'

'Dr King, might I take a final look at the girl?' Holmes requested.

'Help yourself, Mr Holmes,' King answered. 'She won't object.'

While Holmes walked over to the shrouded body, Lestrade drew Sergeant Froggat aside to discuss further lines of inquiry. I followed Leonard King to a steel sink where he was pouring himself a glass of water. I could not help but note the brittle look of his sparse grey hair and the parchment-like pallor of his dry skin. Forty-odd years among the dead had not been kind to the man and the death of his son in France in 1940 had aged him even further. It wasn't hard to see why some of his colleagues referred to him with morbid humour as *King of the Dead*.

'That's another one shuffled off to the undiscovered country,' he lamented. 'I wonder if there's anything out there?' He sucked in his sallow cheeks and shrugged. 'I doubt it. If there was, we'd have heard something by now.'

'Some people claim they have,' I said, attempting to inject some sort of hope into his tragic world-view.

'Loonies most of them,' King said dolefully. 'The rest are just wishful thinkers. Can't say as I blame them. Who wouldn't hope for something better than this?'

His eyes drifted back to the corpse, as though its wounds symbolised the ruined state of a fallen world. He popped a pill into his mouth and washed it down with a swallow of water that made his Adam's apple bob beneath the wrinkled skin of his neck.

'Ulcers,' he explained. 'Inevitable really.'

'Perhaps you need a rest,' I suggested. 'A few days in the country, a spot of fishing.'

He shook his head and replaced the glass precisely on the edge of the sink. 'With all the bodies that pass through here these days, they'd pile up into a crowd if I wasn't here.'

'Surely, though,' I pressed him, 'you've already done as much as can be asked of you, no matter how dedicated you are.'

'I do this business because somebody must in the interests of justice.' Now his voice dropped so that the police officers would not overhear, and his tone became that of a confession. 'But after a while a certain morbidity
of the soul sets in. It's almost as if every corpse I examine drains away some of my own life. One day, I'll have nothing left and I'll be laid out on the slab myself.'

As we departed, I was left with the macabre image of the ageing pathologist lying here in the very place where he had for so long carried on his lugubrious trade, just one more body among the many. Would he even then be at rest, I wondered.

Holmes and I returned to Baker Street with copies of the files and photographs Lestrade had compiled on both murders. Holmes settled himself into his favourite chair surrounded by this information as well as his own reference books and back issues of recent newspapers. He perused the Scotland Yard documents once more before leaning back and puffing on his cherrywood pipe.

'Do you see any light in this?' I asked.

'I see points of interest to which we must give deep consideration,' he replied. 'For a start, the differences between the two murders.'

'The first a prostitute, the second a perfectly respectable young woman,' I recalled. 'Is it possible that the murderer, in spite of her appearance, took her for a street-walker also?'

Holmes shook his head. 'If he wished to kill another prostitute, there are more than enough of those to be found, as Lestrade pointed out. No, this second victim was singled out for some other reason.'

'Might she not have been chosen at random? A mere chance encounter that led to murder?'

'Both were killed in the shadows of an obscure back street,' said Holmes, 'which is just where the first victim might expect to carry on her trade. The second girl set out along a major road on her way home, but for some reason she turned round and was murdered in a dark alley in an area no woman with a grain of sense would enter at night unless accompanied by someone she trusted.'

'By someone known to her?' I suggested.

Holmes jabbed the air with a finger to emphasise his conclusion. 'Either that or someone who would be instinctively trusted, such as a man in uniform.'

'Well, there are plenty of those around,' I said, 'not just British, but also Canadians and Americans.'

'Note also that, although she turned back and headed for Covent Garden after setting out for home, she was not dressed for a night out, nor was she made up for any sort of date. There was therefore no assignation made beforehand.'

Holmes paused to take a puff on his pipe before continuing. 'I suggest that shortly after leaving the cinema she encountered someone who suggested a late supper in that part of town, then deliberately led her into an obscure and narrow street. If by this time her suspicions were aroused, it was already too late.'

'You are suggesting that the killer was lying in wait within view of the cinema, ready to approach Clara Bentley as soon as she was alone.'

'Everything points to that,' said Holmes. 'And if she was targeted deliberately, then his first victim, Margaret Hopkin, was deliberately targeted too.'

'But Holmes, what connection could there be between

the two?' I asked, spreading my palms out before me. 'They would not have moved in the same circles and they lived and worked in different parts of the city.'

'Yes, the choice of victims marks a striking divergence from the original Ripper, on whom we believe our own killer models himself.' He removed the pipe from his mouth and waved the stem slowly back and forth, as his thoughts moved between the original Ripper and his imitator.

'We can also note that, gruesome as these two crimes are, they were carried out in a coldly clinical fashion. The victims were strangled, so they had no chance to cry out. The throat and stomach were then cut post mortem to minimise the amount of blood spilled. The organs removed were those most easily accessible.'

'But surely, whatever the cool efficiency with which he carries out his crimes,' I said, 'this man is motivated by a hatred of women.'

'It is true that hatred can often be a cold thing,' Holmes agreed. 'A twisted passion is not necessarily accompanied by reckless savagery. It is clear to me from the way he strikes quickly and then departs, this man is making every effort to ensure that he is not caught.'

'In that case why sign his name in the vicinity?'

'To make clear his identification with Jack the Ripper. And yet, it is in the telling differences that our best hope for exposing him is to be found.'

After such a day it was small wonder that thoughts of death haunted me as I prepared for bed that night. Before turning out the light, I paused to stare at the photograph of my dear Mary that stood upon my bedside table, a carefree smile upon her lips, her eyes bright with the joy of summer. I had taken it one day when we were picnicking in the New

Forest, our happiness unclouded by any premonition that in only a few months' time she would be caught in the fatal grip of tuberculosis.

Such joy, I knew, could never be mine again, nor could I imagine any trial worse than what followed. For all my medical training, for all my experience of overcoming dangers of every kind, I could only watch helplessly as she slipped away into that cold and nameless night leaving me bereft of all but the memory of her.

As I gazed upon that beautiful face, my heartbeat slowed and my breath faded to silence, as if I were drawing closer to the realm of the departed in search of even one momentary glimpse of whatever lay beyond. Not for the first time there passed through my mind the words of Poe's famous poem, in which he longs helplessly for the lost Lenore. *Tell me*, he appeals to the raven, *is there balm in Gilead?*

Many were the times I wondered myself if there was indeed some miraculous cure that could mend all the sorrows of the world. Given the dread tides of war that crashed about us on every side, it seemed too much to hope for. Sleep, when it finally came, brought its measure of relief, but I knew in my heart that there would be for me no surcease of sorrow.

8

THE CHAMBER OF WAX

Over the next few days I was too much occupied with my duties at St Thomas's to keep track of Holmes's progress, if there was any. We sometimes crossed paths when I was setting out for the hospital while he returned from one of his expeditions, sometimes in his normal clothes, at other times in the sort of shabby attire that allowed him to pass unnoticed through the lower parts of the city. In spite of the circumstances, it did me good to see him fully engaged in a mystery, when only a few days before I had feared that he was sinking into a lethargic melancholy.

'If I can only find a connection between those two women,' he told me in passing, 'that might give me a clue as to the identity of the next victim – even the next two victims if our man holds true to the pattern of his predecessor.'

I could not help but feel that if the current killer was as mad as the original Ripper was generally deemed to be, then my friend's usual method of rational analysis might not be a sufficient instrument to probe his sick motivations. Holmes's own dedication to reason might in this case be misleading him in directions which would prove quite fruitless.

I spent that Thursday night at the hospital, catching what little sleep I could following a large influx of injured from a fire at the docks. When I returned home mid-morning I was greeted by the sight of a familiar face emerging from our front door.

'Tommy!' I greeted him. 'I haven't seen you in months.'

Thomas Wiggins was the last of the Baker Street Irregulars, the young ragamuffins who used to serve Holmes as scouts, spies and lookouts, often penetrating areas of the city even he was hesitant to enter undisguised. Now that they were grown up we had lost touch with most of them. Some, I knew, were serving in the army, while one or two had been sucked down into the undertow of criminal life. Only Wiggins now remained to assist the man he continued to idolise and – I suspected – regarded as a substitute for the father he had never known.

That homely face, with its crooked nose and small, darting eyes, still retained the cheeky self-assurance of youth. He was dressed in the uniform of a volunteer fire warden and gave me a lopsided grin from beneath the brim of his metal helmet. Hooking a thumb into the strap of his gas mask case, he threw me a brisk salute.

'Cheers there, Dr Watson. Quite a shocker you and the great man have got tangled up in, eh?'

'So serious that Mr Holmes has called upon the services of his brightest protégé,' I complimented him. It had a been a blow to Wiggins's pride that he had been rejected by the military on health grounds, and I took every opportunity to bolster his confidence.

'I wouldn't call myself that, doctor,' he responded modestly, 'but I'm right glad to be of use to Mr Holmes, specially with the army turning me down like they did on account of my asthma. I'll show them they've passed up on a bloke that might have done them good service, eh?'

'No doubt, Tommy. So what task has Mr Holmes assigned you? Chasing a barge full of smugglers down the Thames? Keeping watch on an opium den?'

Wiggins let out a short, high laugh. 'Nothing as exciting as that, doctor. Just wants me to keep my ear to the ground and pick up what I can from my contacts on the shadier side of the street, anything that might tie in with these horrible killings.'

'I'm sure any information you can turn up will be welcome,' I assured him. Then, lowering my voice, I asked, 'And tell me, how is your mother?'

'Struggling along, Dr Watson.' He was suddenly deflated and his shoulders drooped. 'You know how it is. We do what we can for the pain, but the end can't be far off. Mr Holmes has given me some extra cash for the medicine, God bless him.'

'If there's ever anything I can do,' I offered.

'I know that, doctor, I know that, but she's beyond any help now.' Eager to change the subject, he suddenly exclaimed, 'I'm betting you had your hands full with that blaze at the docks last night! See it for miles, you could!'

His evident relish for disaster struck me as rather inappropriate, but I let it pass. 'There were some terrible burns among the survivors,' I told him gravely, 'and those suffering from smoke inhalation are still in a bad way. I suppose we're lucky it wasn't worse. I hear that you've volunteered at St Thomas's yourself on occasion.'

'I'm too busy for that now,' said Wiggins, 'what with this new case to work on. Just between the two of us, doctor, with all the tips I've picked up from working with Mr Holmes, I fancy I could take up the detective lark myself and make a proper job of it. What do you think of that?'

'I think the more soldiers we have in the war against crime the better,' I said encouragingly.

'If you ask me,' Wiggins waved a disgruntled finger, 'the real crime is Mr Holmes being robbed of the credit he deserves, year after year. He's the greatest man in the world, I say, but where are his honours? Where are the riches, I ask you?'

'You know as well as I do, Tommy, that such things have little meaning for Mr Holmes. His concern is that justice should be properly served to poor and rich alike. And, of course, he craves the mental stimulation of cracking a puzzle that leaves others baffled.'

Wiggins drew closer and spoke in a confidential tone. 'That's exactly right, sir. He's been needing a case like this, if you don't mind me expressing an opinion, one that's a worthy challenge to his brains.'

'His primary concern is that no more women die at the hands of this fiend,' I corrected our young friend.

'But if Mr Holmes was to capture Jack the Ripper,' Wiggins positively beamed at the prospect, 'why, that would set a real crown on his career. There would be no way for them dim plodders at Scotland Yard to thieve the glory, not this time.' He toyed with the warden's whistle that hung around his neck as though it were a trumpet through which he might broadcast the fame of his patron.

'You are aware, Tommy, that this cannot actually be Jack the Ripper,' I advised.

'As good as, doctor, as good as,' Wiggins insisted brightly. 'And you know, if we need to corner the blighter, Mr Holmes can count on me to do my part. I'll not duck out of a scrap.'

In the face of his enthusiasm, I felt it necessary to utter a word of caution. 'Remember, it is vital that we keep the possible Ripper connection confidential for the present. You mustn't mention it to anyone.'

'Too late for that,' said Wiggins, marching off with a jaunty wave. He disappeared down Baker Street, whistling to himself, while I entered 221B and climbed up to our lodgings. I could not but wonder what he meant by that parting remark.

From beyond the door at the top of the stairs came the sharp, agitated strokes of the *Tambourin Chinois* by Kreisler being played on the violin. The sweep and slice of the piece lent itself to the venting of frustration and I could hear that it was being performed with a malignant fury. This did not bode well for the mood I would find my friend in. Indeed, as soon as I entered he whirled sharply to face me without interrupting the piece. He finished with an angry flourish and pointed to a newspaper on the table with his bow, as though he wished to stab it.

'There, Watson, do you see? The board is upended and the pieces go flying!'

It was a copy of the *London Bulletin* emblazoned with the headline: RETURN OF THE RIPPER!

I quickly scanned the article below, noting that it contained only a few bare details of the deaths of two women but made great play of the dates being coincident with those of the infamous Whitechapel murders. The fact that both were mutilated was recorded, though there was no mention of the killer's menacing signature.

Does the Ripper live again to terrorise our streets? the journalist wondered, adding, *We demand Scotland Yard answer that question!*

Holmes plucked irritably at the strings of his violin. 'It is a bad turn of events, Watson. From now on this investigation will be beset with cranks, hysteria and sensationalism.'

'Might it not at least alert women to take care on the future dates?'

Holmes dismissed the suggestion with a flick of his bow. 'People who continued to go about their business at the height of the Blitz in defiance of the Luftwaffe will not be deterred from doing so by one lone man with a knife. Many of those who have survived thus far fancy themselves inoculated against the sudden strike of death and pay no heed to even the most serious warnings.' He resumed playing in such a fury of frustration I was afraid he might damage his precious Stradivarius. Mercifully he was interrupted by the jangling of the telephone. I picked it up.

'Baker Street. Dr Watson here.'

Lestrade's voice came over the line. 'Dr Watson, would you and Mr Holmes please meet me at the Chamber of Wax. There's been a development.'

'A development?' I repeated. 'At the Chamber of Wax?'

'That's right, in Lombard Street. Summers will be along to collect you in a few minutes.'

With that he hung up, leaving me completely baffled. I passed on the message to Holmes, who quirked a sardonic eyebrow. 'It seems our friend Lestrade is seeking inspiration in some unusual places. I suppose we had best humour him.'

We found WPC Laurel Summers waiting for us downstairs. She opened the back door of the saloon for us then got in behind the wheel.

'Any idea what this is all about, Summers?' I asked.

'None at all, sir,' the young policewoman replied. 'A call came in from that wax museum that had the inspector spluttering like a firework. And that on top of that story in the papers this morning.'

'I anticipate that Inspector Lestrade will be in a temper hot enough to melt some of those waxwork figures if he gets too close to any of them,' Holmes remarked drily.

When we reached our destination we saw a restless crowd milling around before the entrance to the Chamber of Wax. I had visited the place years ago with Mary and admired the skill with they had rendered likenesses of Henry the Eighth and Napoleon Bonaparte as well as familiar stars of stage and screen. I was aware that custom had dropped off in recent years and was surprised to find it still open.

Summers waited in the car while Holmes and I disembarked. As we made our way through the crowd, we saw a poster outside that promised the horrors of the Spanish Inquisition and the crimes of history's most notorious villains. This was followed by a warning that small children and those of a sensitive disposition should approach with caution. Two policemen were blocking the entrance, much to the chagrin of the public.

'When are they gonna let us in, eh?' some indignant citizens grumbled. 'Come on, constable, we want to see it before they take it away!'

One of the policemen on guard recognised Holmes and opened a path for us through the crowd.

''Ere, ain't that Sherlock 'Olmes?' cried a voice. 'Maybe they're gonna do him in wax.'

'They'll need a big gob of it for that hooter!' joked another.

We ignored the gust of crude laughter and entered the foyer.

Here we met with a leering effigy of Genghis Khan (for so the figure was labelled) who threatened us with a blood-stained scimitar. On the other side of the foyer Vlad the Impaler gloated over a turbaned Turk skewered through the belly on a sharpened spike. A large woman with a bag of change secured around her midriff and a roll of tickets in her hand blocked our way, demanding payment of two and sixpence each.

'We are here on police business,' Holmes informed her curtly as we swept past.

'This is a business too, you know!' she called after us in shrewish aggrievement. 'We don't do it for free.'

Following the buzz of voices we could hear from the passageway ahead, we entered a gallery of waxwork tableaux illustrating only history's bloodier moments. Here was an elaborately wigged Marie Antoinette, her neck pressed down on the guillotine awaiting the fatal blade. Next Cleopatra clasping the deadly asp to her bosom, then Joan of Arc, tied to a stake with artificial flames licking about her feet. Another depicted in gruesome detail the torment of a female victim of the Spanish Inquisition.

Given the crimes we were investigating, I could not help feeling repulsed by the notion that people would pay money to see these images of women facing agonising death. There was worse to come in the chamber beyond. It bore the title *The Dungeon of Crime*.

Here the figures of Burke and Hare were digging up a grave, while facing them was a grisly tableau of the hanging of Charles Peace. Similar deathly scenes surrounded us on every side. In the midst of these waxen villains we found Lestrade interrogating a small, paunchy man with grey hair and thick wire spectacles who was wearing a brightly patterned waistcoat.

'I swear to you that's just how I found it this morning,' the little man bleated unhappily. 'I locked up as usual last night and I've got the only key.'

There was relief in Lestrade's face when he caught sight of us. 'Ah, Mr Holmes, Dr Watson, this is Cedric Chalfont, the owner of this establishment.'

Chalfont executed a bobbing bow and summoned up an ingratiating smile. 'Sherlock Holmes, eh?' An avaricious gleam sparked in his eye. 'I don't suppose, Mr Holmes, that you would consider modelling for a . . .'

Holmes cut him off abruptly. 'Indeed I would not. Lestrade, what on earth are we doing here?'

'Especially at a time like this,' I pointed out, 'when we are immersed in genuine horrors.' I gazed at the gruesome waxworks with undisguised distaste. 'I seem to recall that when this exhibition first opened it did not consist solely of the morbid and the grotesque.'

'I did initiate a change in direction,' Chalfont admitted shamelessly. 'If you want to stay in business, you have to give the public what they want.'

'The crowd outside certainly seem to be excited about something,' Holmes noted acidly.

'There has been a *development*,' Lestrade told us uncomfortably, directing our attention to the tableau directly behind him. It bore the caption *Jack the Ripper Claims Another Victim*.

The scene was a dark, dingy alleyway where stuffed rats lurked among the refuse. A fake street lamp dimly illuminated the bloodied body of woman stretched out on the cobbles, her clothing disarrayed, a scarlet gash glaring in her throat. Over her loomed a figure in a black cloak and top hat. The face had been strikingly rendered into an expression of bestial savagery as he gloated over his victim. In one hand he held a medical bag, while the other was menacingly upraised and clenched around a bloody knife.

'Are we supposed to be enlightened by this crude and inaccurate mockery?' Holmes's voice dripped with disdain.

'The knife, Mr Holmes,' Chalfont explained in breathy excitement, pointing dramatically at the Ripper's weapon. 'That's not the fake knife I put there when we set the scene up weeks ago. Somebody sneaked in during the night and replaced it. That's a real knife, sir – and real blood!'

9

THE DISPLACED KNIFE

I approached the Ripper tableau and peered closely at the red streaks on the knife. 'Unless I am much mistaken, Holmes, this is genuine blood.'

Joining me in my inspection, Holmes leaned in close and took a fastidious sniff. 'Indeed it is,' he agreed. With a fingernail he tapped the lower, unbloodied part of the blade. The dull metallic clink confirmed that it was of steel.

Chalfont produced another knife from his pocket and bent the rubber blade to demonstrate its harmlessness. 'Normally Jack's holding this dummy knife here, see, with a patch of red paint smeared on to it.'

Holmes took the fake knife and subjected it to a cursory glance. Handing it back, he resumed his examination of the waxwork Ripper, giving close attention to the hand.

'And where did you find the original knife?' I inquired.

'It was just tossed on the floor back there,' said Chalfont, indicating the shadowy background of the imitation alley.

A flicker of movement drew my attention to a nearby tableau representing the mad monk Rasputin casting a hypnotic spell over the Russian tsarina. An incongruous figure stepped out of the darkened recesses of the tsarina's boudoir and stood before us, smiling. A short, stocky specimen, he was dressed in a loud houndstooth jacket and trilby. Small, crooked teeth like a rodent's showed beneath his pencil-thin moustache.

'Good day to you, gents,' he greeted us with a doff of his hat. 'Charlie Deeds, *London Bulletin*.'

'Here! How long have you been skulking about back

there?' demanded Lestrade.

Deeds's ratty face assumed an unconvincing expression of innocence. 'Just keeping out of the way, Inspector. And taking some notes of course.'

'I called Cha— Mr Deeds before sending for the police,' Chalfont explained, 'him being an expert on crime.'

Lestrade glowered at the reporter. 'Expert, eh? I suppose you're the one that's responsible for all that tosh in this morning's paper.'

'Just keeping the public informed of the facts,' Deeds retorted airily.

His smug attitude aroused my ire. 'You fashioned a garish horror story out of the personal tragedy of two lost lives,' I accused him. 'Your responsibilities as a journalist extend to more than just concocting an eye-catching headline.'

Deeds had the effrontery to grin. 'Oh, I've got headlines aplenty now, Dr *Watson*, is it?'

He pulled out a notebook and jotted in it with a stubby pencil. 'First the new Ripper breaks into the Chamber of Wax and leaves his calling card right here, bloody evidence of his crimes. Then the great Sherlock Holmes arrives on the scene. Very juicy stuff.'

Holmes turned from his examination of the wax Ripper and fixed a contemptuous eye on the reporter. 'How fortunate for you that Mr Chalfont thought it correct procedure to contact you before the police, Mr Deeds.'

'Well, I am the chief reporter for the Bulletin.' Deeds puffed out his chest. 'I even have my own column – *Deeds Not Words*. I expect you've read it.'

'I may have overglanced it once or twice,' Holmes conceded contemptuously.

'Mr Chalfont rightly feared that when Scotland Yard showed up they would do their best to suppress the facts,'

Deeds continued in an attitude of gross self-righteousness. 'He obviously had heard of my reputation for honesty and invited me here to make sure the public are fully informed.'

Lestrade took a long stride forward to loom over the reporter like a thundercloud. 'You'd best mind what you write in that rag of yours,' he warned. 'There's rules in wartime about misinformation.'

'This isn't war business,' Deeds retorted. 'Or is it?' He tapped the end of his pencil against his crooked teeth. 'Yes, now that I think about it, that might be a fresh angle. There's a rumour that Hitler's developing a new terror weapon.'

'What are you havering about, man?' Lestrade growled.

'Maybe this is it,' Deeds continued with schoolboy enthusiasm, 'bringing our nightmares to life to break our spirit. First Jack the Ripper, then Dracula, then . . . well, who knows what? It hardly bears thinking about.'

'You publish anything as harebrained as that,' said Lestrade, 'and I'll lock you in a cell myself and chuck the key in the Thames.'

Deeds ignored him and scribbled furiously in his notebook. 'Of course, we'll need a name for this killer. How about the Blackout Ripper? Or Jack the Black? What do you think, Mr Holmes?'

'I will spare you my thoughts,' Holmes retorted caustically, 'since they do not flatter you. Come, Watson – we've wasted enough time here.'

'I will need to take that knife, Mr Chalfont,' said Lestrade, 'so it can be examined properly.'

'Oh no, you can't do that without damaging my figure,' Chalfont objected. 'I have my rights, you know. I'll sue.'

'Don't waste your time with it, Lestrade,' Holmes advised. 'It's an obvious fraud.'

Chalfont clenched his fists with a splutter of indignation.

Deaf to his protests, Holmes made for the exit and I followed close behind.

'You sound very sure of yourself, Mr Holmes,' Deeds called after us. 'You could be overlooking a vital clue, you know.'

I laid a hand on Holmes's sleeve. 'Unlikely as it seems,' I muttered, 'it is still possible that knife has some connection to our killer.'

Holmes gave a loud snort and turned back to face the gathering in the Dungeon of Crime. 'That knife has no more connection to the killer than any of the other props in this chamber of horrors,' he declared roundly. 'The instrument now in the wax Ripper's hand has a larger hilt than the rubber one it replaces. This means that it could only be fitted between the fingers by someone who had the skill to recast them without damaging them, in other words Chalfont himself.'

Ignoring an outraged squeak from the owner of the establishment, he pressed on. 'There are one or two minuscule cracks, fresh ones, showing where the alterations were made. Also, upon examining the blade, one can tell from the slight tell-tale strokes, which are still visible, that the blood was applied with a brush. It is almost certainly animal blood acquired from a butcher.'

With that he strode off down the horror-lined passageway towards the front entrance, leaving Chalfont stammering and Deeds in a state of apparent amusement.

'What a disgusting hoax!' I exclaimed. 'Why, the man should be driven out of business.'

'Oh, I am quite sure that Deeds is the brain behind the scheme,' said Holmes.

'Really?' I exclaimed. 'They gave the impression that they were strangers to each other.'

'Although Deeds tried to conceal the fact, Chalfont let it slip that they are on first name terms. They have obviously colluded on this fraud for their mutual self-interest – an increase in custom for one, and sensational headlines for the other.'

In the aftermath of Deeds's story and the scene at the Chamber of Wax, Scotland Yard was besieged by the press. Lestrade gave out an official statement to the effect that no connection had been made between the two recent murders and the crimes of the individual commonly referred to as Jack the Ripper and that such lurid speculations were baseless and unhelpful.

This did nothing to halt the deluge of letters that now flooded into Scotland Yard from concerned citizens, helpful cranks and would be amateur detectives. Worse still were the taunts and confessions variously signed Your Friend Jack, Saucy Jack, and The Ripper.

'I've got three poor sods shut away in a stuffy back room,' Lestrade told us glumly, 'with orders to read every single word of every single letter and report anything that might be a lead. Not that I expect it to do any good, but we have to keep at it on the chance that there may be a clue somewhere amongst all the rubbish and ravings. Lord knows we've got little else to go on.'

Some of the mail which was deemed by Lestrade's unhappy triumvirate of readers to be worthy of further attention was forwarded to Holmes for his assessment. It was on a rainy Thursday afternoon in Baker Street that a break in the case finally came.

Holmes and I were seated in our favourite chairs on either side of a card table on which lay a loose pile of assorted envelopes – WPC Summers' most recent delivery. From the gramophone came the soothing music of Heifetz playing one of Bach's violin sonatas. Heifetz's perfect technique and intellectual approach were well suited to my friend's temperament, but today that was not enough to calm his growing aggravation.

As soon as the music finished, he brandished a letter in the air with the suppressed howl of a man tried to the very limits of his endurance. 'Just listen to this, Watson!' he exclaimed, and proceeded to read it aloud.

'*Dear Scotland Yard, In investigating this case you would do well to make use of the principles of numerology. Taking the numerals of the year 1888 and adding them together gives us 25. When you add those two digits together the result is 7. Now, when we follow the same process with the current year, 1942 reduces to 16 which also reduces to 7. You would do well to seek out any other murders carried out in years which also have the numerological value of 7.* Did you ever hear such humbug?'

He tossed the letter aside and threw himself back in his chair with a groan. 'There is more, but I can't bear to go on. Have you anything better to show?'

I gave a despondent shake of the head and read from the letter in my hand.

'*Dear Police, I think I can put you on the track of this mad killer. My brother-in-law Arthur is always reading those lurid American crime magazines and I find his interest in such matters to be quite unhealthy. Once I caught him standing in front of a mirror talking to himself like a character in one of those dreadful gangster films. I believe he was imagining himself to be Edward G. Robinson. I think it more than likely that his obsession has taken him over the brink and you should arrest him before he claims another victim.*'

'Pah!' Holmes leapt from his chair in a fit of disgust and stalked over to the window to gaze upon the rain-drenched street below. 'I need solid matter to work on, and instead all I have is this piffle.' He waved a dismissive hand in the direction of the abandoned letters.

'The trouble is, of course,' I said, 'that somewhere among all the nonsense there might be one tiny chink of light. The fact remains that the killer must be somebody's neighbour and it's possible he's been spotted returning from one of his nocturnal jaunts.'

Holmes suddenly stiffened and a hard gleam came into his eye. 'I think your chink of light may be here. I see Lestrade getting out of his car down there and he appears more animated that I have seen him in some time.'

Once Mrs Hudson had admitted the inspector and we heard his familiar heavy tread on the stairs, Holmes was there to meet him in the doorway.

'Lestrade, there has been a fresh development?' He was as keen as a hound catching the scent of a fox.

The inspector strode into the room, shaking the raindrops from his bowler hat. 'There has indeed, Mr Holmes.'

I shot to my feet. 'Not another body, I hope?'

'Nothing like that, thank God. But a letter was handed in to us no more than an hour ago. I'd like to know what you make of it.'

Delving into an inner pocket of his overcoat, he produced a small manila envelope which he handed to Holmes with a strange mixture of reverence and revulsion.

Holmes accepted it and we returned to our seats. Lestrade pulled up an extra chair to join us and watched my friend expectantly as he turned the envelope over in his hands.

'Another anonymous letter, Lestrade, claiming credit for the crimes?'

'Not anonymous,' Lestrade answered grimly. 'This one is signed *Crimson Jack*.'

10

A LINEAGE OF BLOOD

Holmes first examined the envelope itself. 'A London postmark,' he noted crisply, 'and a typewritten address: *Miss Abigail Preston (For Scotland Yard), Morley Manors, London, sw1.* Who, may I ask, is Miss Abigail Preston?'

'An American lady,' said Lestrade, 'a journalist employed by the NBC radio network. She broadcasts regularly from London on the course of the war.'

Holmes tapped the envelope against his palm. 'And what connection does she have to Scotland Yard?'

Lestrade shrugged his broad shoulders. 'None apart from this. She had the good sense and discretion to bring it to us without opening it. I've left her back at the Yard with a pot of tea and some digestive biscuits in case you want to interview her.'

'Fingerprints?' Holmes inquired.

'None but Miss Preston's own,' Lestrade reported resignedly.

The envelope had been neatly sliced open and Holmes now carefully withdrew a single sheet of notepaper. He read it through once then offered it for my inspection. The message consisted of a short, typewritten rhyme:

An artist is Jack no less
Next to die is anybody's guess
Removed like a piece in chess
Killing tarts is the family business

This was followed by a signature in black ink, scrawled in crude, almost child-like capitals: *CRIMSON JACK*

'Lestrade, are you quite certain that no hint of this name has leaked out?' Holmes asked.

'It's been hushed up good and proper,' Lestrade assured us. 'Only a handful knows about it, all of them trusted men.'

'This too must remain confidential,' Holmes instructed, tapping the paper with his forefinger.

'You believe this is authentic then, Holmes?' I asked, handing the paper back to him.

He nodded slowly. 'The formation of the letters in the signature is broadly the same as that scrawled on a wall at both murder scenes, allowing for the difference in the materials used. Both were written by a man, and from the slope of the letters we can see that he was using his left hand.'

'A left-hander then?' said Lestrade, excited at any possible lead.

'No, a right-handed man using the left hand to cover up any semblance of his normal script.'

Lestrade gave a disappointed grunt. 'Well, that hardly narrows it down.'

Holmes examined the envelope and the letter, even to the extent of placing them beneath his nose and sniffing. 'Both the stationery and the ink are quite commonplace,' he concluded, 'and could be purchased in any one of a thousand outlets.'

Snatching up his magnifying glass from a nearby table, he began a closer examination of the letter. 'Of course, it may be possible to discern the exact model of typewriter by using the system recently developed by Ordway Hilton.'

'And who's he when he's at home?' Lestrade inquired.

'Ordway Hilton is the head of document analysis at the Chicago Police Scientific Crime Detection Laboratory,' Holmes replied without looking up. 'The size of typeface, the design of the lettering – whether monochrome, script or shaded – tells us much. This was definitely typed on a portable machine.'

'One easily concealed then,' I supposed.

'Further examination of the spacing of lines and characters leads me to believe that the model was an Aurora Speedline No. 3,' Holmes concluded, setting down the glass. 'Quite common. Of course, if we could find the individual machine itself, we could tie it to this letter by the slightly raised *e*, the sticky *s* and other distinctions.'

'Well, as Dr Watson points out,' said Lestrade, 'it will be easily hidden. We need something else to go on.'

'There's the rhyme itself,' I hazarded. 'The lack of punctuation would seem to indicate a poor education.'

'Not at all,' Holmes corrected me. 'It reveals a man who is aware that how he uses punctuation might be as incriminating as his handwriting. Barton-Finch's excellent book *The Styles of Punctuation in Notable English Authors* demonstrates quite clearly that, given enough examples, you can identify a man by his use of commas, colons and dashes almost as accurately as by his handwriting.'

I found myself perplexed. 'Well, what can we say about the sender of this message?'

'There is this,' said Holmes. 'Odd as these few brief lines are, they are unquestionably the product of a well-ordered mind.'

'Well-ordered?' snorted Lestrade. 'But he's a lunatic!'

'Observe that we are presented here with four compact lines, each consisting of precisely six words,' Holmes explained. 'Such regularity cannot be the result of pure chance, though it may be done unconsciously.'

He handed the letter over for my inspection and I counted the words.

'Six, six, six, and yes, six again.'

'Six-six-six? Here, isn't that something biblical?' wondered Lestrade.

'In the book of Revelation,' I recalled, 'six-six-six is the number of the Beast.'

'The number of the Beast!' Lestrade scowled. 'With an extra six thrown in for good measure. Here, do you suppose he's telling us he's some kind of devil worshipper?'

'If he worships anything at all,' said Holmes drily, 'it will be his own cleverness.'

'Well, leaving that aside,' said Lestrade, 'he's still given us some pointers to his identity.'

'Yes, I believe he has,' I agreed. 'But why would he do that, I wonder?'

'Why, to taunt us, doctor,' Lestrade answered. 'He's so cocksure we'll never catch him, he thinks it's funny to toss a few tidbits our way. We'll just see about that.' He jabbed a finger at the letter. 'For a start, this talk about tarts – that shows us his motive is a hatred of women.'

'As you say, he does reveal a few things about himself,' I agreed. 'We can guess that he sees himself as an artist, whether amateur or professional, perhaps a painter or a sculptor. Also that he plays chess, again either as a hobby or at the competitive level, and that he has applied that game-playing skill to the business of murder.'

'But don't you see, Watson,' Holmes objected, 'that these hints demonstrate a glaring inconsistency? He says that the next to die is anybody's guess, suggesting that the choice is a random one. And yet, on the other hand, he tells us that the victim is removed like a piece in chess. Now there is nothing random in chess, where each move is a carefully considered part of a larger strategy.'

'Yes. You're correct, of course.' I felt as though a fog of

uncertainty had closed around us again. 'So what are we to make of it, then?'

Lestrade leaned forward, the chair creaking beneath his shifting weight. 'I believe you gentlemen are missing the biggest clue of the lot,' he said. 'The blighter tells us in plain English that his family business is killing women. That can only mean he comes from a line of murderers . . . or that there is at least one other killer in the family.'

'Yes, yes, go on,' Holmes encouraged.

Lestrade's voice grew husky with the dramatic import of what he was about to say. 'Suppose he's telling us that he's a blood relative of the original Jack the Ripper.'

'That is an intriguing suggestion, Lestrade,' Holmes commented approvingly, 'most intriguing.'

'And yet hardly very helpful,' I reminded them both. 'We can scarcely follow up on this hint when the true identity of Jack the Ripper has remained a secret for decades.'

Holmes assumed a wounded air. 'You do me a disservice, Watson. Of course I know the true identity of Jack the Ripper.'

Holmes had surprised us many times over the years, but never before, I believe, had we both turned on him with such utter blank astonishment.

Lestrade's jaw went slack. 'Mr Holmes, are you seriously telling us that you've solved the Ripper murders?'

'Certainly,' said Holmes with complete aplomb. 'You will recall, Watson, that in April of 1931 I was suffering from a debilitating bout of ennui brought on by a lack of crime to provide me with the intellectual stimulation which is as vital to my well-being as the very air.'

'I can recall a number of such occasions,' I admitted, somewhat stiffly, 'though I confess I cannot assign dates to them all.'

Holmes pressed his long fingers together. 'Well, on that particular occasion, rather than resorting to those means of recreation of which you so heartily disapprove, I decided to apply myself to that long unsolved mystery.'

Rising to his feet, he stepped over to one of his bookshelves and lifted down a large folder tied shut with a red ribbon. Returning to his chair, he deposited it on the table in our midst. 'This folder,' he explained, 'contains all the relevant documents I was able to assemble: newspaper reports, police records, witness statements and all other materials with a bearing on the Whitechapel murders of 1888.'

Lestrade uttered an incredulous bleat. 'And you solved the case?'

'Of course,' Holmes affirmed, with no trace of modesty.

My own thoughts were reeling. 'And it did not occur to you, Holmes, to make public your discovery?'

'To what end?' Holmes seemed genuinely puzzled at the notion of courting publicity with this breakthrough. 'The murderer is long beyond the reach of human justice and there is no purpose to be served in causing distress to his surviving family.'

'Really, Holmes,' I pressed him, 'I appreciate your point, but surely in a matter like this . . . of such huge and enduring public interest . . . ?'

Holmes looked pained. 'You know, Watson, I'm beginning to suspect that what really irks you is that I did not turn over all of this to you,' he tapped the bulging folder, 'so that you could weave it into one of those overly romanticised tales your publishers are so fond of.'

'Really, Holmes,' I retorted, 'I will not grant so unworthy a suggestion even the dignity of a denial.'

'Mr Holmes,' Lestrade intervened almost humbly, 'whatever the rights of the public in this matter, might you see your way to sharing your findings with Dr Watson and myself?'

'Of course,' said Holmes with a fleeting smile. Untying the ribbon, he opened the folder and spread out the documents. 'A full account of my investigation would fill a large book, but for the sake of brevity I will confine myself to the essentials.'

PART TWO

INVESTIGATION

While from a proud tower in the town
Death looks gigantically down.

The City in the Sea

11

THE TRAIL OF THE RIPPER

By way of preamble, Holmes took his pipe from the pocket of his smoking jacket and filled it with tobacco. Lestrade fumed silently over the delay but held himself in check, as did I. We both knew from experience that Holmes would not be hurried.

When he got the pipe going to his satisfaction, Holmes sank back in his chair. Gazing into the middle distance, as though through a window in time, he commenced his disquisition.

'Let us briefly review the pertinent facts of the case. To begin with, all five victims were evidently prostitutes operating in the Whitechapel area of London. All of them except the last were in their forties. The victims were first strangled, then laid out flat before their throats were cut and various mutilations carried out.

'At twenty to four in the morning of August the thirty-first, a forty-three-year-old woman named Polly Nichols was found dead in a stable yard in Buck's Row. Her throat had been cut and her stomach incised in several places. The second victim, Annie Chapman, was aged forty-eight. Her body was discovered in the back yard of a house in Hanbury Street at around ten to six on the morning of September the eighth. Her throat was cut and her abdomen sliced open. Her intestines had been removed and placed above her right shoulder. Later examination revealed that the uterus had been removed also.'

Holmes's tone was one of clinical detachment, but below the surface of his composure I detected deep-seated stirrings of emotion. During the Great War both of us had seen our share of dead and mutilated corpses, but the brutal murder of helpless women held a special horror all of its own.

He paused to flip through his files in order to refresh his memory on particular points of detail. He then resumed in the same restrained manner.

'The third and fourth victims both died in the early hours of September the thirtieth; again, both were in their forties. Elizabeth Stride's body was found at one o'clock in the gateway to Dutfield's Yard. One hour later the Ripper claimed a second victim, Catherine Eddowes, who was found in Mitre Square. Both had their throats cut and the uterus and a kidney had been removed from Eddowes' body. It was surmised that the approach of passers-by had startled the killer and caused him to abandon his first victim without taking the time to mutilate her. Driven by his compulsion, he rapidly found another victim on whom to do his bloody work.'

Lestrade was hunched forward attentively, his inner tension visible in his tightly knotted fingers. Even for an officer of his experience, this litany of savage violence was difficult to listen to.

Holmes took a deep draw on his pipe and continued.

'Mary Jane Kelly, aged only twenty-five, was killed in the early hours of November the ninth in her lodgings at Miller's Court, though the body was not discovered until ten forty-five. She had been horribly mutilated. Her internal organs were scattered about the room but the heart was missing. Following this, the most barbaric murder of all, no more was heard of Jack the Ripper. That name the killer had given himself in a letter addressed to the authorities which was headed with the words *From Hell*.'

Even at a distance of more than fifty years it was still impossible not to be seized by a sense of disgust and outrage at the sheer foulness of these crimes. That the killer had evaded justice throughout the course of his rampage rendered it even more appalling.

'It certainly seems, Mr Holmes,' Lestrade commented, 'that behind the brutality lay a certain degree of medical knowledge, enough to single out particular organs.'

'But surely no doctor could have graduated from medical school and carried on a practice,' I objected, 'if he was so demented as to carry out these crimes. His diseased mentality would have revealed itself before he had become established.'

'Well reasoned, Watson,' said Holmes, 'and it was on that basis that a number of medical students were interviewed by the police. Their names are on record, although none of them was ever charged. One of them, however, was a certain Henry Carvel, whose circumstances I have studied very closely indeed.'

I nodded, encouraging Holmes to continue.

'Henry Carvel was born into a medical family. His father, August Carvel, was a doctor as was Henry's elder brother, Adrian Carvel. Henry, who was always closer to his mother than to either of them, went against family tradition and took employment as a Latin master at Chesterly Abbey School.

'During this time he married a local girl named Rosa Langland. She abandoned him after a few months, claiming that he had mistreated her. Reading between the lines, it appears likely that young Carvel suffered from impotence. He told people Rosa was a loose woman and had moved to London to become a prostitute. In fact, she emigrated to America and changed her name to Violet Paulson.'

I found myself fascinated, as ever, by the depth of Holmes's researches, and I saw that Lestrade was following the narrative with an attention as rapt as my own.

'Further misfortune followed,' Holmes went on, 'when he was dismissed from his post on the grounds of impropriety. It would be unhealthy to speculate what exactly so scandalised the school governors that they refused ever to discuss it. Carvel suffered a mental breakdown and spent some months in a sanitarium. When he recovered he saw his only recourse as taking up medicine in hope of winning his father's long withheld favour. And so he enrolled as a medical student at London College.'

'And did he succeed in his intent?' I asked.

Holmes shook his head. 'He was two years into his course when his father died. Henry's hopes of an inheritance large enough to support him were dashed when it transpired that August Carvel had left the bulk of his wealth and property to his two daughters, reasoning that this would make them an attractive match for potential suitors while his sons would have the means to support themselves by their own labours.'

'Very queer that is,' murmured Lestrade, 'but logical in its way, I suppose.'

'Adrian, the elder brother, was already a successful doctor and had moved to Edinburgh, leaving his now disused offices in London's east end to his younger brother, whom he expected to open a practice there once he had graduated. College records, however, show that Henry Carvel's tutors were dissatisfied with his poor progress and lack of attendance.

'Carvel's mother, who had a history of mental instability, now had a complete breakdown and was placed in Wolfenden Sanitarium in Bournemouth. Henry Carvel made a point of visiting her twice every month, even though staff noted that he always left visibly distressed. And here we come to a telling point.'

Holmes paused to relight his pipe. Lestrade and I exchanged an impatient grimace as we were forced to endure the delay.

'Each of the Ripper killings follows close upon a visit made by Carvel to his mother,' Holmes resumed at last. 'The records of Wolfenden Sanitarium are very exact in matters of dates and times. We can suppose that these visits, which so distressed him, stirred up buried resentment against the wife who abandoned him on account of his impotence, and against his sisters who inherited the bulk of what he thought to be his by right.

'I think we can safely surmise that he was seized by the deluded fantasy he had created of Rosa operating as a prostitute in the Whitechapel area and took vicarious revenge upon her by brutally slaughtering women who, because of their profession, were all too easy to lure into the shadows.'

'You say Carvel was interviewed by the police?' I interjected.

'Medical students, doctors, slaughtermen and many others passed through Scotland Yard,' said Holmes. 'Carvel, however, appeared to be a perfectly innocent young man from a respectable family with no history of violence. The police at the time had not the resources to delve so deeply into his personal history as I have done.'

'If these murders followed his visits to his mother,' Lestrade inquired with a scowl, 'then why were there no murders in October?'

'Ah, that is the most decisive point of all,' Holmes stabbed the air with the stem of his pipe for added emphasis. 'Records show that Carvel was hospitalised for the whole of that month with what is described as a severe brain fever. This followed upon the night of the double murder, which we can easily imagine left him in a state of extreme mental and physical exhaustion.

'It was noted that in his delirium he expressed a violent hatred for a number of named women, presumably the long gone Rosa and the two innocent sisters. He was released at the beginning of November and made the first of his regularly bi-monthly visits to his mother in Bournemouth. His sickness had now reached a climax and the murder of Mary Kelly was the most savage of all.'

'But, Holmes, what put an end to his killing spree,' I wondered, 'if the police did not catch up with him?'

Holmes steepled his fingers and related the final part of the tale in sombre tones. 'After this last murder, Carvel was reported as missing by the college authorities. Some weeks later a body was dragged from the Thames. It was badly decayed but identified as Henry Carvel by certain personal possessions. The pockets of his overcoat were filled with stones and it was clear that he had drowned himself, presumably as the only way to restrain himself from any further acts of depravity.'

'Then somewhere beneath the madness,' I speculated, 'there must have gleamed a small scintilla of conscience.'

'Perhaps,' said Holmes noncommittally.

'It still puzzles me, Mr Holmes,' said Lestrade, 'that he was able to elude capture for so long.'

Holmes allowed himself a grim smile. 'Ah, he had been using his brother's disused office in Whitechapel as a base from which to operate. The building appeared to be derelict and was never investigated. A year later, when it was sold off, knives and some items of bloodied clothing were found stored in a closet, but after all this time no one connected these with the Ripper killings. It was assumed that they were typical items to be found in a surgery where some simple operations might have been carried out on impoverished patients.'

I could only marvel at Holmes's orderly marshalling of the facts in a case so long shrouded in mystery. 'The evidence certainly appears decisive,' I complimented him.

'Additionally there are the statements of witnesses,' Holmes added, 'who claim to have seen the killer either before or after the fact. These testimonies are at times contradictory, but when we take them as a whole, a vaguely defined but solid figure emerges from the fog. He is of gentlemanly appearance, though his fine clothes show signs of wear and tear, indicating that he has fallen upon hard times and is declining into shabbiness.

'Assessments of his age fit a man in his late twenties who appears prematurely aged by drink, drugs or illness. The statement of police detective Stanley Walsh, published many years later in a magazine, confirms these details. His description of a man he saw in the region of Mitre Square shortly before the discovery of Catherine Eddowes' body makes a striking fit with this surviving photograph of young Carvel.'

Holmes plucked a photograph from the folder and passed it over to us. It showed a smooth-faced young man with mild, friendly eyes and a small, thin moustache. He was dressed in a blazer and cricket cap, and presented a stark contrast to the grotesque effigy we had seen at the Chamber of Wax.

Lestrade clapped himself on the knees. 'Well, if that don't beat all! Here's the finest brains in criminology scratching their heads over this for years and you've gone and solved it. And just for fun at that.'

'I do not regard the exercise of my deductive faculties as fun, Lestrade,' said Holmes, 'though I admit to enjoying the stimulation of tackling such a puzzle. Without a signed confession the case is as complete as it can be.'

I was struck by a sudden thought. 'Given that Carvel apparently destroyed himself out of guilt,' I suggested, 'do you suppose such a document might exist?'

'If it does,' said Holmes, 'it has never been made public.'

The beating rain casting a grey blur upon the windows muffled the rumble of the traffic beyond. I could almost fancy that this room had transported us back in time, as Mr Wells's time machine had carried its inventor forward. In my mind's eye I seemed to gaze upon the fog-bound Victorian streets with their gas lamps and hansom cabs, not ravaged by war, but poisoned by poverty, social unrest, and the atrocities of a faceless, knife-wielding devil.

My reverie was broken by the ringing of the doorbell and the sound of Mrs Hudson admitting a visitor.

'Who can that be?' I wondered as rapid footsteps ascended the stairs.

'There is only one person it can be, Watson,' Holmes stated with absolute confidence. 'We are about to make the acquaintance of Miss Abigail Preston.'

12

A MEETING WITH AN
AMERICAN LADY

Lestrade started up. 'Abigail Preston? Are you sure?'

'I heard a voice addressing Mrs Hudson in an American accent,' Holmes explained, 'and those footsteps on the stairs are undoubtedly a woman's.'

We all stood up as the door flew open and a lady swept into the room, followed by a flustered Mrs Hudson.

'Aha!' our visitor exclaimed. 'I thought so. The gang's all here.'

In all our years of entertaining clients in this room, she was one of the most striking women ever to cross the threshold of 221B Baker Street. Her honey-blonde hair was cut in a short bob and topped by a navy blue beret set with a silver pin in the shape of a sword. Her large grey eyes were wide set and seemed to take in the whole scene at a glance, while her nose was of that type commonly referred to as pert. Her wide, full-lipped mouth bespoke a forceful nature.

She was dressed in a grey jacket and pencil skirt which admirably outlined a figure that would have been the envy even of a younger woman. Her efficient low-heeled shoes still brought her close to my own height. All in all, she impressed me as a woman who had seen enough of the world to be hardened to its ways whilst being daunted by nothing.

'I'm sorry, Mr Holmes,' Mrs Hudson apologised. 'I asked the lady to wait and be announced, but . . .'

She fluttered her hands in a gesture of helplessness.

'That's quite all right, Mrs Hudson,' Holmes assured our landlady. 'I've been expecting Miss Abigail Preston.'

'Gail is fine,' said our visitor. 'Only my aunt Minnie calls me Abigail.'

Mrs Hudson departed, muttering to herself in a disgruntled Scottish burr.

Lestrade glowered blackly at the newcomer. 'How were you so sure she'd show up here?' he demanded of Holmes.

'I could tell at once that she had steamed open the letter before delivering it to Scotland Yard,' my friend explained, 'then stuck it down again.'

Miss Preston eyed him with impish interest. 'It was that obvious?'

'There were tell-tale dimples around the seal,' Holmes informed her, 'and the gum you used to stick it back down has an odour quite different from that used by the manufacturer of these manila envelopes. As a journalist, you recognised that there was more to this enigmatic message than the ravings of a crank and Scotland Yard's insistence on detaining you without discussing it only heightened your suspicions.'

'You got that right,' the American lady confirmed jauntily. 'I figured that while they were stalling me with tea and biscuits, the inspector was hot-footing it over to Baker Street to hob-nob with his old pal Sherlock Holmes, and there was no way I was going to be cut out of the action.' She added, 'I'd have been here a lot quicker, but most of the cabs were taken because of the rain.'

Lestrade drew himself up in a ponderous attempt at dignity. 'Miss Preston, I can assure you that I had an appointment already arranged with Mr Holmes – for a late lunch, in fact.'

'Don't try to soft-soap me, inspector,' Miss Preston scoffed. 'I can see the letter on the table there. So he calls himself Crimson Jack, eh? I'll bet you've seen that name before and it spooked you.'

'Does it mean anything to you, Miss Preston?' Holmes queried.

'Yes,' Lestrade interposed bullishly, 'it strikes me as mighty fishy, his making you his messenger girl.'

Gail Preston arched a scornful eyebrow. 'What, do you think he's my boyfriend? That's not exactly a love letter, you know.' She cast a glance about the room. 'Say, have you got anything to drink around here?'

It was a very forward request, coming as it did from an uninvited guest, but I retained my good manners. 'Perhaps I might offer you a sherry?'

Miss Preston planted herself on the settee and crossed her legs briskly. 'I was talking about something with hair on its chest.'

'We did bring a bottle of Glenlivet back with us from Scotland,' Holmes reminded me.

As I poured her a drink, she lit a cigarette and assessed Holmes as though he were a museum exhibit.

'So this is the great Sherlock Holmes. It's funny but you look a lot younger than I expected.'

Unsurprisingly, Holmes was gratified. 'I shall take that as a compliment. You are already acquainted with Inspector Lestrade. This is my good friend and associate Dr Watson.'

I handed the lady her glass of whisky. 'And I, Miss Preston, do I meet your expectations?'

'You, doc? You look just as I would have imagined – kind of solid and comfy, like an easy chair.'

I was aware of Holmes concealing a smirk beneath his hand and could not help feeling ruffled. It irked me that people generally assumed Holmes to be the younger of us two, when in fact he was three years my senior. This misattribution was due in part to the fact that he had retained the lean, athletic physique of his youth while I had acquired the somewhat more rounded contours typical of middle age. I also suspected, however, that Holmes had taken to dying his hair in order to remove any tell-tale streaks of grey. It served his vanity well that he was famously a master of disguise.

We pulled our chairs round to face the lady and sat down. In his hand Holmes held the note from Crimson Jack.

'Miss Preston, much as we appreciate your bringing us this letter,' he said, 'you must be aware that this is a private meeting and everything discussed here must remain absolutely confidential.'

Our visitor took an approving swallow of Glenlivet and gave him a steely look. 'If you're trying to throw me out, then you'd better think again. You need me here and you know it.'

'Really, miss, I must insist—' Lestrade began.

Miss Preston cut him off short. 'Look, this joker chose me to deliver his mail. There's got to be a reason for that, right? You don't know when he might contact me again by letter, phone or even in person.'

'In person?' I was appalled at the thought. 'Surely not!'

'So you need me on the inside,' Gail Preston concluded, 'not running loose on the outside, shooting my mouth off.'

Lestrade's cheeks flushed the colour of port wine. 'I'll be blowed if we'll have you spreading this letter all over town.'

'Or anything you've overheard here,' I added.

'Fine, I'll keep my mouth shut.' Gail Preston took a stiff draw on her cigarette. 'But only so long as I'm part of the team. Then at the end I'll have all the inside dope. It'll make a swell story, maybe even a book.'

Holmes had listened to her in silence, but now he spoke. 'Very well, Miss Preston, the points you make are valid.

We shall be delighted to add your undoubted talents to our resources.'

Lestrade subsided with a grumble, and while I might have liked to argue the point, I knew that Holmes had the right of it. If Crimson Jack had singled her out for his attention, we would do well to keep a close protective eye on Miss Preston.

Or Gail, as I soon came to call her.

'For now,' Holmes continued, 'can you think of anyone who might have sent you a letter like this?'

Gail let a wisp of smoke drift from her lips. 'If it was a gag, sure, I can think of a few clowns who might get their jollies this way. But you guys are taking it seriously and that's a whole different ball game. I can't think of anybody I know who would be skulking around with a knife pretending to be Jack the Ripper.'

A sudden thought occurred to me. 'A short while ago, Holmes, you drew our attention to certain inconsistencies in that letter. Might that not point to something deeper?'

Lestrade leaned towards me, his chin resting on his knuckles. 'How do you mean, doctor?'

'I mean that our man might be conflicted against himself to such an extent that he has a divided personality,' I replied. 'He may appear perfectly sane and respectable in his everyday life, yet another personality might inhabit the same body, one that is capable of these terrible acts.'

'I get you, doc,' said Gail. 'You mean like Dr Jekyll and Mr Hyde.'

'Like many people, Miss Preston, you misunderstand Stevenson's novel,' Holmes stated didactically. 'Edward Hyde is not a separate evil personality inhabiting the body of Henry Jekyll. He is merely Dr Jekyll stripped of all the moral constraints that normally govern civilised behaviour.'

'The bloke we're looking for certainly doesn't give a toss for civilised behaviour,' Lestrade commented ruefully.

'Well, assuming he hasn't just busted out of an asylum,' said Gail, 'he's out there somewhere living a normal life. How about we follow up some of the hints he's given us?'

'You mean look for an artist or a chess master?' said Lestrade.

'Well, it's either that or track down a grandson of the real Jack the Ripper,' said Gail. 'A bit of a long shot since nobody knows who he was and it's kind of late to pick up the trail. Hey, what are you smiling about?'

I took some pleasure in her puzzlement and briefly reiterated Holmes's identification of the Ripper.

'Pretty slick, Sherlock,' Gail complimented him. 'So do you have any candidates for our boy Crimson Jack?'

Holmes winced at the uninvited use of his first name and consulted his file. 'There is only one surviving member of the family who carries on the Carvel name. He is the son of Henry Carvel's elder brother Adrian. His name is Dr William Carvel.'

Lestrade's eyebrows shot up. 'A doctor!'

'He has a private practice in Hammersmith,' Holmes noted.

Lestrade perked up at this first scent of a quarry. 'Hammersmith, eh? I think I'll maybe pay him a visit.'

Holmes waved the suggestion away with a wag of his finger. 'Since we wish to avoid giving our friend Mr Deeds any more material for his lurid speculations, it would perhaps be best if Scotland Yard were not to be seen taking an interest in any relative of a possible Ripper suspect.'

'Don't you think a visit from Sherlock Holmes is just as likely to put this guy on his guard?' asked Gail.

'True,' Holmes conceded. 'Perhaps, Watson, you might pay a call on him?'

'Of course, Holmes,' I agreed at once.

'If you really want to get something out of him,' said Gail, 'you'd better let me come along too.'

'Do you really believe that your presence will render him more forthcoming?' said Holmes.

She drained the last of her whisky and tilted her head coquettishly. 'He's a man, isn't he?'

13

A CONVERSATION WITH AN
ENGLISH DOCTOR

So it was that I found myself the next day walking up the path to Dr Carvel's door with our unexpected new ally at my side. It was not the first time I had gone in Holmes's stead to interview a potential suspect and I flatter myself that I was quite capable of drawing out pertinent information and observing anything in my surroundings that might have a bearing on the case. It was a new experience, however, to be accompanied by a female companion on such a mission, and I felt obliged to give her some instruction in the proper conduct of our meeting.

'I shall talk to him medical man to medical man,' I said, closing the garden gate behind us, 'and you may take notes as you wish. Be alert for any evasions or discrepancies on his part.'

'Sorry, doc, that man to man routine won't wash,' Gail responded airily, 'not in a situation like this.' She stepped past me and looked back over her shoulder. 'You leave the talking to me and follow my lead.'

'My dear Miss Preston—'

'Listen.' She cut off my objections. 'I've charmed state secrets out of politicians and had bishops spill the beans to me about their love affairs. Trust me – I'll crack this guy like an Easter egg.'

'I really must insist that there is a certain procedure to be followed . . .' I protested.

But it was too late. She was already ringing the bell and I could hear someone coming to the door. When it opened we were faced with a tall, large-boned man with broad angular features topped by a mane of grizzled hair. Dark eyes peered suspiciously at us from below his heavy brow.

In the twinkling of an eye, my companion's manner underwent a startling transformation from brashness to gentility.

'Dr Carvel?' she inquired diffidently. 'Dr William Carvel?'

I was stunned to hear her adopt what sounded to me like an excessively theatrical English accent, but Carvel appeared quite taken in by it.

'I am he.' In spite of his imposing appearance, Carvel's voice was more of a creak than a rumble. 'I don't believe we are acquainted.'

Gail flashed her eyes at him demurely and made a self-deprecating gesture. 'My name is Edwina Caldwell. *Lady* Edwina Caldwell. Although,' she added bashfully, 'I really prefer not to use the title. People make such a fuss over it. But I expect you will know me better by my other name.'

'Other name?' Scepticism clouded the doctor's brow like a thunderhead. 'What would that be?'

Gail became girlishly conspiratorial, as though imparting a naughty secret. 'My *nom de plume* – Sylvia Swift, author of the Millicent DuMornay mysteries.' She pulled from her bag a green paperback bearing the title *The Mystery of the Silent Priory*, by Sylvia Swift.

'I do drag poor Millicent into the most hair-raising adventures. There's this' – she displayed the book in her hand – 'then there's *The Mystery of the Iron Falcon*, *The Mystery of the Five Windows*, *The Mystery of the Singing Legionnaire*, and so on and so on. Oh, if my father the duke ever got wind of my secret life as an author he'd probably disown me, and that would be just too, too awful.'

Dr Carvel turned his bewildered gaze to me. 'And this

gentleman would be?'

Gail gave a trill of laughter. 'Oh, this is my friend Johnny. He goes absolutely everywhere with me, don't you, Johnny?'

'Evidently,' I concurred stiffly. I could see I had no choice but to fall into line with her colourful imposture.

'He really is quite, quite invaluable,' Gail continued archly. 'However, I find myself in need of your assistance, Dr Carvel.'

Carvel knit his brow. 'Are you ill? These are not my surgery hours and I—'

'Oh, it's not a matter of illness,' Gail assured him. 'Although I *am* a little fatigued by the journey from Norfolk. Might I come in and trouble you for a glass of water?'

She put a hand to her head and swayed slightly as if on the brink of a swoon.

Picking up my cue, I took her by the arm with an expression of deep concern. 'We really must get her ladyship inside before she faints away,' I said, leading her past the doctor, who was now thoroughly nonplussed.

The entry hall beyond was decked out in sombre shades of scarlet. Off to our right, a half-opened door afforded me a glimpse of over-stuffed chairs grouped around a Dutch-tiled fireplace.

'I take it this is the lounge,' I said, and steered the wilting Gail in that direction.

Carvel had no choice but to close the outer door and follow us.

I guided Gail to a cushioned divan to the right of the hearth, then took the opportunity to appraise our surroundings.

We were in a comfortably furnished room, its bookcases filled with works on anatomy and military strategy. There were portraits on the walls of soberly dressed Hollanders with their plain, subservient wives and, above the fireplace, a painting of a ship of war executed in the style of Turner.

Carvel was hovering indecisively in the doorway.

'The water?' I prompted.

'Yes, of course,' he responded, and withdrew, presumably in the direction of the kitchen.

I bent over my companion and demanded in a whisper. 'Miss – Gail, what on earth are you doing?'

'Being charming and eccentric,' she answered with a mischievous smirk. 'Don't you English just lap up that kind of stuff?'

I was at a loss for an adequate rejoinder. Hearing Carvel's returning footsteps, I hastily perched myself on the other end of the divan. When he entered with a glass in his hand, I smiled apologetically. 'I hope we are not inconveniencing you.'

'No trouble,' Carvel muttered.

Gail took a tiny sip of water and batted her eyelashes. 'Thank you ever so much. I don't know what came over me. I do suddenly get these fainting spells, don't I, Johnny?'

'Frequently,' I confirmed.

During this exchange I noted a chess board on a table by the window. The arrangement of the pieces suggested a game in progress.

'You play chess, Dr Carvel,' I observed.

'Yes, I play once a week with a colleague of mine,' he responded. 'As you can see, we are halfway through a game. He is utilising what he calls the Montenegro Defence, but I have a strategy which will quite demolish it.'

He remained standing with his hands behind his back like an officer reviewing an unruly parade. 'I don't wish to be rude, but I must insist that you state your business. Briefly, if possible.'

'Oh, yes, of course.' Gail set the glass down and smiled engagingly at our host. 'You will be aware of an increasing trend in detective fiction towards extensive forensic detail.'

'I was not aware of that,' Carvel retorted. 'I am not a great reader of fiction.'

'Well, that is the direction things are moving in,' Gail continued. 'Nowadays the author is expected to have a compendious knowledge of chemistry, biology, anatomy and Lord knows what else. Honestly, it makes my head spin just to think of it.'

'I'm sure it must be very trying,' said Dr Carvel without sympathy.

I saw Gail start to reach into her bag for a cigarette then think better of it. Instead she folded her hands demurely in her lap.

'The fact is, Dr Carvel, I need your help. Without the guidance of a medical amanuensis it is certain that I, and consequently dear Millicent, will wander into a maze of errors whenever we touch upon matters of poison, autopsies and other such vital elements.'

Carvel appeared anything but gratified. 'That may be so, but I hardly think that I am the man you seek.'

'Oh but you are!' Gail leaned forward with an earnestness that would have touched the heart of a hanging judge. 'You were particularly recommended to me by – who was it again, Johnny?'

Rapidly I searched my memory and plucked out a name. 'I believe it was Sir Tolliver Smedley.'

'The eminent surgeon?' Carvel was impressed in spite of himself. 'I am not personally acquainted with him.'

'Oh, he speaks very highly of you,' Gail assured him breathlessly. 'In fact, he says you come from a family of distinguished physicians.'

Carvel's reserve was now melting to the extent that he sat down in an armchair and demurred gruffly. 'I would not go so far as that.'

'Was not your father consulted by the police when they were investigating those awful murders in Whitechapel?'

Carvel was immediately on his guard. 'You are referring to . . .'

'The Ripper killings,' I filled in for him.

'I am quite sure Scotland Yard never consulted my father.' Carvel drummed his fingers agitatedly on the arm of his chair. 'He was, in fact, living in Edinburgh at that time.'

'Oh, it wasn't your father then,' said Gail with a concentrated frown. 'It was an uncle, I believe, by the name of . . .'

She made a show once more of looking to me for assistance.

'Henry Carvel,' I provided.

Dr William Carvel stiffened at the name. In a tight voice he said, 'My uncle, as far as I am aware, never qualified as a doctor. In fact he died quite young.'

Gail put a shocked hand to her mouth. 'Oh, really? How tragic! What happened?'

Carvel's words grew shrill. 'Why would you think that I have any inside knowledge of his circumstances? He died before I was born and his unhappy life was not such as to gild the family annals.'

Gail made a soothing gesture. 'Of course, I quite understand. But it does put me in mind of something.'

'In mind of what exactly?' Carvel stared at her in the suspicious manner of a man faced with a species of poisonous insect.

'Well, I have recently been considering a change in direction, literarily, I mean.'

'Indeed.' The doctor folded his arms and exuded an almost palpable lack of interest.

'Yes, I thought I might try my hand at an historical novel,' Gail confided. 'My agent has in fact suggested a detective story set in Victorian times.' Gail paused to gauge Carvel's reaction but he maintained a stony silence.

'Yes, perhaps even based on some real case,' she continued, unfazed. 'Given your family history, I wondered if you might have some documents that might help me create a plot, atmosphere, characters.'

Carvel sprang upright. 'I have no such documents nor do I have any advice to offer you,' he stated frostily. 'And now I must ask you to leave. My time is valuable.'

'I quite understand,' I told him. Rising, I turned to Gail and said pointedly, 'We should be on our way, your ladyship. Don't you have a fête to open?'

The bite in my voice only brought a glint of amusement to her eye. Taking hold of my outstretched arm, she let me help her to her feet. 'You're quite right, Johnny. We've taken up enough of this charming gentleman's time.'

We were escorted out into the hall, and the doctor extended a hand in the direction of the front door.

To my embarrassment, Gail was not to be so easily ejected. She spotted a back stairway and drifted towards it. 'I don't suppose Mrs Carvel is at home?'

The doctor immediately blocked her way. 'My wife died some years ago in a boating accident,' he informed her brusquely.

'I sympathise,' I told him. 'I am a widower myself.'

'Then you will appreciate the impropriety of treading on so painful a subject,' said Carvel.

He escorted us to the front door, where Gail paused and treated him to a kittenish smile. 'So may I consult you from time to time upon medical matters?'

'I very much hope that you will not,' Carvel stated flatly. 'And now I bid you a good day.'

The door was closed behind us with some force.

Once we were beyond the view of the doctor's windows, I gave vent to my feelings.

'That was the most absurd imposture I have ever witnessed. And I do not appreciate being referred to as *Johnny*.'

'You don't think he might have recognised the name Dr John Watson,' Gail pointed out, 'and cottoned on to your connection with Sherlock Holmes? That would have spooked him worse than a visit from Scotland Yard. As far as he's concerned now you're just the sidekick of a screwy lady writer.'

'Lady writer!' I scoffed. 'What a lot of nonsense – and in that overblown accent.'

Gail chortled. 'I suppose your approach was going to be something like this.' She adopted the ridiculous manner of a dithering fogey and spoke in a waffling voice that was intended to be comic. 'I say, old chap, speaking as one medical man to another, were you aware that your poor old uncle was Jack the Ripper? And while we're on the subject, maybe you'd like to confess to being a murderer yourself.'

I regarded her with a cold stare. 'I'm quite sure I sound nothing like that.'

She slapped me playfully on the shoulder. 'Come on, doc, can't you take a little ribbing?'

She delved in her handbag for a cigarette, lit one and sucked in the smoke with obvious pleasure.

'I'm surprised you were able to restrain yourself from smoking during the entire charade,' I commented.

Gail shrugged. 'There were no ashtrays anywhere in that

mausoleum, so I figured he wouldn't appreciate my lighting up a Chesterfield.'

I decided to return our focus to the purpose of our visit. 'So what have we learned as a result of your impersonation?'

'Well,' Gail responded thoughtfully, 'he got real touchy at any mention of Jack the Ripper or his uncle. Also, it might be worth poking into exactly what happened to the late Mrs Carvel. There's a skeleton somewhere at the back of his closet that's rattling so loud it must be doing the Lindy Hop.'

'You're right about that,' I agreed. 'And when he thought neither of us was looking his gaze drifted briefly to the naval painting over the mantelpiece.'

Gail grinned. 'Say, that's pretty sharp. Sounds like you could give Millicent DuMornay a run for her money.'

'I am struggling to take that as a compliment.'

Gail patted the paperback in her bag. 'You know, whoever Sylvia Swift is, she spins a pretty good yarn. You should give them a try. So should your pal Sherlock. He might pick up a few tips from old Millicent.'

'I beg you never to suggest any such thing in his presence,' I cautioned her. I could only imagine the violence of Holmes's reaction to such a notion.

'I'll leave you to report back to Sherlock,' Gail said, flagging down a taxi. 'I've got other fish to fry.'

'Not red herrings, I hope?'

'I'm interviewing some lady munitions workers for my next broadcast, getting their stories to share with the folks back in the USA. You know, good human interest stuff.'

She gave me a parting wave as she ducked into the cab. 'I'll catch up with you later, Johnny – at the fête.'

When I arrived back at Baker Street, Mrs Hudson was handing Holmes a newly delivered note. When he had perused it, he settled into his chair and invited me to be seated while I related all that I had learned from our visit to Dr Carvel.

He listened in concentrated silence, interrupting only rarely to clarify a particular point. As a skilled actor himself, he was amused by my disapproving account of Gail Preston's performance.

'Really, Watson, I believe you are taking more of a liking to that lady than you care to admit.'

'That note you have there, Holmes,' I said, pointedly changing the subject, 'does it have a bearing on the case?'

'It may, old fellow, it may.' He picked it up and glanced over it once more. 'This is a summons to Whitehall. It appears we are to have a meeting with the government.'

I at once understood that by *the government* he was referring to his brother, Mycroft Holmes.

14

A TALE OF TWO BROTHERS

The following morning we presented ourselves outside Admiralty House at the appointed time. The building was bolstered with a wall of sandbags and surrounded by barbed wire, while the windows were taped over to secure them against the concussion of any nearby explosions. There was a visible police presence, and from the uppermost floor security officers at the windows kept a close watch on the street below.

We identified ourselves and were escorted upstairs to a waiting area littered with magazines and newspapers. I sat down and absently fingered this week's copy of the *Radio Times* while Holmes paced impatiently between the door and the bay window.

'This can only be in connection with our current investigation,' he surmised, 'though it is not like Mycroft to involve himself in the affairs of Scotland Yard. I can only assume that these crimes have prompted unsettling questions in government circles.'

When preparing me for my first meeting with his august brother many years ago, Holmes had explained that Mycroft possessed a finely honed intelligence and deductive acumen the equal of his own, but lacked the inclination to pursue matters actively in his own person. Instead he preferred to surround himself with the warmth and comforts of a well-appointed club while others came to him with reports and information on which to exercise his unsurpassed powers of reasoning.

His Majesty's Government had decided to make use of

his gifts by appointing him to a post which was only vaguely defined but consisted in being passed all information relating to matters financial, industrial, economic, and military. Mycroft would ponder these diverse data and draw conclusions upon which government policy would be based as unshakably as on a foundation of solid marble.

'In effect,' Holmes had told me then, 'Mycroft *is* the government.'

After a short wait we were escorted to a large office looking out upon St James's Park. Shelves of reference books and filing cases filled with civil service reports surrounded us. A large photograph of King George and Queen Elizabeth hung on the wall opposite the door. I noticed that it had been personally signed by both of Their Majesties.

The imposingly corpulent figure of Mycroft Holmes rose laboriously to greet us from behind the well-ordered expanse of his desk. The capacious, velvet-covered chair with its silk cushions was the one that had for years occupied the place of honour directly in front of the fireplace in the rigidly enforced silence of the Diogenes Club members' lounge.

There still hung about him an air of heavy melancholy over the fate of the Diogenes Club, that refuge of privileged and prominent misanthropes, which was the only place where he had felt entirely comfortable. During the Blitz, the building had been so badly damaged by German bombing that the reclusive members were flushed out into the sunlight and forced to commingle with their fellow man.

Mycroft emerged from behind his desk like a galleon leaving harbour, and, steering his way past an oakwood table spread with an array of daily newspapers, advanced towards us.

'Dr Watson.' He acknowledged me with a small bow, which for him required considerable effort, and then turned to his brother. 'Sherlock, you are keeping busy, I hear.'

'Not so busy as you, I'm sure,' Holmes responded.

Mycroft inclined his massive head. 'Yes, the war. But of course, there is never a ceasefire from crime. I assume you have been following the Appleby case.'

'Yes. It was murder, of course.'

'And the identity of the murderer quite obvious.'

'Gentlemen,' I interrupted, 'I too have been following that case with some interest, and the police have concluded that it was suicide. It says so in today's *Times*, which covers the affair in some detail.'

I pointed to the day's edition, which was prominent among the newspapers on display.

'Really, doctor?' Mycroft raised a sardonic eyebrow. 'Perhaps you would care to reacquaint us with the facts as recorded there so that we may reassess our verdict.'

I fetched *The Times* and, opening it to the Appleby story, summarised the details out loud.

'According to this article, Sir Arthur Appleby had for many years lived at Harrower's Lodge in Strood, Kent, with his younger brother Hugh, both of them bachelors. The only other resident was the butler, a former military man named Poole. For some weeks, according to his testimony, Hugh Appleby had noted that his elder brother was increasingly depressed, apparently troubled by some unspecified financial difficulty.

'On the afternoon of the seventeenth, the Thursday of this past week, matters came to a head. While Poole the butler was out purchasing groceries for the weekend, Sir Arthur uttered an exclamation along the lines of "It's all up! I'm done with it!" With those words he shut himself in the upstairs study. Hugh knocked repeatedly on the door, encouraging Sir Arthur to unburden himself, but there was no response. When he tried the door he found it was locked with a key from the inside.'

I paused to gauge the reaction of my listeners. Both of them appeared quite impassive, as if this evidence in no way dented their murder theory.

'Knowing that the reliable Poole had in his possession a spare set of keys for every lock in the house,' I continued, 'Hugh awaited the butler's return with some anxiety. He prowled about, taking a drink to calm his nerves, and when Poole entered the house he found the younger brother in a state of extreme agitation, so much so that he was actually spilling his drink.'

This detail prompted an amused snort from Holmes. Ignoring this, I pressed on.

'Doing his best to calm the younger man, the stalwart Poole attempted to unlock the study door but was frustrated by the key still in the lock on the other side. Putting his broad shoulders to good use, the butler broke down the door to be greeted by a shocking sight. Sir Arthur lay dead on the floor, blood flowing from a stab wound to the chest. A quick search of the room turned up a bloodied letter opener lying under a nearby chair. On later examination the dead man's fingerprints were found on the hilt and no other prints. Have I got it right so far?' I challenged the brothers Holmes.

'I can find no fault in your summation,' Sherlock Holmes commented drily.

'Please go on, doctor,' Mycroft encouraged.

'The window, like the door, had been secured from the inside and there was no other means of entry or exit,' I continued, with growing confidence in the official verdict. 'It was concluded that, while in an unbalanced state of mind, Sir Arthur committed suicide by stabbing himself in the chest. In a last moment of lucidity he pulled the fateful weapon from his chest and flung it aside in horror. He then fell dead, insensible to the noise of his brother beating on the door.'

I became aware that both Holmes brothers were gazing at me with an expression that bordered on condescension.

'You see,' I declared with conviction, 'there was no way for anyone else to have entered and left the room and there was no one else present there. It simply must be suicide.'

'And yet it is not,' said Mycroft.

'It is murder,' said Holmes.

With a supreme effort of will, I did my best to remain civil. 'I suppose, Holmes, you're going to tell me the murderer was hiding behind the door disguised as a soldier.'

Mycroft eyed me with concern. 'What an extraordinary suggestion! I fear, doctor, that Sherlock has been overtaxing you of late.'

'Watson alludes to a matter we recently investigated in Scotland,' Holmes explained, 'but really this is quite different.'

'Or perhaps you will say that the butler did it,' I said. 'That he somehow used his spare key to lock the door after murdering his master, in spite of the fact that there was a key inserted from the inside.'

Mycroft tutted like a disapproving schoolmaster. 'Really, doctor, we must deal in facts not fancies.'

'What motive could the estimable Poole have for murdering his master?' Holmes queried. 'Let alone then to contrive to lock him in his study before calmly setting out for a spot of grocery shopping.'

'As a medical man,' said Mycroft, 'would you not consider stabbing oneself in the chest to be an unlikely means of self-immolation? Sir Arthur had been in the military, after all, and must certainly have possessed a pistol.'

'And, as an active participant in the annual grouse shoot, he would also have a shotgun in his possession,' added Holmes. 'Either one of those would have served his purpose better if he seriously proposed to do away with himself. And bear in mind that we only have Hugh Appleby's word for it that his brother was in any way melancholic. There is no medical testimony to that effect.'

'Are you saying then that the younger brother is the killer?'

'Of course,' said Mycroft. 'Why else do you think that Poole found him in such an agitated state that he was spilling his drink?'

'What on earth has spilling his drink got to do with it?' I demanded.

'I think we can safely assume that his drink of choice was red wine,' said Holmes, 'or a dark sherry, and that he spilled it on the carpet outside the study door.'

'In order to cover the blood stains,' Mycroft concluded.

'You mean that Sir Arthur was stabbed outside the study rather than inside?' I was beginning to see where Holmes's logic was leading.

'Let us suppose,' said Mycroft, 'that while Poole was absent, Sir Arthur fetched the mail from downstairs and was opening it on the way to his study. He encountered his younger brother and an argument ensued.'

'Over money, most likely, or perhaps a woman,' Holmes speculated. 'The dispute became violent and whether deliberately or no, Hugh Appleby stabbed his brother in the chest with his own letter opener. Sir Arthur pulled himself free of the blade and staggered into the study, locking himself inside to escape further assault.'

'But it was already too late,' said Mycroft. 'The wound

was fatal and he expired within seconds. When there was no response to his hammering on the door, Hugh guessed that his brother was dead, but circumstances had offered him a trick card. If his brother Sir Arthur was found dead and alone in the locked room, the verdict would probably be suicide, but only if the instrument of his death was found there too. That instrument, unfortunately, he still gripped in his own hand.'

'He might have broken in himself and dropped the letter opener beside the body,' I suggested.

'Bear in mind, Watson, that he stood to inherit the house and the family fortune,' Holmes pointed out. 'Under the circumstances you describe suspicion would inevitably fall upon him. No, it was vital that the door remain locked until a witness should arrive in the shape of Poole. Poole it was who broke open the door and rushed at once to his stricken master.'

'He paid no attention to Hugh Appleby,' said Mycroft, 'who came in behind him. It was child's play for Hugh to drop the bloodied letter opener under a chair then draw Poole's attention to it, knowing the butler would assume it had been lying there the whole time.'

'But the fingerprints,' I objected.

'When Poole left to call the police,' said Holmes, 'Hugh took the opportunity to press the hilt into the hand of his dead brother to leave a clear set of prints before returning it to its place under the chair.'

I gazed back and forth between the two of them, exasperated to hear them treating this as some sort of game, a continuation of the competitions of their childhood.

'I don't suppose either one of you has seen fit to inform the Kentish constabulary of your conclusions?' I inquired.

'I seek no plaudits from the police,' Mycroft sniffed.

'I also see no advantage to having my name entangled in so simple a matter,' said Holmes.

'I suppose then that it is incumbent upon me to see that justice is served,' I concluded testily.

'Yes, once we are done here, doctor, do inform the police of the true state of affairs,' said Mycroft.

'If they examine the area of the carpet where Hugh Appleby quite deliberately spilled his drink,' said Holmes, 'they will still be able to detect a blood residue. We can assume that he had the letter opener in his pocket, but even if it was wrapped in a kerchief or rag, enough blood would have seeped through to his clothing to be detected by chemical analysis.'

'I shall be sure to so direct the police.' I tossed the newspaper on to a nearby chair in a gesture of disgust. It seemed that when both brothers were in a room together, everything else paled into insignificance beside their lifelong rivalry.

Recovering my composure, I turned to Mycroft. 'Perhaps, now that the pair of you have disposed of the Appleby case, we can proceed to the business for which you summoned us here.'

'You are quite correct, doctor,' he responded, not in the least chastened. 'Sherlock, it is time we had a serious talk about your mysterious friend Crimson Jack.'

15

MATTERS OF LIGHT AND DARKNESS

'I have just come from a meeting of the Intelligence Inner Council,' Mycroft Holmes continued.

'Yes, I thought I detected the symptoms of fatigue,' said Holmes.

'These meetings, while tedious, are necessary,' Mycroft retorted, 'but they do not normally involve a discussion of crime and its ramifications as regards our national security. Which brings me to the business of this so-called new Ripper.'

'The fact that the coincidence of dates and methods has become a matter of frenzied interest to the public is most unfortunate,' said Holmes.

'I do not believe you appreciate the full ramifications,' Mycroft opined caustically. 'Why, just this morning the Prime Minister was forced to grant an audience to that bulwark of moral rectitude Sir Carlton Jessop.'

'The chairman of the Committee for Public Decency?' I said.

'The same. He informed the PM that these murders of women are the product of the government's own moral laxity and their failure to cleanse our streets of prostitution. So you see, we are assailed on all sides, as if winning the war were not burden enough.'

He took two slow steps to where a copy of the *London Bulletin* lay on the newspaper table and treated it to a contemptuous sneer. With nimble fingers he whipped it open to the offending page.

'Have you read the column paradoxically entitled *Deeds*

Not Words?'

'I am familiar with the author,' Holmes acknowledged with distaste.

'See the headline for today – TURN ON THE LIGHTS! This is only one of many strident voices calling for a relaxation of the blackout in order to deny this monster the cover of darkness.'

I was shocked that any Londoner should demand anything so rash. 'But without the blackout, London would be an easy target for night-time bombing raids.'

Mycroft returned to his desk and lowered himself into his chair with the ponderous dignity of a Manchu emperor assuming the throne. 'The fact that there has been no major air raid on London for some months,' he said, 'has led to a certain complacency which might prove disastrous if this campaign continues. Even one night with the streets lit might enable the Luftwaffe to target our most important institutions and deliver a ruinous blow.'

He waved to us to be seated in the chairs set out in front of his desk. Once we were settled, Holmes eyed his brother hawkishly. 'Are you suggesting that is the actual intent behind the murders?'

'I am suggesting that whatever the intent, this is one of the more troubling results,' answered Mycroft. 'The effect on public morale is serious enough, but this . . .' He gestured towards the offensive newspaper before swallowing his outrage and turning upon his brother. 'How close are you to cornering this beast?'

'There are lines of inquiry being pursued,' Holmes returned.

'There are always lines of inquiry being pursued,' said Mycroft acidly. 'That is the sort of stock answer I expect from Scotland Yard, not from you, dear brother.'

'I assume you know about the letter,' said Holmes.

'A copy of that ill-constructed doggerel was forwarded to me as a matter of course. However many suspects there may be, I believe we can safely cross Messrs Eliot and Auden from the list. I take it there is no question as to its authenticity?'

'It is authentic,' Holmes affirmed. 'It points us in several directions, some of which may be worth following.'

'You are aware, of course, of the hidden acrostic?' Mycroft raised an interrogative eyebrow.

'Of course,' said Holmes with a barely perceptible nod.

'An acrostic?' I repeated, irked that my friend had not seen fit to mention this to me. 'I know that you are referring to a poem in which the first letter of each line spells out a word or a name, but that is not so in this case.'

'Is it not?' Mycroft responded.

As I had the four lines memorised, it was no great task to spell out the initial letter of each. 'A-N-R-K. It is quite meaningless.'

'I did make a point of referring to it as a *hidden* acrostic,' Mycroft reminded me.

'Yes,' said Holmes. 'You must read it this way, Watson – take the first two letters as a single word then read out the whole. An-R-K. It is homophonous with the word *anarchy*.'

'Quite correct,' said Mycroft. 'I think it no coincidence. No, these brutal murders, specifically fashioned to invoke the memory of the most feared killer London has ever known, may be part of a larger plot to provoke terror and panic and so ultimately bring chaos to the streets of London.'

'Surely you exaggerate,' I protested. 'Our people have held firm through the worst the Germans have thrown at them. The resilience of the Londoner has become almost a byword for courage.'

'A large proportion of Herr Hitler's success thus far can be attributed to his skilful use of propaganda to inspire his own people and demoralise his enemies,' Mycroft pointed out.

'It is difficult to believe, however,' said Holmes, 'that he is quite so devious as to somehow engineer the return of a legendary murderer in order to bring terror to our streets.'

'Yet that aspect of the affair cannot be entirely discounted,' Mycroft persisted. 'If the people should become more afraid of the dark than they are of the enemy's bombs, well, the hazards are only too obvious.'

His heavy-lidded eyes fixed upon Holmes with a hint of remonstration.

'You cannot doubt that I am already applying myself to the problem with the utmost vigour,' said Holmes.

'That goes without saying,' Mycroft conceded, 'but a little further help would not go amiss, surely.'

'I believe our resources are quite adequate to the task,' I asserted, bristling at any implication of incompetence on our part.

'As Watson says,' Holmes confirmed, 'we already have Scotland Yard and one or two other useful persons at our disposal.'

Mycroft affected a dismissive wave. 'I suppose you are referring to that reformed urchin Wiggins and the American woman Preston. No, no, with matters of national security at stake I must insist on assigning one of my own operatives to your little band.'

Holmes's jaw tightened visibly. 'I require no bureaucratic interference to spur me on.'

'I assure you this man is no bureaucrat.' Even as Mycroft spoke, there came a firm knock upon the door. 'That will be him now. Do come in, Commander Rayner!'

I recognised the name at once as that of an officer we had become briefly acquainted with the previous year when Mycroft had brought us in to help expose a Nazi espionage ring. Holmes and I rose to greet him as the door opened, but Mycroft took full advantage of his superior authority to remain comfortably seated.

In spite of his rank, Commander Philip Rayner entered in civilian garb: a single-breasted grey suit, an Oxford Blue tie and custom-made black shoes. He was a good-looking chap with sharp intelligent features. Even though, as I knew, he was long returned from service abroad, his complexion still retained its darker hue from lengthy exposure to the tropical sun.

'Mr Holmes, Dr Watson.' He acknowledged us with a short military bow. 'It's a pleasure to be working with you again.'

'You will recall Rayner's instrumental role in the Vosperian affair,' Mycroft reminded us. 'All your efforts at tracking down that particular nest of vipers would have been in vain if Vosperian had succeeded in escaping.'

'Yes, we can be grateful that Commander Rayner is such a crack shot,' Holmes admitted.

'I just did the mopping up,' said Rayner. 'It was Mr Holmes who discovered the clues that led us to the secret rendezvous.'

'You yourself took a bullet in the arm, Rayner,' I recalled. 'All healed up now?'

'Couldn't be better,' Rayner answered cheerfully. 'Though I doubt my bowling will be quite so devastating in future. Bit of a blow for the department's cricket eleven.'

'Your field is military intelligence, Rayner,' said Holmes tightly. 'This is still, I believe, a criminal investigation.'

'As I have already made clear,' said Mycroft with forced

patience, 'there are security implications that cannot be ignored. It would be remiss of either of us to neglect that aspect of the matter. It would in fact smack of incompetence.'

'I'm sorry if my presence feels like an imposition, Mr Holmes,' said Rayner affably. 'I'll do my best to stay in the background and let you carry on with your work unimpeded.'

I felt that I should make some amends for Holmes's coldness. 'Not at all, commander. I'm quite sure you will make a significant contribution to our efforts.'

'No doubt,' said Holmes. With some reluctance he added, 'Welcome aboard, Rayner.'

Mycroft clapped his hands together to indicate that the whole matter was now amicably concluded. 'Now, commander, you should go and finish filing your report on that Westonbury business. Report to Mr Holmes first thing tomorrow.'

'I look forward to it.' Rayner gave a small farewell bow, and departed.

We sat down as the door closed and I saw Mycroft gazing at us with satisfaction.

'As you know,' he said, 'Rayner spent many years abroad, carrying out the most delicate and hazardous missions. It was only the threat of war that compelled us to summon him back to London to bring his skills to bear in the interests of protecting the homeland.'

'He's certainly done that,' I concurred.

'What you may not be aware of,' said Mycroft, 'is that both his parents and his sister – his whole family – were lost with the *Lusitania* when the Germans sank her in 1915. I know of no man more dedicated to the defeat of Germany.'

'We are tracking down a murderer,' said Holmes, 'not planning a commando raid on Berlin.'

'If this killer of yours should turn out to be a mere lunatic,' said Mycroft, 'all well and good. But I suspect that we did not manage to eliminate all of Vosperian's organisation. If the man you seek is carrying on that work by other means, then it is not justice we seek but elimination.'

Holmes stiffened. 'We are not executioners.'

A hard gleam flashed in Mycroft's normally lazy eyes. 'Has that always been your opinion?'

I felt an unprecedented tension charge the air between the two brothers, as if something unspoken had passed between them that I could not even guess at. Did it concern some incident in their youth – of which I had heard very little – or was Mycroft alluding to more recent events? I could almost fancy that, if I were rash enough to intervene, the very air itself might shatter.

Holmes broke the brittle silence. 'We shall do our duty, you may be assured of that.' Rising to his feet, he turned to me. 'Come, Watson, we have much to do.'

Mycroft did not raise his voice but his words carried clearly as we walked out of the door. 'If you will not conclude the matter in the best interests of the country, Sherlock, be aware that Rayner has his orders.'

'I am quite sure of that,' Holmes retorted. 'You excel at giving orders.'

As we walked down the stairs in silence, I was aware that some cloud hung over my friend, and that something in his past, still hidden from my sight, had returned to haunt him.

16

THE TORN PAINTING

My next direct involvement in the case came a few day later when I went calling once more in company with Gail Preston. This time we were to visit an artist by the name of Damon Sardinas.

'This painter chap, Sardinas,' Lestrade informed us, 'we had him in a few weeks ago. One of his models claimed he came after her with a knife. Chased her out into the street, so he did.'

'And no charges were brought?' I asked in some surprise.

'It seems these sorts of rows are pretty common among your arty types,' Lestrade sniffed, 'and nothing came of it. He paid her a few extra quid and the matter was dropped.' His eyebrows elevated knowingly. 'Sounds as if he's worth a visit, though. Artist – knife – hot temper.'

'A job for you, Watson, I think,' said Holmes. 'And I suggest you take Miss Preston along with you.'

'Really?' I could not help but be suspicious of his motives.

'It will afford you the opportunity to observe his reaction to a woman,' Holmes explained.

'Yes, of course. Very logical, I'm sure,' I conceded. 'I'll phone Miss Preston and see if she's available.'

Sardinas' studio occupied the top floor of a tenement in Bloomsbury. While Gail and I were mounting the stairs, I experienced a pang of apprehension. As we climbed the last few steps I said, 'I hope you're not going to pass yourself off as another overly mannered English aristocrat.'

'Relax, doc,' she chuckled. 'I've got it covered. Here, grab hold of this.'

She handed me a box camera and rang the doorbell.

The door was opened by a tall man with a thick, squat body perched atop long, thin legs, like some ungainly species of waterfowl. He was wearing a loose artist's smock streaked with shades of red like a butcher's apron and brandished a long-handled sable brush coated in a lurid shade of pink. There was a foreign cast to his dusky, mustachioed features suggestive of the Eastern Mediterranean, and his small black eyes surveyed us with displeasure.

Gail flashed a dazzling smile. 'Mr Sardinas?'

'The same,' he responded testily and wagged the brush at us. 'Why do you interrupt my work?'

'My name is Gail Preston and I'm a reporter for the American National Broadcasting Company,' Gail introduced herself brightly. 'I'm doing a feature on British artists for next week's broadcast – you know, how they're doing their bit for the war effort and helping to boost the public morale.'

I watched the prospect of his name's being spread across the airwaves of America overcome Sardinas' initial hostility. 'And you have come to interview me?' His voice was now as oily as his hair.

'That's right,' said Gail. 'So how about it – can we come in?'

Sardinas stepped aside to admit us. 'And who is this who accompanies you?' His voice was prickly with suspicion.

'Oh, this is just Johnny,' said Gail, 'my photographer. You know, I want to get some shots of your paintings so I can describe them on air.'

Sardinas yanked the camera from my grasp as we stepped through the doorway. 'No, no, no, I can't permit photographs. If people wish to see my work, they must come to the show I am planning for the end of the month.

I will not have my art reduced to a few grainy black and white snapshots.'

Much as I disliked his manner, I was relieved not to have to act the role of a professional photographer.

'I quite understand,' said Gail as he led us down a short hallway. 'Rembrandt would have felt the same way, I'm sure.'

We passed through a bead curtain into the studio beyond where Sardinas set the camera aside on a wicker chair. I was somewhat taken aback as I gazed around me at the paintings illuminated by the overhead skylight. It was difficult to see how Sardinas' work would boost the morale of the public or anyone else.

'These look . . .' I searched for a word, 'distressing.'

Sardinas appeared gratified. 'Exactly right!' he exclaimed. 'You have an eye for art, I see.'

'Well, he is a photographer,' said Gail with only the barest trace of a smirk.

'You recognise the subject matter, of course.' From Sardinas this was more of a challenge than an assumption.

I walked from canvas to canvas, noting the similarity of theme. Each depicted an attractive young woman in a classical Greco-Roman robe that was disordered and torn. Every one of them was either sinking to the ground in an ecstasy of terror or attempting to scramble away. Their hands were either thrust out before them in a defensive posture or pressed modestly to their partially bared breasts. Beneath dishevelled hair their faces were contorted into extremes of fear and horror.

'They are classical figures,' I opined. 'Perhaps Vestal Virgins?'

Sardinas snorted. 'Have you never heard of the Sabines?'

Unexpectedly, Gail interjected, 'Romulus and his brother

Remus kidnapped a bunch of women from their neighbours, the Sabines, so they could use them to populate their new city of Rome. Right?'

'Correct.' Sardinas sounded pleasantly surprised. 'It is a mythological prototype of the fundamental relationship between men and women, one of dominance and submission.'

I felt compelled not to appear an ignoramus. 'The so-called Rape of the Sabines has been represented by many artists, has it not?'

'In the past unimaginative daubers such as Rubens and Poussin have always represented them as a group,' said Sardinas, 'as did Degas and David. My bold innovation is to present them afresh in a series of striking individual portraits.'

'They are certainly *striking*,' I agreed drily.

'Each illustrates a stage in the tale,' Sardinas explained gesturing at the paintings. 'From their youthful innocence to the horror of their abduction, their initial fear, the awakening of sexuality, then sensuous pleasure leading to acceptance and fulfilment.'

'You've definitely cooked up an angle that'll make a splash,' said Gail, taking a pack of Chesterfields from her bag. 'Is it okay if I smoke?'

'Normally I would object,' said Sardinas, narrowing his eyes at her, 'but I'm intrigued by the shape of your mouth. I'd like to see you put something in it.'

'Sure you would,' said Gail. She slipped a cigarette between her lips and lit it. 'Is there some place we could sit down? I'd like to take some notes.'

Sardinas gestured to an ugly piece of furniture padded in gold brocade. 'Might I suggest the divan? My models tell me it is *very* comfortable.'

Leaving Gail to beguile the artist, I took the opportunity

to explore the studio unnoticed. The only reading material was books of mythology, copies of *Art Alive* magazine and a pamphlet entitled *A Futurist Manifesto*. I could hear Gail encouraging Sardinas to speak of his ambitions for the future, a topic he was happy to elaborate on at length.

Drifting past various work tables, I noted the paints, brushes, solvents, palettes, and stacks of blank canvases. Also the selection of craft knives, scrapers, and other potentially harmful items. Taking care not to draw attention to myself, I sidled over to where a row of canvases were shrouded in white sheets to conceal them from view. Here I thought to find some evidence of Sardinas' obsessions that would link him to the crimes.

Casually I took a corner of one sheet between thumb and forefinger and lifted it slowly. As the painting beneath was revealed, I held my breath in anticipation of being met by the face of one of Crimson Jack's victims. But no such revelation was granted me. Instead there was an incomplete painting, the body in the expected attitude of fear, the face only a vague outline devoid of feature.

I was startled from contemplation of the faceless woman by an angry exclamation from Sardinas. He strode towards me and slapped my hand away, causing the cover to drop back into place. 'I did not give you permission to view this work!' he stormed.

His dusky face was suffused with passion, like that of a spoiled child throwing a tantrum. I decided my best course was to play the penitent.

'I'm dreadfully sorry, old man. I couldn't help being curious. Your other paintings are so fascinating.'

Gail took my arm and tugged me away. 'Johnny, I've told you before not to go sticking your nose where it's not wanted.'

'You should choose your companions more carefully,' Sardinas advised her haughtily.

Gail blew a cloud of smoke in his direction and he sniffed at it as though it were perfume.

'Look, it's probably a gag,' she said off-handedly, 'but I'm pretty sure somebody told me you went after one of your models with a knife and chased her out into the street.'

Sardinas scoffed so hard I was afraid he might choke on his own disdain. 'I needed that stupid girl to show me real fear, not in some wooden melodramatic pose, but through her face, her eyes. I wanted the very quaking of her heart to be visible.'

'And she refused to cooperate?' I guessed.

'No more than a block of wood refuses to sing. For all her outward beauty, within she was merely an empty shell, happy to bare her body for a guinea or two, but with a soul as inert as granite. I had to present her with a mortal threat to stir any emotion out of her at all.'

'Well, you're a man of action, that's for sure,' said Gail. She took a step closer to him, as though drawing him into a mischievous conspiracy. 'I don't suppose you've got a picture of her?'

An expression of malicious amusement lit Sardinas' dusky features. 'I do indeed.'

He stalked over to one of the concealed paintings and whipped the sheet aside with a sneering flourish. The canvas beneath had been viciously slashed into pieces so that it was hardly possible to discern a human form among the hanging tatters.

'Would I wish anyone to witness such a failure?' Sardinas struck a dramatic pose. 'No! This is her monument – this nothingness.'

I'd had about as much as I could take of his insufferable

ego, and I sensed that Gail felt the same way.

'Well, this has been a real eye-opener,' she said, retrieving the camera and handing it to me. 'I can't wait to share it with my listeners.'

'It has been an unexpected stimulus for me too,' said Sardinas. 'I don't suppose you would consider sitting for me? I would make it worth your while. There's something suggestively Etruscan about your features.'

'Etruscan, eh? That's a new one.' Gail started for the door. 'I'm flattered, of course, but I find it hard to sit still for more than a minute at a time. I'd probably drive you crazy.'

'I expect you would.' Sardinas did not sound at all displeased at the prospect. 'I am quite sure you would.'

Once we were safely back downstairs, Gail glanced over at me. 'So what do you think, doc? Is he nuts?'

I considered for a moment. 'Clinically no. But I would advise any woman to keep well clear of him. His interest in you was as obvious as it was distasteful.'

'Yeah, he was eyeing me up all right,' Gail agreed. 'Don't let it rattle you. I get that a lot.'

'What concerns me is that if he is our killer, then he sent that rhyme to you with the precise intention of luring you to his studio.'

'Spider and the fly, eh? Don't worry, doc – I pack a hefty sting.'

I found her disregard for her own safety deeply troubling. 'None the less,' I advised, 'you should not return here unaccompanied.'

'Okay, I'll take that advice, seeing as it comes from a professional.' She flashed a carefree smile. 'What do you say we hustle over to Baker Street and see if Sherlock has dug anything up?'

17

A NIGHTMARE IN INK

Arriving back at Baker Street, we found Rayner lounging in a chair smoking a cigarette. As we entered he rose smartly and straightened his jacket.

'Dr Watson.' Even as he greeted me, his attention gravitated to my companion. 'Hello, Gail. I was wondering when we'd run into each other.'

'Oh, hi, Phil.' Gail raised a curious eyebrow. 'I didn't know you were in on this caper.'

'I'm just here to follow Mr Holmes's orders,' said Rayner, 'and lend a hand where I can.'

'I wasn't aware you two were acquainted,' I said.

'You can't attend many embassy receptions or official banquets without bumping into Phil Rayner Secret Agent,' Gail joked.

Rayner feigned a pained expression. 'Really, Gail, that sounds like the title of one of your American radio dramas.'

'A murder case is pretty small potatoes for you, isn't it, Phil?' Gail took out a cigarette and searched in her bag for a light. 'I thought you were more a cloak and dagger kind of a guy.'

Rayner laughed modestly and produced a silver lighter. 'Honestly, Gail, you make me sound like some sort of swashbuckler. I'm just as much a civil servant as the chaps who collect the taxes.'

Gail took a light from him and let a thin stream of smoke filter through her lips. 'I'm betting there's a string of tough customers from Barbados to Shanghai who would call you something else.'

I stepped between them to interrupt their banter. 'Is Holmes about, Rayner?'

Rayner pointed his cigarette at the door to the back room where Holmes carried out his more noxious chemical experiments. 'He's through there.'

At that moment Holmes emerged, gripping a small leather-bound book in his hand. 'Ah, Watson, Miss Preston. What did you make of Mr Sardinas?'

I glanced aside at Gail. 'He certainly has an unhealthy interest in painting terrified women,' I reported. 'I suppose it is possible this obsession has spilled over into more extreme actions, but we found nothing that would stand up as evidence.'

'The guy is a serious creep,' Gail added, 'but I don't suppose you can arrest him for that.'

'Inspector Lestrade will be disappointed,' said Holmes, 'but perhaps the fellow does bear watching.'

'So what do you think, Mr Holmes?' Rayner indicated the book my friend was holding.

Holmes nodded in evident satisfaction. 'I've tested the paper and the ink and both definitely date from the 1880s.'

Rayner gave a low whistle. 'It's genuine then, not some sort of forgery?'

'Quite genuine,' Holmes affirmed.

'Evidently we've missed something,' I said.

Gail took another draw on her cigarette. 'Yeah, I feel like I just walked in on the middle of the third act.'

'I asked Commander Rayner to pay a visit to Dr Carvel's home while he was absent visiting a cousin in Strood,' Holmes informed us. 'I recalled he has rather a knack for this sort of thing.'

'It wasn't hard to find the safe,' Rayner reported. 'It was behind that painting of the *Victory*, as you suspected.'

'It was Watson who observed Dr Carvel's more than proprietary interest in that particular painting,' Holmes acknowledged.

'Well, it didn't take long to crack,' said Rayner. 'There were some dull legal papers, a few heirlooms of no great value and a velvet bag containing that small book Mr Holmes now has in his possession.'

Holmes displayed the item and opened it for our inspection. The black leather cover was stained with wax, its edges frayed, and the yellowing pages covered in an untidy scrawl.

'This book is pertinent to the case?' I asked.

Holmes gave a noncommittal tilt of the head. 'It is the personal journal of one Henry Carvel, covering the months from March to November of 1888.'

He ran a long finger down one of the pages before continuing. 'The entries are sporadic but revealing. Mostly he bemoans his unhappy lot, the disdain of his father, the madness of his mother. He speculates that his elder brother left London primarily to evade his family responsibilities. His two sisters are described in unflattering terms.'

Gail blew out an astonished puff of smoke. 'Hold on a second, Sherlock – are you telling me that's the diary of Jack the Ripper?'

'If my deductions are correct, then yes. The name Henry Carvel is written on the flyleaf and the entries are consistent with what we know of his troubled life.'

'There's poetry too,' Rayner informed us meaningfully.

'Of a sort.' Holmes passed the book to me. 'See for yourself.'

I read aloud from the page in front of me.

'*My bloodstream is in spate,*

My heart is filled with fire.
A fist beats at the gate
Of unconstrained desire.'

I felt Gail press against me as she gazed down at the contents of the journal. She flicked the page over and read another entry aloud.

'*I hate to think of her smiling ever. I prefer to imagine her face twisted in terror as some dread fate overwhelms her, the justice of her betrayal.*' Her voice faltered at the horror of it. 'Wow, this guy and Sardinas should get together and do a picture book for bored psychopaths.'

I handed the journal back to Holmes.

'There is no outright statement of guilt,' he said, 'but it does confirm Carvel's tortured state of mind. Here is the last entry: '*I have had enough, enough of blood, enough of darkness. Whatever devil claims my soul, may he keep silent as regards those matters of which I cannot bear to think. So I shall make an end of it and cast myself upon that invisible sea. I have little hope for this life and even less for the next.*'

He snapped the book shut, as if to lock up the madness that lay within its pages.

'We can guess that Dr Adrian Carvel found this among the personal effects of his deceased younger brother. Whether he made any connection between it and the recent murders or whether he retained it simply as a memento, I do not say. Clearly it was passed on to his son William, who sets enough store by it to keep it safely locked away.'

'Some might take it as confirmatory evidence of Henry Carvel's guilt,' I said. 'Perhaps it is for that reason that the present Dr Carvel wishes it to remain out of sight.'

'I wonder, Mr Holmes,' Rayner suggested, 'if Dr Carvel places a value upon this beyond the purely sentimental.'

Holmes frowned. 'How do you mean?'

Rayner paused to choose his words. 'Might he perhaps be reading it and absorbing the madness into himself? Might he be identifying himself with his dead uncle and recreating his actions?'

'It is a possibility,' Holmes agreed, 'but no more than that for now. There is no more to be learned from this.' He handed the book back to Rayner. 'Please put this back before Dr Carvel returns from his excursion and ensure that you leave no trace of your visit.'

'It will be as though a ghost passed through,' said Rayner with confidence.

'Well, this has been fun,' said Gail, tossing the remains of her cigarette into the fireplace, 'but I'd better get back to work. I need to whip up a piece on British artists and the war effort for my next broadcast, just to keep up the story I told Sardinas.'

I felt moved to caution her. 'Whatever you choose to say on air, be careful not to provoke him. There's no telling how he might react.'

'The one thing that would really get him riled would be not to mention him at all,' Gail chuckled. 'Believe me, I'm tempted.'

As she started for the door, Rayner said, 'We really must have that drink sometime, Gail.'

'I'll take a rain check on that, Phil. My dance card has been pretty full since Uncle Sam started shipping our boys over here.'

'Of course, entertaining the troops is very important for morale,' said Rayner with mock gravity. 'I expect you remind them of mother's apple pie and the World Series.'

Gail looked back from the doorway. 'That's me – "Home On The Range" and "Take Me Out To The Ball Game".

Kate Smith's got nothing on me.'

With a cheery wave she left.

Following her departure, I gave Holmes a full account of our visit to Damon Sardinas, making no effort to conceal my disgust at his manner and his pretensions.

Holmes listened attentively throughout. When I had concluded, he asked, 'Tell me, Watson, how did Sardinas react to Miss Preston?'

The mere recollection aroused my ire. 'His interest in her was as obvious as it was offensive,' I answered with restraint. 'Only my status as an observer prevented me from upbraiding him for his insolence.'

'You were correct not to indulge in a confrontation,' said Holmes, 'difficult as I know that must have been for you where a lady's honour was concerned.'

'It crossed my mind,' I continued, 'that he might have sent her that poem for the express purpose of drawing her to him. He may well have come across her at some time in the past and set his sights on her without her being aware of it.'

Rayner was obviously intrigued. 'You think so, doctor?'

'It's only a speculation on my part,' I admitted, 'but I am concerned for her safety.'

'And yet, as she herself pointed out,' Holmes reminded me, 'we cannot exclude her from the investigation. She may hold some clue we do not as yet suspect.'

'Speaking of clues,' said Rayner, slipping the journal into his pocket, 'I'd better get this little item back in its hiding place.'

As he headed out of the room, he gave an almost imperceptible tilt of the head to indicate that I should accompany him to the front door. Leaving Holmes absorbed in his files and maps, I followed Rayner downstairs.

'Dr Watson, your friend Mr Holmes is entirely focused

on the victims and the suspects,' he said gravely. 'It's up to you and me to keep an eye on Gail.'

'I'm sure I share your concern, Rayner. But it's not as if we can stand guard over her day and night. She's too independent, too . . .' I paused to select a world.

'Stubborn?' Rayner suggested. 'Headstrong? Bloody-minded?'

We shared a smile.

'Yes, all of those,' I agreed.

At the bottom of the stairs he stopped and faced me with grim resolve in the firm set of his jaw. 'I don't want to see her running headlong into this lunatic, whoever he turns out to be.'

'You're convinced he's insane, then?'

'Completely off his trolley. What other explanation is there? His actions aren't those of a rational man. The crimes themselves, the signature, the letter. When we catch him, he'll probably end up in a padded cell instead of on the gallows.'

'You sound very confident of catching him,' I noted.

Rayner squared his shoulders. 'Doctor, it's only a matter of time. There's no way a mental case can stay one step ahead of a properly organised pursuit.'

'Jack the Ripper did,' I reminded him.

Rayner merely smiled. 'That was then. We're a lot cleverer now.' He offered me his hand as he opened the door. 'It's a great honour to be working with the two of you.'

We shook hands and I watched him walk off down the street, reflecting on the alliance we had formed as guardians of Gail Preston's welfare. There was no doubt in my mind that he had romantic designs upon her.

Which was, of course, entirely his business and none of mine.

18

MR DEEDS SPEAKS HIS MIND

Though he knew nothing of the arrangement I had made with Rayner, Holmes likewise made it clear that he wished me to keep in close contact with Gail Preston.

'There is some connection between her and our killer that she is not as yet aware of,' he said. 'You must be on the lookout for any indication that she has had contact with a possible suspect and keep a wary eye out in case he is shadowing her even now.'

The very thought chilled me to the marrow. It was at Holmes's insistence, therefore, that I made so bold as to telephone Gail and suggest a drink in town. I had it in mind that perhaps an informal meeting outside our investigation might bring to light some hint of why she had been selected to act as a messenger between Crimson Jack and Scotland Yard.

I was gratified to find her so agreeable that she suggested we rendezvous at a public house named the Nag's Head in Poulter's Lane. This was, she informed me, 'a favourite watering hole for newshounds'.

On my way out of Baker Street I paused before a mirror and found myself carefully adjusting my bow tie. I ceased at once and chided myself for behaving so foolishly. This was strictly business and business of the most serious kind.

I took a taxi to my assignation and was unlucky enough to have one of those talkative drivers who are as much a part of London life as double-decker buses and the Underground. At no instigation of mine, he started upon the topic of the new Ripper killings.

'Want to know what I think?' he offered knowingly.

'I'm sure you have your views,' I responded with an air of indifference which I hoped would discourage him. It did not.

'I think it's as simple as pie. This Jack character – he's the old Jack, the original himself, back in business. Makes sense, don't it?'

'There are difficulties,' I pointed out politely.

'Oh, you mean that he'd be an old geezer?' He swerved sharply to avoid two drunk sailors staggering across the road. 'That's not a problem. There are some tough old birds out there could easily tackle a younger man, let alone a woman. You take Crusher Crown, for example.'

'I'm afraid I'm not acquainted with Mr Crown,' I felt forced to confess.

'Crusher – the wrestler,' he expanded, as though pressing me to admit some acquaintance.

'Oh, yes, of course,' I conceded reluctantly.

The cabby beamed into his rear-view mirror. 'Crusher was sixty-five if he was a day when he mopped the floor with the Battersea Bulldog. Kept himself in shape, did Crusher.'

'Even so—' I began hesitantly, only to be cut off.

'You still think the Ripper'd be too old, too feeble?' the cabby persisted. 'Well, there's other ways to keep fit, ways that don't hardly bear speaking about.'

'I'm sure they don't,' I said hopefully. But I was not to be spared.

The driver grinned broadly over his shoulder. 'I've been reading about voodoo rituals that give a bloke super'uman strength. That's *super'uman*. And what was those mutilations of his, if not voodoo rituals? That's what's kept him going for all these years. Yeah, that's what I think,' he concluded triumphantly, 'and I'd like to see somebody prove me wrong.'

'It's certainly a bold theory,' I temporised.

'Of course, my wife's cousin Arnold takes a different view,' the cabby confided, his expression darkening. 'He says the Ripper froze hisself in a big fridge in order to dodge the bobbies. He only thawed out when the coast was clear and he could get back to work. What do you make of that?'

'It sounds highly unlikely,' I offered tentatively.

'Bollocks is what it is!' the driver expostulated, shaking his fist at a cyclist who had cut across his path. 'It's voodoo, you mark my words. And that's all I have to say on the subject.'

Unfortunately this last statement proved to be far wide of the mark, for my new acquaintance had several more points to express, most of them of so lurid and fantastical a nature I have no desire to repeat them.

By the time we stopped in Poulter's Lane, I was so glad to escape that I accidentally tipped him the equivalent of a second fare. He thanked me heartily and drove off in search of more passengers in need of his particular brand of enlightenment.

As soon as I stepped through the door of the Nag's Head I found myself immersed in an atmosphere thick with cigarette smoke and jocular ribaldry.

From a radio in the corner came the rhythmic sounds of Jack Payne and his Orchestra, but it was no match for the spirited cries of the competitors at the dart board, the loud opinions being expressed about the progress of the war in various quarters, or the coarse blandishments being rained down on a pair of ladies standing at the bar, whose feigned indifference only stimulated their admirers to increase their efforts.

Peering through the murky atmosphere, I spotted Gail playing cards with three men, who at that moment were throwing their hands down in disgust while she raked in the pot. Before interrupting their game, I walked over to the bar where a threadbare Union Jack and a framed photograph of the late King Edward the Seventh were fixed to the wall above the bottles of spirits and the chalked price list.

I ordered a pint of best bitter for myself and, knowing her tastes, a Scotch whisky for Gail. I then made my way across the room, doing my best not to be jostled. I passed a table where a friendly game of dominoes was giving way to a heated argument over our alliance with Russia, the debaters emphasising their points of view by rapping loudly on the table with their playing pieces.

Seeing me approach, Gail waved away the hand that was being dealt her and swept her winnings into her handbag.

'Sorry to break up the game, boys,' she said, rising to her feet, 'but it looks like my date is here.'

Ignoring the other players' demands for a chance to recover their losses, she led me to an unoccupied table by the window. She raised her glass in a toast and took a small sip. 'Are you sure Mrs Watson doesn't mind your hanging out with strange women?'

'I am afraid Mrs Watson passed away some years ago,' I said.

Gail set her glass down and gazed at me thoughtfully. 'Well, however long it's been, you're still wearing the ring and you still come across as a married man.'

'I hope that is true. And what about you, Gail? You strike me as being determinedly single-minded, as much in your personal life as in your professional activities. Have you never considered marriage?'

She pulled out a cigarette and took her time lighting it. 'Believe it or not, I was engaged once, right here in London, to an English guy who took pictures for *The Times*. He was killed when a 500-pound German bomb flattened his apartment.'

'I am very sorry to hear it,' I told her sincerely.

'Don't be.' She flicked some ash from her cigarette. 'That louse was in bed with some floozie when it happened. I should write Hitler a thank-you note for saving me the trouble of plugging him myself.'

She took a swallow of whisky as though washing a bitter taste from her mouth. I decided to change the subject.

'I confess I was not expecting you to accept my invitation so promptly in view of how in Commander Rayner's case you . . .' I searched for a polite phrase.

'Gave him the brush-off?' Gail suggested. 'Phil's not such a bad guy, I guess, but something about him rubs me the wrong way. He reminds me of this jerk Bill Miller that I dated a few times when I was working on a newspaper in North Dakota – a real stuffed shirt. Turned out he had a wife he wasn't through divorcing.' She gave a throaty laugh and levelled her clear grey eyes at me. 'You must be starting to think I've got lousy taste in men.'

I met her gaze frankly. 'Maybe it's just that there are too few good men in the world for a woman of character to choose from,' I suggested.

'That's a cute way of putting it.' She flashed a brief smile then leaned in confidentially. 'So how's the manhunt going?'

Obscurely I felt as though we had just stepped back from a very steep edge. Tugging at my bow tie, I said, 'Lestrade has pulled in every thug who has ever so much as raised his fist to a woman and subjected him to rough questioning.'

'But no dice, huh?'

'None. It seems to me unlikely that any common criminal would suddenly take it into his head to set out on a course of murders as brutal as these.'

Gail took a long moment of thought. 'Could it be they're so brutal because they're a warning to women to keep in their place? You may have noticed that there are a lot of women doing men's work now, from munitions to flying aeroplanes. Some guys feel threatened by that.'

I took a swallow of beer and shook my head. 'I hardly think the killer's motive is likely to be anything so sociological.'

'I can tell you what's behind it,' a familiar and thoroughly unwelcome voice interrupted.

It was the reporter Deeds whom Holmes and I had encountered at the Chamber of Wax. Sporting the same loud jacket, he inserted himself at an adjacent table along with two others whom I took to be fellow journalists.

'Okay, Charlie, why don't you tell us about it?' invited Gail. 'Not that there's much we could do to stop you.'

Deeds puffed out his chest. 'Well, as usual,' he began, 'while everybody else is stumbling about in the dark, old Deedsy has cracked it.'

I found his cocksure manner irksome. 'If you have any pertinent information,' I told him, 'you should report it to the police at once.'

'The police?' Deeds sneered. 'I don't think so. Isn't it obvious that this is an inside job?'

'Come on, Charlie, let's hear it then,' said one of the other reporters, stifling a long-suffering yawn.

Deeds gulped some beer and leaned towards us confidentially, as if imparting a deep secret.

'Now, it doesn't make sense, does it, that some lunatic is running about killing women for the sheer fun of it? No, there's bound to be more to it. And if he's nuts, how can the police, the army – lord knows there are enough of them in town – and the RAF not catch him? It's because they're not allowed to. It's because there's no such person as the new Ripper.'

'Here, Deedsy, have you gone off your rocker?' one of his fellow journalists scoffed. 'Somebody's killing those girls. They sure as hell aren't just playing dead, not with all the blood and all.'

With the back of his hand Deeds gave his associate a slap on the chest. 'What I'm saying, you thick lump, is that it isn't one bloke, let alone one loony. It's a conspiracy reaching up' – he stretched a hand high above his head – 'way up here.'

His companions exchanged derisive glances. 'Oh, I suppose it's a satanic cult carrying out human sacrifices right on the street,' mocked one of them.

'That would be less scary than the truth,' Deeds sneered. 'Now listen, you mugs, you all remember the last king, Edward the Eighth, him that had to abdicate?'

There was a spark of genuine interest at the mention of so famous and controversial a figure.

'The press was never allowed to let on about it,' Deeds continued, 'but we all know young Eddie was a bit of a lad back when he was Prince of Wales. Had an eye for the ladies, he had, especially the older ladies.'

I could not help bristling at so disrespectful a reference to our former king, but I contained myself. I was duty bound to listen to any theory that might shed light on these dreadful crimes.

'Now, my guess is that he got stuck on a common bit of fluff,' Deeds theorised with a salacious leer, 'but the only way he could get inside her bloomers was to marry her – in secret, naturally. Course as soon as the palace gets wind of it, they break it up and drag him back home by his ear. But it's too late, because there's already a nipper sprung from the royal loins.'

He paused dramatically and leaned back in his chair, taking a long swallow of his beer while the audience digested this outrageous concoction.

Gail appeared more amused than anything else. 'So, Charlie, I suppose you've got a big heap of proof tucked away someplace and you're just waiting for the right moment to break the story?'

'Not as such,' Deeds replied with a barefaced grin, 'but it fits the facts, don't it? You mark my words, there's a genuine royal heir out there who could knock King George off the throne. Just think what Goebbels and Lord Haw-Haw would do with that meaty piece of propaganda if they got their hands on him.'

One of Deeds's companions squinted through his glasses and wrinkled his nose. 'So you're saying old Churchill is having these girls bumped off because they know about this little prince of yours.'

'Make sense, don't it?' Deeds shrugged as if the matter were settled. 'A few poor girlies that isn't married to barons or earls, what are they worth to the nobs that are running the show?'

At this final outrage my indignation overcame my self-restraint. I stood up and seized him by the lapel of his houndstooth jacket.

'You unmitigated swine! While better men than you are fighting and dying for this country, you sit there casting the most foul aspersions on our highest institutions. There was a time you would have been jailed as a traitor for such talk and whipped to within an inch of your life.'

Deeds shook himself loose and slid his chair back a few inches. 'It seems to me, doctor, that what's being fought and died for is a man's right to speak his mind without being whipped for it by those that fancy they're his betters.'

I seethed, my fist still clenched, until I felt Gail's hand on my arm.

'Cool off, doc. He's just blowing hot air because it's all he's got inside.' She threw back the last of her whisky and stood up. 'Come on, you can walk me home. It's only a few blocks.'

With a final glare at the disreputable Deeds, I left my beer unfinished and turned to go.

'Maybe you could help me with a different story, doctor,' Deeds piped after me. 'Tell me, what's the inside dope on your friend Sherlock Holmes? What makes him tick?'

I swung about on my heel. 'That is not a subject I care to discuss, Mr Deeds,' I informed him scornfully, 'least of all with you.'

'No need to be so formal,' the reporter retorted cheekily. 'Call me Charlie.'

'Even on so brief an acquaintance as ours, Mr Deeds, I am quite persuaded that you and I shall never attain such a degree of informality. Good evening to you.'

With that I yielded to Gail's tug at my arm and let her lead me out of the door.

19

A TRACE OF THE PHANTOM

Once we were outside the cool night air took some of the angry flush out of my face.

Still holding my arm, Gail gave it a squeeze. 'Doc, you slay me. You stick up for your country like it was a pretty girl.'

'I'm pleased to say I will always stand up for a lady's honour,' I declared, 'if that doesn't sound too priggish to you. At times like this I will not have those values and institutions that are our bulwark against tyranny besmirched by that smirking weasel.'

As I allowed her to steer me through the darkened streets I became pleasantly aware of the faint, sweet scent of her perfume, which came as a welcome balm after the stifling atmosphere of the Nag's Head.

'Don't be too hard on Charlie,' Gail said. 'He's just doing his job.'

'His job,' I said, not at all mollified, 'seems to be the promotion of scurrilous falsehoods in order to keep his name in the public eye.'

'The fact is,' Gail continued, 'he used to be a pretty hot crime reporter. He's the one who tracked down and cornered the creep that murdered those two girls in Ipswich last year. The killer held Charlie at gunpoint while he explained how and why he did it, then turned the gun on himself and blew his brains out. Now that's a scoop.'

I refrained from comment, but my disapproval was written on my face.

'Yeah, I know,' said Gail. 'You have to be pretty cold to

watch a man go through with something like that.' It was the first time I had seen her so subdued. 'Look, it's a messed-up world and we're all trying to find our own way to get through it. Not everybody can keep their hands clean – not even Sherlock Holmes.'

Affronted as I was by that suggestion, I chose not to shake loose of her clasp. 'What on earth do you mean by that?'

Gail kept her eyes fixed ahead. 'I mean I've heard it said that once or twice, when he's caught up with the crook he's after, he's let him go. Have you got any comment to make on that, Dr Watson?'

I recalled all too clearly the incidents alluded to and my wholehearted agreement with Holmes's motive in each case, but I was not prepared to enter into a discussion of such sensitive matters. 'All I can say is that – on occasion – the interests of justice go beyond the strict demands of the law.'

'Yeah, that's what I thought you'd say.'

I did my best to appear unruffled. 'It wasn't my expectation that you would spend the evening trying to worm a story out of me.'

'Sorry about that. Habit.' Gail sighed. 'Maybe it was a mistake to try to relax in the middle of all those professional snoopers.'

The sound of a raucous sing-song interrupted us. Four servicemen in a state of mild inebriation were rolling up the street towards us, their arms locked around each other as they sang 'Show Me The Way To Go Home'. When they emerged from the dark I recognised the uniforms and badges of the United States Army Air Forces. One of them gave a start of recognition and broke away from the others.

'Hey, Gail! What's a nice dish like you doing on a plate like this?'

'Hi, Gerry. You flyboys out keeping the civilians awake again?'

Turning to his companions so quickly he nearly overbalanced, the airman announced loudly, 'Fellas, it's Gail, good old Gail.'

The other three called out in unison, 'Hello, Gail!'

'Who's this?' one of them asked, peering at me as though I were a fish in a tank. 'Your uncle?'

Gail gave my arm a squeeze. 'Believe it or not, boys, this is my doctor.'

'Good evening, gentlemen,' I greeted them, doffing my hat.

'Doctor?' Gerry queried. 'Say, you're not sick, are you?'

'Only lovesick,' Gail replied, batting her eyelashes.

Gerry clutched a hand to his heart. 'For me?'

'No, for Tyrone Power.' Gail struck a languishing air. 'What do you think of my chances?

The airman rubbed his jaw. 'I dunno. Can you sing as good as Alice Faye?'

'Maybe not,' Gail confessed, 'but I can dance like Ruby Keeler.'

'Dancing! Say, that's a swell idea!' exclaimed one of the others. 'We're headed for the Palatine Club. They've got a hot band there playing jitterbug music. Why don't you come along?'

'Yeah, come on, Gail!' they all pleaded. 'It'll be fun.'

'Sorry, boys,' said Gail as we moved past them. 'It's been a long day and I'm bushed.'

'It's your loss,' Gerry called after us. 'You'll be sorry when you hear I hooked up with Myrna Loy.'

Linking arms again, they four of them headed off in an ungainly march, singing, '*Got the St Louis blues, just as blue as I can be. That gal got a heart like a rock cast in the sea.*'

'You certainly have some boisterous friends,' I commented with amusement as the song faded into the distance. 'I hope they manage to make it back to their barracks before morning.'

'They're bomber crew,' said Gail. 'If even half of them are still alive when this dust-up's over, it'll be some kind of miracle. So I guess it's okay to cut them some slack.'

There was a minute or so of silence between us until I said, 'I'm not treating you to a very jolly evening, am I?'

'Don't worry about it,' said Gail brightly. 'How about next time we have a night off we go catch a flick?'

I cast her a questioning glance. 'Catch a flick?'

'Go . . . to . . . the . . . pictures,' she translated, slowly enunciating each word. 'We could go see that Spitfire movie with Leslie Howard.'

'Howard – yes, I remember him in *The Scarlet Pimpernel*. He was very good.'

'This one's a little more up to date – not so many powdered wigs. What do you say?'

'I haven't been to the cinema in some time,' I admitted. 'I suppose it would make a pleasant change.'

'Well here we are.' Gail released my arm as we arrived at the front entrance of a large apartment house. She threw a glance at an upper window. 'I've got a bottle of bourbon upstairs. What do you say to a nightcap? I could put on some music and we could pretend we're dancing at the Ritz.'

I suppressed my first impulse to accept her unexpected invitation and smiled apologetically. 'I'm afraid that under the circumstances, given that we are . . . well, it might be considered indiscreet.'

Gail tilted her head at me. 'Come on,' she coaxed, 'take the starch out of your collar. You do know Queen Victoria's dead, right?'

'Contrary to what you might think,' I informed her gravely, 'I'm not actually old enough to have known her socially.'

Gail gave a throaty chuckle. 'There you go. I knew you had a good crack in you. All I had to do was poke you hard enough.'

She prodded me gently in the chest with her finger.

'Really,' I said, 'I have to be at St Thomas's for my rounds in the morning.'

Gail shrugged. 'Oh well, maybe next time, eh?' She made a half turn towards the door, then stopped and gave me a sidelong glance. 'Doc, I don't say this to many guys,' her voice had lost its teasing air and she paused before continuing, 'but you're okay – you know.'

With that she disappeared inside. I spent some moments staring at the door, reflecting how curious it was, given her colourful vocabulary, that those few, simple words represented the highest compliment she could pay a man. Then I set off in search of a taxi with a certain lightness of step.

Over breakfast next morning I recounted to Holmes in detail my conversation with Gail Preston, all except the words we exchanged on her doorstep, which I judged to have no relevance to our case. Whether Holmes discerned any indication of a connection to Crimson Jack, I could not tell.

He also insisted that I recount in full the absurd theories of the garrulous cabbie and the obnoxious Deeds. 'Any theory, no matter how foolish it sounds,' he said, 'may yet contain some suggestive hint of the actual truth.'

'If either of those gentlemen has struck upon any element of truth,' I told him, 'it would be like a blind man hitting the centre of a dart board.'

Holmes paused in the act of lighting up his first pipe of the day. 'Even so, their wild fancies may, by reaction, set my own thoughts on a path more direct and fruitful.'

I let the matter rest and turned my attention to the copy of *The Times* that was laid out at my elbow. 'I see there is a statement here from the Prime Minister's least favourite philanthropist.'

'I take it,' said Holmes, 'you are alluding to Sir Carlton Jessop.'

'Indeed.' I ran an eye over the article. 'Speaking on behalf of the Committee for Public Decency, he upbraids the government for perpetuating the blackout. He claims it has created a festering darkness in which every form of vice thrives unchecked. This, he says, is a greater danger to the public welfare than Hitler's bombs.'

Holmes poured himself a fresh cup of coffee and sipped at it. 'Perhaps, as the saying goes, he would be better advised to light one candle than to expend so much effort on cursing the darkness.'

'He has always ridden a moral high horse,' I recalled, for Sir Carlton had long been a public figure, 'but since the death of his daughter he has become an outright puritan.'

'A dead daughter, you say?' Holmes's interest was momentarily piqued.

'The official story is that she died of pneumonia, but there have been rumours that she was a drug addict. Very tragic.'

Holmes gave the article a sceptical squint. 'Unfortunately no amount of moral outrage will do anything to stop these killings.'

'Have the police turned up anything of value?'

'Inspector Lestrade has his men running hither and yon in pursuit of all manner of geese, as if such frenzied activity was its own justification.'

'And what of your own researches?' I inquired.

'I have, in a variety of guises, been making the acquaintance of some of the city's ladies of the night,' he informed me, 'in particular associates of the late Mags Hopkin. I managed to glean some small scraps of information while at the same time declining their wares.'

'And?' I prompted, eager to hear anything that might take us a step closer to our quarry.

He hunched forward in an attitude of utmost concentration. 'Last night, while masquerading as a merchant seaman, I spoke with a certain Agnes French, who recalled her last conversation with Hopkin the evening before her murder. It seems that the previous day, while she was off the clock, as Agnes put it, Mags had run into a man she recognised from a previous meeting some weeks before.'

'A client?' I suggested.

'Not to hear Agnes tell it, no. Mags suggested that the first encounter was quite innocent but also memorable. Once he had overcome his initial surprise at being hailed by her, he became very friendly. Mags Hopkin's exact words, as related to me by Agnes, were, *He wanted to talk to me about the others*.'

'The others?' I blurted. 'What others?'

Holmes grimaced. 'Before she could say any more the women were interrupted by the approach of two customers and went their separate ways.'

'You think, Holmes, that this unnamed man may be our killer?'

'I very much think that he is. Recall that we have already deduced that Clara Bentley, on her way home from work, must have encountered someone she recognised and trusted enough to follow through a dark and lonely area of town.

It seems certain that she was one of those whom Mags's gentleman wished to speak about.'

'You believe then that they had all encountered this man before?'

'Yes. Some incident brought them all together.'

'And for some reason this unknown man fixated upon these women, casting them as potential victims.'

'I do not think so, Watson. We have no reason to suppose that he gave them as much as a second thought until that accidental second meeting with Mags Hopkin. Something occurred then to set this murderous train of events in motion.'

'But you have no name or description?'

Holmes shook his head in frustration and took a calming draw on his pipe. 'And yet it is progress. Before we had only a phantom. Now we have a figure that, though still indistinct, is at least solid.'

20

THE MONTENEGRO DEFENCE

I spent a long night at St Thomas's standing in for another doctor who was laid up with influenza. In the morning I decided to clear my head by taking the air in Kensington Park before returning to Baker Street.

There was a refreshing autumnal snap in the air and the sun cast a sheen over the leaves as their greenery melted into the yellow and gold of September. I spotted a familiar figure seated on a bench, ignoring the hopeful pigeons who pecked the ground at his feet. He raised a small silver flask to his lips and took a long swallow. The birds dispersed at my approach and I sat down beside him.

Leonard King blinked at me once and thrust the flask back in his pocket. I noticed that in his lap lay a piece of paper covered in some sort of shorthand notation. 'Watson? Fancy meeting you here.'

I had not seen him since receiving his autopsy report on Clara Bentley and his appearance had not altered for the better. The flesh of his once round face was pale as ash, his cheeks were sunken, and dark circles surrounded his eyes, as though some inner emptiness was physically consuming him. I tried to recall a time when he had appeared hale and hearty, but it seemed so long ago that I could not summon the memory.

'I was working overnight at St Thomas's.' I waved a hand in the direction of the hospital and ignored the bitter scent of gin on his breath. 'But what brings you here?'

'Oh, I only live down the road there.' He gestured vaguely towards a cheerless row of tenements. 'Thought I'd get a bit of air on my way home.'

'I take it you too had a long night.'

King's sallow features seemed to take on a deeper shade of grey as his hand reached instinctively for the flask in his pocket. He stopped himself at the last moment and rested the hand on his knee instead.

'Some kids came across an unexploded bomb yesterday. They started mucking around with it and it went off. If they'd just gone home for their tea instead of staying outside to lark about . . .'

He rubbed his eyes as though to erase the memory of what he had seen before returning his attention to me. 'You're lucky, John. You get to patch up the living. All I do is carve open the dead. Sometimes I wonder if they're not the lucky ones. They're done with all the pain and struggle.'

'In these times more than ever,' I said, attempting to divert the stark pessimism of his words, 'we need to focus on what's good.'

'What's good?' He tried to laugh but it broke down into a brief convulsive cough that left him short of breath. 'Sometimes I think it must be a comfort to be mad. Better than seeing the world as it is, eh?'

'Look, Leonard, you get back to your wife and let her put a full breakfast inside you.' We had never been on first name terms before, but I felt the need to reciprocate his attempt to reach out. 'It will all seem less bleak then, I'm sure.'

'Wife?' He made a noise in his throat somewhere between a laugh and a sob. 'She left months ago. Can't say I blame her.'

I had lost my share of patients over the years, and just then I felt as though King was one of them, drifting towards death like a boat cut loose from its moorings. Still, I made the best effort I could to draw him back to shore.

'I'm sure that when the war is over a lot of things will go back to the way they were. Life's bound to be hard in these sorts of times, but we've found our way through them before.'

He made no response. I noticed that he had picked up the paper from his lap and was rubbing it absently between thumb and forefinger.

'What's that you've got there?' I asked. 'It looks like some sort of code.'

He glanced at the symbols scrawled on the scrap as though only now realising it was there. 'Oh, it's some chess moves I jotted down, that's all.' He folded the paper and slipped it into his pocket. 'I meet up with my friend Bill once a week or so to play chess. Sometimes takes us weeks to get through a game. Neither of us is in much of a hurry. I thought I'd stymied him with the Montenegro defence, but he's cracked it like a walnut.'

'Montenegro defence,' I heard myself murmur under my breath. I knew exactly where I had heard that before.

King hauled himself to his feet with a weary groan. 'I'd best go and try to catch a few winks, I suppose, before the next wagonload of bodies comes in.'

With a half-hearted wave he set off down the gravel-strewn path, his footsteps crunching as though he were crushing the very life out of the ground. My own heart sank to see him like this, but there seemed nothing I could do to haul him out of his downward spiral. I decided to focus my mind instead on some area where it might do some good and redirected my thoughts to Crimson Jack's cryptic letter.

Holmes had too easily dismissed the teasing rhyme, which might have been the killer's intention all along – to flaunt his identity before us but in such a crudely flamboyant fashion that this genuine clue would be cast aside. If Holmes had a weakness, it was his intellectual pride, and in this case I was quite sure it had blinded him to what was right in front of his eyes.

I recalled the words: *an artist no less . . . a move in chess*. I thought of the two men hunched over a chess board, each one haunted in his own way by a spirit of death. Then I looked up and caught a last glimpse of Leonard King as he disappeared from view.

And the light of a terrible revelation dawned upon me.

I returned to Baker Street in a state of some excitement. As soon as I walked through the door I burst out with my discovery.

'I've found our man, Holmes – I've found him.'

My friend was deeply ensconced in his leather chair surrounded by photographs, police reports and maps, puffing on the calabash pipe he reserved for only the most intractable of problems. He looked up with a puzzled quirk of the mouth.

'I sincerely hope you have, Watson, but I must say . . .'

'It's Leonard King,' I told him. 'The pathologist.'

'I am aware of who he is. And you are telling me that he is Crimson Jack?'

'Yes, Holmes, I'm quite sure of it.'

Holmes's hooded eyes regarded me through a deepening haze of pipe smoke and scepticism. 'And you base this upon what?'

'The clues were there all along in that infernal rhyme. The first line, *Jack's an artist*. Surely the most famous artist of all is Leonardo da Vinci. You see – Leonard. Then there is the chess reference. King not only plays chess regularly but his very name is that of a chess piece, the most important one of all.'

'You've been working hard through the night, Watson,' Holmes commented. 'Have you had sufficient sleep?'

I waved his patronising question aside. 'I caught a few hours in a cot in the dispensary. I assure you I am well rested and my mind is perfectly clear.'

Holmes peered down his nose at me. 'And yet you hang your case – if we can call it such – upon the flimsiest of clues, ones intended by the killer most probably to mislead and misdirect.'

'I agree that a few words taken from the letter are a shaky foundation,' I admitted, 'but there is more, far more.'

Holmes sank back in his chair and took a long draw on his pipe. 'I'm intrigued. Do go on.'

I planted myself in an adjoining chair and leaned towards him intently. 'I have just been speaking to King and found him in a shocking condition, descending further and further into a state of mental depression. The very work he does has unsettled his mind to the point where he has become utterly obsessed with death and the futility of human life. He actually sees madness as something to be desired.'

'I fear we can hardly arrest him on that basis,' said Holmes.

'Let me finish,' I told him impatiently. 'He was pondering a particular chess stratagem called the Montenegro defence. That is the very stratagem Dr William Carvel told us was being employed by his regular chess opponent, a fellow doctor. Can we doubt that King is the man Carvel referred to and that the two are closely acquainted?'

'I would grant that is a logical inference,' Holmes conceded.

Pleased to have scored a point, I continued eagerly. 'Is it then not possible, in fact, given their common medical interests, highly likely that Carvel might have shared his relative's diary with his chess companion and related its bloody history?'

Encouraged by a thoughtful nod from my friend, I set about describing the sequence of events as I envisaged them in my mind's eye. 'Given access to the diary, King reads it through. His morbid imagination is kindled. He reads it again and a dangerous fantasy takes hold. Absorbing the spirit of the deranged young Carvel, he sets out to re-enact the Ripper's murderous work. But subconsciously he retains sufficient remnants of conscience to provide his colleagues in the police force with clues to his identity in the hope that someone will stop him.'

My exposition complete, I confronted my friend in expectant silence. He removed the pipe from his mouth and pointed the stem at me with a nod of approval.

'Bravo, Watson! I am tempted to applaud. It is all most ingenious.'

Though I felt a brief flush of pride at the compliment, I said, 'I do not seek applause, Holmes, not even from you. All I want is to bring about an end to this dreadful business.'

'As do I,' Holmes agreed roundly. 'However, it grieves me to say that this is not it.'

This came as a shock. 'You do not intend to investigate this further?'

Holmes shook his head. 'There is no need. I already had Lestrade investigate Dr King's whereabouts on the nights of the murders. On the night of September the seventh he was at home with no alibi, but on the night of August the thirtieth when the first murder took place, he was at a medical conference in Brighton from which he could not have absented himself without his disappearance's being noted.'

'So you did investigate King as a possible suspect?' I was

somewhat mollified that my suspicions were not after all so far-fetched.

'Tenuous as those indications are, there was some small chance that the references in the killer's rhyme pointed to Dr King, as you say. Our man does have some degree of medical knowledge, and given the fact that he has so far evaded detection he may also have a familiarity with police methods. I too have noted Dr King's morbid frame of mind and speculated that someone whose very livelihood involves examining those who have died by violence might nurture a fascination with such crimes. But he is not our man.'

I flopped back in my chair, deflated and exhausted. 'I was so sure I had the solution and now I feel a perfect fool.'

'Not at all, my old friend,' Holmes assured me warmly. 'It was your concern for the victims that drove you to grasp at a solution, and that is entirely to your credit. It is not your fault that what appeared to you so solid turned to smoke in your hands.'

He drew once more on his pipe and stared into the embers sputtering in the fireplace.

'At every turn we seem to find ourselves dogged by the ghost of Jack the Ripper, but we must not let that distract us,' he murmured. 'There are facts, there are discrepancies, there are patterns – these must be our guide, and we must not allow them to be obscured by a fog conjured up from a bygone age.'

The ticking of the clock on the mantelpiece brought to my mind the inexorable passage of time. Tomorrow was September the twenty-ninth. If the pattern Holmes had discerned held true, Crimson Jack was about to strike again.

PART THREE

JUSTICE

'No beast so fierce but knows some touch of pity.'
'But I know none, and am therefore no beast.'

SHAKESPEARE,
Richard III

21

A COUNCIL OF WAR

The mood in London as the fateful night approached could not have been described as one of terror. Without the corroboration of the chalked name and the taunting letter, details known only to a restricted few, it was easy to dismiss the two murders as just two more crimes among the many spawned by the concealing obscurity of the blackout.

That the *Bulletin* had made such play with the supposed connection to the Ripper was widely regarded as a typical journalistic ploy intended to boost their circulation. And, of course, there were other, weightier matters occupying the minds of the populace – the progress of the war on so many fronts, separation from husbands fighting overseas, and children evacuated to the safety of the countryside.

Those of us who knew of the existence of Crimson Jack, however, were gathered in Inspector Lestrade's office, preparing for a long and perilous vigil. Scotland Yard's official position was that there was no proven link between the two recent murders and the historical crimes of Jack the Ripper. On this night, however, they were deploying all the resources at their disposal under the command of Inspector Lestrade.

Particular attention was paid to those areas where the ladies of the night were to be found in great numbers, on the suspicion that Crimson Jack might still have a preference for the exclusive prey of his predecessor and because they were most at risk through the nature of their trade.

Rayner had arrived earlier to discuss strategy with Lestrade and to give instructions to the constables and plain clothes men who would be out on the street tonight. They had all been equipped with electric torches and given as much information as was deemed necessary. Now we had a closed meeting of what might be styled our own Intelligence Inner Council.

'I suppose tonight, for better or worse, we'll find out if you were right all along, Mr Holmes,' said Lestrade.

'Believe me, inspector,' Holmes responded grimly, 'I have never before wished so heartily to be proved wrong, but I fear that will not be the case.'

'I see the *Bulletin* is still sticking it to Downing Street for not switching on the lights,' said Gail, waving the paper she had brought with her.

'They're flogging a dead horse with that,' rumbled Lestrade.

Rayner was seated in a corner, smoking a Turkish cigarette. 'The *Daily Crier*'s taken a different line,' he noted, referring to the *Bulletin*'s great rival. 'They claim these supposed Ripper killings are simply a hoax designed to publicise the Garrick's new production of *Sweeney Todd* with Miles Davenish in the lead role.'

'Davenish?' Lestrade bristled with disapproval. 'I thought that lunatic was still locked away in a sanitarium.'

'No, he's out now and back on the stage,' I said. 'According to the reviews his performance is making audiences gasp.'

'I don't doubt that at all,' said Rayner, rising to his feet and stubbing out his cigarette. 'The man's notoriously unhinged. Half the actors in London refuse to work with him, but he does draw in the crowds.'

'I met him once back before he cracked up,' said Gail. 'He was blacked up to play Othello then and wouldn't let anyone see him without his makeup. I'll never forget how he leered at me – and I've been leered at by experts.'

We gathered around Lestrade's desk where a large map showed the areas thought most likely to prove the scene of an attack. Laid out before us were lists of personnel and where they were to be deployed.

'We've got Dutfield's Yard and Mitre Square staked out,' said Lestrade, 'just in case.'

'Because those are the locations of the original Ripper murders on this night,' I surmised.

'Correct, doctor,' Lestrade confirmed. 'Up until now, our bird hasn't stuck to the same locales as the Ripper, but it occurs to me that, if the sickness in his head keeps growing, he might be getting more like the Ripper all the time.'

'It is a reasonable precaution,' Holmes agreed, though without enthusiasm.

'I've also sent Constable Coleman in plain clothes to keep watch on Dr Carvel's house,' Lestrade continued, 'in case he decides to sneak out.'

'And what about Damon Sardinas?' I inquired.

'I'm going to be on him like glue,' said Rayner. 'I've done some checking up on Mr Sardinas. Did you know that during his time at art school he was had up for a drunken assault on a fellow student? I'll be shadowing him all night, and if he's out to bag himself a Sabine, then he's in for a fatal shock.'

There was an edge to Rayner's voice which prompted me suspect that my account of Sardinas' behaviour towards Gail had engendered in him a cold antipathy towards the artist. This did not bode well for Sardinas, for I was aware that Mycroft's instructions gave Rayner a dangerous degree of leeway in dealing with a suspected killer.

'Commander,' said Lestrade, as Rayner made for the door, 'I know you've got quite the reputation in your own circles, but tonight you're under my command. I expect you to follow the same rules as any other police officer.'

Rayner paused and made a point of adjusting his shoulder holster. 'I'll bear that in mind, inspector.'

No sooner was he gone than there came a tap at the door. It opened to admit WPC Laurel Summers dressed as I had never seen her before. She wore a low-cut floral frock and red high heels, with entirely too much makeup defacing her pretty features.

'So, Summers,' Lestrade addressed her with a gruffness intended to cover his discomfiture at her appearance, 'are your girls all ready for a night on the town?'

'Every one of them has a cosh in her handbag and a whistle to raise the alarm.' Summer produced these items from her own bag and displayed them proudly.

Lestrade grunted his satisfaction. 'Each of them will have a constable hanging about the area,' he informed Holmes and me, 'keeping enough distance to avoid spooking our man, but close enough to rush in when he hears the signal.'

'Are we trying to scare him off or lure him in, sir?' Summers inquired.

'The best thing would be if we could bag him,' said Lestrade, 'but I don't want your girls taking any stupid chances. You'd better have a last word with them about that and make sure they've got it straight.'

'I'll do that, sir.' Summers left the room with a quick salute that appeared quite incongruous coming from someone dressed as a good-time girl.

'It might be there's enough coppers out there to throw him off his game,' Lestrade suggested to the rest of us. 'Maybe even get him to chuck the whole business.'

'No. If we are fortunate enough to frustrate him tonight,' Holmes was sombre and assured, 'he will kill again at the very earliest opportunity.'

'You seem very sure of that, Mr Holmes.' Lestrade was clearly disappointed at having even this thin hope brushed aside. 'Do you really think we're in for two murders tonight?'

'To duplicate that bloody feat doubles the risk,' Holmes stroked his chin meditatively, 'and our man is noted for his caution.'

'Caution?' Lestrade stared at him. 'I wouldn't exactly call him cautious.'

'Oh no?' Holmes eyed the inspector sardonically. 'He imitates the Ripper, but not to the extent of duplicating the murder locations. That would make it too easy for us to set a trap for him. He mutilates, yes, but in a fashion that is restrained and precise, not with the brutal savagery of the Ripper. In this way he lessens the chance of picking up any tell-tale spatters of blood on his person and minimises the time he leaves himself exposed to possible discovery.'

'You think then that there will be only one murder?' I concluded.

'No, I think whatever motivates him to follow the pattern of the Ripper's murders is too important for him not to persist in it, whatever additional risk that poses.'

'Then that gives us a better chance of laying hands on him,' said Lestrade, 'if we're quick enough.'

He glanced at the clock on the wall, which showed that nine p.m. was approaching. 'We'd best get moving then. Now remember that Mr Holmes and I will be coordinating from my command car, which will maintain radio contact with several of our points around the city. As soon as we pick up on something Mr Holmes judges might be our man, we'll be there in a flash.'

Gail eyed the papers on the desk. 'Well, doc, it looks like you and I are going for a romantic stroll around Marble Arch.'

'Hardly very romantic,' I said, slipping my old Webley service revolver from my overcoat pocket to demonstrate that I was armed.

'We still do not know your connection with our man, Miss Preston,' said Holmes, 'but you should remain alert for a familiar face.'

'I will,' Gail assured him. 'But, doc, go easy on the trigger finger. I don't want you blazing away at some guy just because he says hello to me.'

'I shall be the very soul of restraint,' I said. 'But you be sure to keep close.'

'Right, good luck, everybody,' said Lestrade as the meeting broke up. 'Be careful and stay in touch. Let's hope this whole thing blows over or that we bag our man before he can do any more harm.'

We dispersed to join the roving army of police officers, both uniform and plain clothes, who were spread across the city. Holmes and I had discussed earlier that Gail might prove a lure to the killer, in which case I was determined to thwart whatever intentions he might have towards her.

As Holmes, Lestrade, Gail and I emerged in a group, we ran straight into Tommy Wiggins, who had clearly been lurking in the street outside.

'Tommy, what on earth are you doing here?' I exclaimed.

'I wanted to know if I could be of any use, sir.' Wiggins addressed Holmes with the innocent loyalty of a puppy.

'You have your duties as a fire warden to carry out, Wiggins, and they have not ceased to be of importance,' Holmes assured him. 'But you should be alert for any man who appears to be following or accosting a woman.'

Wiggins nodded enthusiastically. 'Right you are, Mr Holmes. I'll do anything at all to help you crack the case.' He added, '*And* see that you get the credit for it.'

He glared pointedly at Lestrade, but the inspector was climbing into the back of his command car and was quite oblivious of his criticism. Wiggins threw Holmes a salute as his idol got in beside the inspector, and then he set off down the street whistling to himself.

'Come on, doc,' said Gail, taking my arm. 'The subway's over this way.'

As we set out for the nearest tube station, I wondered that I felt so protective towards a woman who seemed more than capable of taking care of herself. I recalled Holmes's maxim that a detective must never let his emotions override his logical faculties, and I knew that I had to be on guard. If there truly was a connection between Gail and our killer, this night might well be the proof of it.

22

THE WATCHES OF THE NIGHT

We emerged from the Tube at Marble Arch and walked out into the London streets. Even on a Tuesday night with the blackout in force, there was still an air of gaiety wafting from the clubs, restaurants and public houses. This was a city where for long, dreadful months bombs had fallen like rain from the sky, the detonations as relentless as thunder and the raging fires more ruinous than lightning. During such dark times men and women learned to take their pleasures filled to the brim, knowing that any given night might be their last.

Even now, when the worst horrors of the Blitz had largely passed, that embattled spirit remained, for death still stalked the world in jackboots and armour, and however the war might be finally resolved not everyone alive now would live to see what peace lay beyond. Better to embrace the joys of this world now, many thought, than to put one's hope in the promise of the future.

There was ample evidence of this to be heard, if not seen, all around us. Every place of entertainment we passed seemed full to capacity, the blackout curtains doing nothing to muffle the sounds of revelry within. Some of the pedestrians around us sported white scarves and handkerchiefs or carried newspapers to make themselves more visible to drivers crawling past in cars whose lights were reduced to mere slits. The kerbs and crossings in this part of the city had been painted white as an aid to navigation, but many people, like ourselves, also carried torches to help them pick out helpful landmarks.

Every now and then a door would open, briefly spilling light into the street as patrons came and went. Each time it happened, I made a point of closely examining anyone caught in the illumination, determined to commit the faces to memory. If Holmes was correct, then Crimson Jack was known to his victims under a more mundane name. In some earlier meeting lay the root of his murderous purpose which led him to track down these particular women.

'Cripes, doc,' said Gail presently, 'you need to take it easy with the eyeballing.'

'What do you mean?'

'I mean when you give a passing couple a gander, you need to be more subtle about it. That sailor you were checking out back there was getting set to slug you when I pulled you away.'

I was taken aback. 'Really?'

'Yeah, really,' Gail assured me. 'You were so fixed on his mug you didn't notice him clenching his fists.'

'You're right, I suppose. I just can't help the awful fear that we might walk right past our killer hand in hand with his next victim and never even suspect.'

'Well, it won't do any good to spook every innocent slob who passes by. Look, try to relax, act like you're out for a good time with a pretty girl on your arm. Or am I not pretty enough?'

The question sounded only half teasing. 'You are very attractive, to be sure,' I told her with complete candour. 'However, under the circumstances, it is difficult to act as though we're having a good time.'

'Do your best. Haven't you picked up any tips on acting from your pal Sherlock?'

'I don't believe I have ever had it in me to be an actor. Dissimulation doesn't come easily to me.'

'No, you're straight and honest, aren't you?' Her voice was warm. 'True steel is what you are. Sherlock's lucky to have you watching his back.'

I trusted that the darkness would hide my blushes at the compliment.

We set a course away from the more populous quarters towards the warren of back streets which were the pitch black haunt of our quarry. En route I used my torch to direct Gail's attention to a nearby ruin.

'That used to be St Godfrey's church,' I told her. 'Before the Blitz I knew it well.'

We halted before the remains of a wall in which lancet windows were still visible. 'I attended my friend Trotter's wedding there back in '32,' I recalled. 'A beautiful place it was. Interestingly the only thing that wasn't damaged when the bomb hit was a wooden figure of the archangel Michael that's now been moved to Holy Trinity.'

Gail took advantage of our brief stop to light a cigarette. 'Well, I hope he does a better job of protecting that place than he did this one.'

We pressed on, using our torches sparingly to maintain our course. As we turned a corner, Gail fetched up short and clutched my arm. Pointing to a wall on the other side of the road, she breathed, 'Look, doc, there's something written there.'

I led the way across the street, bracing myself to confront that dread name chalked in large red letters. Instead my torch revealed a quite different message daubed there in bright yellow paint: TURN ON THE LIGHTS!

'Looks like Charlie Deeds has really set something rolling,' Gail commented with grudging admiration.

'It's a terrible thing,' I reflected, 'that while darkness

brings death on the streets, light would bring it raining down from the sky.'

Could it be, I wondered, that this was the purpose lurking behind what were on the surface the acts of a madman? Might Mycroft's fears prove well founded? It appeared to me entirely plausible that the enemy were preparing a final, ruinous air raid and only required the lights to guide their way for one single night of terrible destruction.

I reserved the thought for the time being, conscious of the need to keep on the move. Passers-by were few and far between in this quarter, but at a minor crossroads we spotted a woman standing alone at a corner. Was she here for an assignation with an acquaintance who had only just re-entered her life and might he even now be closing in on his target?

At the sound of someone approaching, the woman flicked on a lowered torch to illuminate a pair of dirty white high heels. Transferring the beam to me, she struck a provocative pose and smoothed her cotton top tightly over her large bosom.

From her slatternly dress and lewd demeanour it was clear that her nocturnal activities were of an entirely professional nature. She gave me a pouting smile that vanished abruptly when she caught sight of Gail and realised I was not alone.

'Wot you after?' she challenged. 'I'll tell you right off, I don't do none of that funny business, see?'

'My dear woman,' I addressed her with as much dignity as I could summon under the circumstances, 'I assure you we have no need of your services.'

'Look, sister,' Gail interposed, 'you should be safely locked away indoors tonight. Don't you know there's a killer on the loose?'

'Killer?' the woman snorted derisively. 'Everybody knows

that's just a story cooked up by those prigs on the public decency committee to scare us off the streets. Well, we ain't scared, see? We've got as much right to make a living as anybody else.'

With a haughty toss of her head she strutted off into the darkness, her heels clacking loudly on the pavement.

'Well, I guess that's us told,' said Gail with an ironic shrug.

'No doubt there are many such women on the streets tonight with a similarly careless attitude,' I said pityingly.

We had now entered the dingier regions of Bayswater and were walking down a narrow street of closed shop fronts. The neighbourhood looked as though it had seen its share of hard times, but here and there our torches picked out a touch of fresh paint laid on in defiance of the fortunes of war.

Gail stopped to lean against a rusty railing. She removed her left shoe and rubbed her stockinged foot. 'I don't know about you, doc, but I could use a break.'

I checked my watch by torchlight and saw it was almost midnight. Redirecting the beam up the street, I spotted a late night café that was open for business. 'Allow me to buy you a coffee,' I offered, pointing the way. 'With any luck they'll have a public telephone and we can check in with Scotland Yard.'

Gail replaced her shoe. 'I suppose a drink's out of the question?' she inquired perkily.

'Perhaps a small brandy,' I conceded, 'to ward off the cold.'

I broke off short at the sound of three urgent blasts of a police whistle echoing down a nearby alleyway. Exchanging a swift glance, we took off into the darkness. Three more blasts on the whistle guided us round a corner to where we saw a uniformed officer crouched beside a figure lying on the pavement.

By the light of his lantern I recognised him as a young constable named Mullen. As we drew closer he recognised me also and his relief at our arrival was palpable.

'Dr Watson – thank God it's you!'

I crouched down beside him and examined the person he was tending.

'She's still alive, sir,' Mullen gasped desperately. 'But only just.'

The woman had been stabbed in the chest and her breath was so shallow as to be barely detectable. I unwrapped my scarf and pressed it down to staunch the blood that was seeping from her wound.

'What happened, man?' I checked her pulse and felt it fading rapidly.

Mullen's jaw quivered. I could see he was almost paralysed with shock, but with an effort he recovered his voice. 'I heard a sort of muffled scream and came running round the corner there. I saw two people struggling. When I blew my whistle he stabbed her and ran off in that direction.'

He pointed a shaking finger.

I was barely aware of Gail standing over me until she reached into my overcoat pocket and pulled out my revolver.

'You take care of the girl, doc,' she ordered, pivoting on her heel and tossing her cigarette aside. 'I'm going to nail the son of a bitch.'

'Gail, no!' I cried, but it was no use. She was already racing off into the darkness.

Mullen hauled himself to his feet. 'Don't worry, sir, I'll go after her.'

I grabbed him by the sleeve to hold him back. 'No, you get to the nearest phone and call for an ambulance.' I felt myself torn three ways at once, but in spite of my fears for Gail's safety, my patient's welfare demanded priority. The young constable was riven by a similar conflict of duties, I could tell, but he nodded and set off to find a telephone.

I gently brushed some dark hair from the girl's face. At my touch her eyes opened and she coughed weakly. A dribble of red at the side of her mouth told me that blood was filling her lungs. Even if an ambulance should arrive in the next few minutes it would take a miracle to save her.

I felt her hand clutch weakly at my arm and her face convulsed in pain as she strained to speak.

'Remain quiet and keep your eyes fixed on me,' I instructed her in my most reassuring, professional voice. 'An ambulance will be here soon.'

Whether she believed me or not she spurned my advice and continued trying to form a word. Her lips trembled and finally she forced a sound from her constricted throat.

'Conrad Brown.' The name came out as a strangled choke, but it was clear none the less. 'It was Conrad Brown.' This last was an exhausted gasp that was barely audible, but the meaning was clear. She would not die without naming her killer.

The effort of making her fateful accusation drained the last of her strength and a cold tremor passed down her limbs. Her eyes closed and I felt the final vestige of life pass out of her. Still pressing my scarf uselessly to her wounded breast, I hung my head in sorrow and could only admire her heroic determination.

It was then that I heard a gunshot echo in the distance.

23

THE DARK LABYRINTH

At the sound of that shot cracking the cold night air my heart skipped a beat and there came a rush of blood to my head. I felt the impulse to dash off into the gloom in search of Gail, but the inviolable ethics of my profession compelled me to remain on my knees at the side of my late patient. This poor young woman deserved at least the respect of a prayer – though I was at a loss to find the words.

I was still kneeling when Gail materialised out of the darkness, the pistol at her side issuing a faint smell of cordite. My sense of relief almost made me too weak to stand, but as she drew close I struggled to my feet. It was all I could do not to fling my arms about her.

'Gail, that was a foolish risk to take.' My concern for her safety lent a hard edge to my voice. 'I heard a shot.'

'He got clean away,' Gail told me ruefully. 'I just loosed a round off into the air to make myself feel better.'

Her expressive grey eyes turned to the victim at my feet and I shook my head to indicate that she was gone. Handing the pistol back to me, Gail knelt down beside the body. She placed a tender hand on the dead woman's brow and gently closed her eyes.

'You rest easy, honey,' she said in a husky murmur. 'You're through with this lousy, hard-hearted world. You're going to a better place now, where nobody will ever hurt you again.'

I was surprised to hear such a sentiment from one whom I had taken to be more cynical. 'Do you really believe that?' I asked.

'Sure I do.' Gail looked up at me with moistened eyes. 'I may not be the most devout Methodist ever to come out of Scranton, but I know there's got to be something better than this.' She rubbed away a tear and gazed around at the dark, war-scarred street. 'There's just got to be.'

A rush of booted feet heralded the return of PC Mullen.

'There's an ambulance on the way, sir,' he reported, 'and word's been passed on to Inspector Lestrade.'

'Too late for an ambulance now, I'm afraid. But you did all you could, Mullen,' I assured him.

The young constable glanced over at Gail and gave a sigh of relief. 'Glad to see you're all right, miss. That was very bold of you, but . . .'

Gail stood up and groped in her handbag for a cigarette. 'No need to worry about me, sonny. I'm tough as nails.'

I did not comment on the fact that the damp smudge on her cheek told a different story.

In the next twenty minutes the ambulance arrived, as did more officers responding to the sound of a whistle and the gunshot. They kept at bay those denizens of the night who were drawn to the scene by a ghoulish attraction, threatening them with arrest if they didn't move off.

Presently the command car arrived and Holmes leapt out, followed by Lestrade. As Mullen gave his report to the inspector, Holmes crouched over the body, his keen eye taking in every detail.

'Made a clean getaway, did he?' growled Lestrade.

'All I saw from the distance was a shadowy figure,' said Mullen, 'and I had to stop to tend to the victim.'

'You did right, of course,' Lestrade conceded gruffly.

'This lady here chased after him,' said Mullen.

Lestrade turned his attention to Gail and raised a bushy eyebrow. 'Is that so? That was very rash of you, Miss Preston.'

Gail shrugged and blew out a plume of smoke. 'I guess I've seen too many cowboy pictures. I heard somebody lamming out ahead of me, but I lost him in that maze out there.'

She waved her cigarette at the network of narrow streets and alleyways that ran between here and Kensington.

Holmes gathered himself to his feet and thrust his hands deep into his pockets. 'This was a brave young woman,' he declared. 'When the killer looped the garrotte over her neck, she was quick enough to get her fingers underneath before it closed around her throat. The cuts can be seen on the fingers of her right hand. While they struggled, she was able to scream, alerting a constable, the sound of whose whistle alerted the killer to the imminent danger of discovery. He needed to escape at once, so, abandoning his usual methods, he made one quick stab at the heart and fled, unaware that his victim yet lived.'

'Yes, the blade was aimed under the rib cage up towards the heart,' I said. 'An awkward stroke to make from behind.'

Holmes nodded. 'He probably would have preferred to cut her throat, but, as already noted, her hand was in the way, thanks to her quick reactions. As a nurse, perhaps her instinct for life-threatening danger was sharper than that of the other victims.'

'A nurse, you say, Mr Holmes?' Lestrade grunted.

'The practical footwear and the fact that she wears a watch on her breast,' I explained, 'both carry over from her profession, even when she's off duty.'

'Exactly, Watson,' Holmes affirmed. 'Again, our killer follows the pattern of his predecessor neither in location nor in the nature of his victim.'

'If only she could have lived long enough to tell us something,' Lestrade sighed mournfully.

I gave Holmes a meaningful look and drew him and the inspector aside. Gail followed and stood close by, hugging herself against the chill of night.

'She did say something.' I kept my voice low so that no one else would overhear. 'She spoke a name: Conrad Brown. She said that Conrad Brown had killed her.'

Lestrade's beefy face lit up. 'Why, that's it then! There can't be many of that name living in London.'

Holmes's attitude was altogether more restrained. 'We must keep this information confidential until we can investigate further. Otherwise, after another murder such as this, any man of that name is liable to be lynched by a vengeful mob.'

'As you say, Mr Holmes,' said Lestrade, resuming a grave demeanour, 'we'll keep it under our hats until we can track him down. Then he clapped his hands together in satisfaction. 'But this is a real lead at last!'

After three weeks of chasing after shadows, there was no mistaking his sense of triumph at having something solid to grab hold of.

'Inspector! Inspector!' Perkins, Lestrade's driver, was yelling from the car. 'A call's just come in, sir – WPC Summers has been attacked!'

The shock in Lestrade's face was evident and I too felt my heart sink at the thought of that dedicated young officer sharing the grisly fate of the poor woman here.

'Come along, Mr Holmes!' Lestrade exclaimed as he raced to the car. 'This may be a fresh trail.'

Holmes darted after him at once and I hesitated only long enough for Gail to wave me on. 'Go get him! I'm keeping this poor girl company until they take her away. She deserves that much.'

Holmes and I piled into the car behind Lestrade and

Perkins. With the siren screeching we raced south past Hyde Park at a dangerous speed.

'Holmes, if he's made a victim of that girl . . .' I could scarcely find words to describe an adequate revenge.

'Yes, I know, my friend, I know,' said Holmes with rigid calm.

We pulled up in a backstreet of Earl's Court where three uniformed officers were already on the scene. We bundled out of the car and to my great relief I saw WPC Summers standing in their midst. She appeared unharmed, though she was examining her right wrist with a wince of pain.

Lestrade bolted to her side with almost fatherly concern. 'Summers, are you all right?'

'This lout thought he'd try it on,' said one of the constables with evident pride in his colleague, 'but he hadn't reckoned on our Laurel.'

He indicated the brawny figure lying at his feet, whose stentorian breathing indicated a state of drunken unconsciousness.

'When he came for me, I raised the alarm,' explained Summers, 'but the whistle didn't scare him off. When he made a grab for me I twisted him by the arm and bashed his face into the wall.'

Lestrade tipped back his hat and grinned at her. 'A neat job, I must say.'

'He's unarmed, though,' said Summers half apologetically, 'and too plastered to be much of a threat. Seems he's just an over-amorous drunk trying to force himself on a doxy.'

'You certainly dealt with his advances very efficiently,' I observed, unable to restrain a smile of relief that the brave young policewoman had not fallen victim to the man we pursued.

'Just a reflex, I suppose,' said Summers modestly.

'Sprained my wrist doing it, though. I'm afraid you and Mr Holmes will have to drive yourselves for a while.'

'You'd best get that seen to, Summers,' Lestrade advised. 'And, er, take the rest of the night off.'

'Thanks, sir,' said the young WPC. She added, 'Sorry it wasn't him.'

Holmes had kept his distance, chafing over the distraction. I knew that his brain was racing through the possibilities of the murderer's next strike, trying to second-guess him.

As we returned to the car, Perkins's head popped out.

'Sir, there's a body been found at Notting Hill, just behind Peel Street. This time it's him for sure!'

We piled into the vehicle and Lestrade gave his driver a sharp poke in the arm. 'Well, get moving man, for God's sake! There's no time to hang about.'

Perkins slammed his foot down and with a roar we jolted into motion. Once again we were racing through the blackened streets, our hooded headlights barely illuminating the road ahead.

24

THE DEVIL UNLEASHED

'What do you think, Holmes?' I asked my friend. 'Has he carried out the double killing as you feared?'

Holmes stirred himself from a solemn reverie. 'I did point out the increased risk,' he reminded me, 'and I have been attempting to work out what stratagem he might employ to circumvent the hazard of striking twice in one night.'

'He doesn't care about risks!' Lestrade exclaimed with sudden violence. 'He's a killer, plain and simple, and that's all there is to it. Thanks to that plucky young nurse back there, though, he's undone for sure.'

I could tell from the grim set of my friend's jaw that he did not share the inspector's bullish confidence.

We arrived at a small yard at the rear of a textile warehouse. When we climbed out of the car we found our way blocked by a crowd of about twenty men and women, all agog with excitement and horror. A single harried constable was struggling to keep them back and he greeted the arrival of reinforcements with a renewed burst of authority.

'Right, back you lot!' he bellowed. 'Make way for the inspector!'

'Inspector, eh? Got here a bit late, didn't you?' taunted a voice from the crowd.

Lestrade ignored the jibe and shouldered his way through, with Holmes and myself pressing behind. My hackles rose when I saw that the ubiquitous Charlie Deeds had arrived before us with a photographer in tow.

The harassed constable was quick to apologise. 'Sorry, sir, they were already here when I showed up,' he told Lestrade.

'I've had my hands full keeping this lot from tramping all over the scene.'

A sudden flash from the photographer's camera lit up the wall before us, revealing one of the reasons for the hubbub. Scrawled across the brickwork in large, red chalk letters were the words *CRIMSON JACK DID THIS*.

'Holmes, is it authentic?' I muttered through gritted teeth.

My friend answered with a terse nod.

Lestrade was bearing down on the newsmen. 'Here, you, hand that over!' he ordered, reaching for the camera.

Deeds nimbly interposed himself. 'Not so fast, inspector,' he chided. 'The public's got a right to know about this. Freedom of the press, I say.'

From the crowd came a rumble of agreement as Deeds and his companion backed away from the looming bulk of Lestrade.

Holmes suddenly pounced on an individual in a shabby uniform and peaked cap who was loitering nearby. 'And you, who are you?' he demanded.

The man started at the sharpness of Holmes's question. 'Albert Wheeler I am, the night watchman here. It's me that found the body.'

'The body?' I echoed. I stared into the far shadows of the yard and saw a human form laid out there.

Wheeler nodded. 'Soon as I saw it and them words on the wall, I went and phoned the *Bulletin*.'

'The *Bulletin*!' Lestrade exploded. 'This is a police matter!'

The watchman shrank before the inspector's wrath. 'They've offered a reward,' he stammered. 'And Mr Deeds said he'd see the police was called in.'

'Which I did,' Deeds affirmed with self-righteous pride.

'Only once you were sure of beating them to the scene,' I accused him.

At this point another police car arrived and four officers leapt out to begin dispersing the crowd. Deeds and his companion began to slink away.

'Deeds!' thundered Lestrade. 'Get back here, you worm!'

Quickening his pace, Deeds slipped off into the cover of the dark. 'You'll not cover this up,' his voice floated back to us. 'The Ripper's struck again and signed his name to it. It's written on that wall as plain as the song of Nebuchadnezzar.'

The inaccuracy of his biblical allusion did nothing to lessen the horrid significance of his discovery. By morning the name Crimson Jack would be on front pages all over London.

'The body, Watson,' Holmes prompted as the protesting crowd were herded back to where they would have no view of our activities.

Together we knelt beside the dead girl and I played my torch over her.

I judged her to be no more than nineteen years old, which rendered her fate all the more tragic. Other points of interest caught my attention, however, beginning with the brutal wounds. The cut throat and abdominal incision were the same as those of the first two victims, but there was a notable lack of blood. Once again, the lower intestine had been removed and laid beside the body.

'Holmes,' I said, examining the pale limbs, 'she's stone cold and rigor mortis has long set in. She must have been dead for twelve hours at least.'

Holmes nodded. 'She was not killed tonight then, nor is this the scene of the murder. I was prepared for something like this. I expect she followed the same profession as our first victim.'

'Really, Holmes?' I could barely contain my surprise. 'But she is so young.'

'Youth is no protection against vice. Our man would select an easy victim whose absence for a day or more would stir up no great alarm.'

'You're saying then that he killed this girl some time back and kept her hidden somewhere?' I was appalled at the methodical coolness of it.

'Most likely wrapped up in a tarpaulin and locked in the boot of a car,' Holmes surmised dispassionately.

Lestrade had been hovering near, listening to us. 'Well, that's a turn-up and no mistake. Rather than do the double proper, so to speak, he played it safe and hedged his bets.'

'Which only further illustrates that he wishes to create the illusion of the Ripper killings,' Holmes declared, 'but is not concerned to imitate them with any faithfulness. These murders are like forged paintings signed by the forger himself.'

Lestrade rubbed the back of his neck. 'Well, if what you say is true, then I can't make head nor tail of it.'

We stood and I gazed at the letters on the wall, barely visible in the gloom. They were like a challenge cast in our faces. By adding the words DID THIS to his signature, he ensured that anyone who set eyes on his message could be in no doubt that it was written by the murderer of the girl whose pitiful body lay alone on the cold, dank ground.

Lestrade was also staring morosely at the wall. 'There will be merry hell to pay now,' he predicted sourly.

'Yes, the devil's loose,' I agreed.

As dawn broke across the city we gathered in Lestrade's office, like a defeated army with nothing left to do but lick our wounds and count our losses. The two women had been identified from their ration books as nurse Emma Wainwright, and Bronwyn Hughes. Lestrade had dispatched men to their home addresses to gather as much information as they could before the press began crawling all over the story.

The inspector had recovered a measure of resignation. 'Much as I wish I could have stopped that weasel Deeds from running off with his pictures,' he said, sipping on a tepid cup of black tea, 'it's maybe not entirely a bad thing that the cat's out of the bag.'

'What do you mean by that, Lestrade?' I asked, setting aside a half-eaten digestive biscuit, for which I had scant appetite.

'Well, now that the public knows the killer is real and calls himself Crimson Jack, somebody out there might twig who he really is.'

Holmes was standing at the window gazing out at the blood-red sky. 'The more likely result,' he suggested, 'is that Scotland Yard will now be deluged with letters signed Crimson Jack.'

Lestrade refused to be daunted. 'Ah, but we've got something solid to go on,' he declared. 'We've got his real name – Conrad Brown.'

'Has it occurred to you, Lestrade,' I said, 'that there is every likelihood the man made himself known to these women under an assumed name?'

'Granted that's possible, doctor,' Lestrade conceded, 'but might it not be the case that he's killing them because they actually know his name?'

Gail was slumped wearily in a hard chair beneath a map of London, but at this she stirred. 'Why would he kill them just because they know his name?' she asked.

Her grey eyes were dulled by the long night and only her

lipstick lent any colour to her face.

'I couldn't say,' Lestrade responded. 'Perhaps Mr Holmes could shed some light on that.'

Holmes remained at the window with his fingers knotted together behind his back. I knew that the death of two more women weighed heavily upon him and I could think of nothing to say that would ease his troubled mind.

The unhappy silence was broken when the door flew open and Rayner stalked in. He flung himself into the nearest chair with an exclamation of disgust. 'Well, that was a bloody waste of time!' he grated.

'I take it, then, that Mr Sardinas is not our man,' Lestrade presumed.

'Not unless there are two of him,' said Rayner. He had about him the frustrated air of a professional hunter denied his prey. 'I stuck so closely to him, I could smell the oil on his hair. Followed him around various night spots all over town, watched him drink cocktail after cocktail, laugh with his arty friends and try to pick up a couple of women. It was about two when he slunk off home to bed. I kept watch from the street until I was sure it was futile.'

Gail leaned forward and offered him the consolation of a cigarette. Rayner jammed it between his teeth and snapped a flame from his lighter.

She said consolingly, 'You didn't miss anything, Phil. We were stumbling about in the dark all night and the rat stayed three steps ahead of us.'

Rayner eyed her sharply through his first puff of smoke. 'I heard you went running after him, Gail. Damn fool thing to do.'

'I may never have been in a gunfight with drug runners the way you have, but I know how to shoot,' Gail asserted. 'If I could just have gotten a bead on him for one second.' She stubbed out her cigarette and mimicked firing a gun with her right hand.

'Well, the night's not a total loss.' Lestrade attempted to strike an optimistic note. 'We'll soon have background on the new victims, and Len King is performing the post-mortems right now. Plus I've got Otley checking directories, files and phone books for anybody named Conrad Brown.'

'Didn't you have a man keeping watch on Dr Carvel?' I asked.

'Yes, Coleman,' said Lestrade. 'He hasn't reported in, so I sent Perkins and a couple of the lads to check on him. He's probably dozed off.'

Holmes abruptly turned away from the window. 'You haven't heard from him, you say?'

Lestrade stood and placed his big hands flat on the desk in front of him. 'That's right. Say, you don't suppose . . .'

Before he could finish the ominous thought, there was a rap at the door and Perkins stumbled in, gasping.

'Coleman, sir, it's Coleman. He's . . . we found him . . .'

'Take a breath, man, and get a grip on yourself,' Lestrade commanded firmly.

Struggling to regain his composure, the officer stood to attention and reported, 'He's dead, sir. We found his body stuffed behind some bushes across the street from Carvel's house. He'd been strangled.'

'And what about Dr Carvel?' Holmes's question was as sharp as a sword thrust.

'He didn't answer the door, so we broke in,' said Perkins. 'He's gone, sir. He's done a bunk.'

25

CONFESSIONS BY FIRELIGHT

'Well, that settles it then,' declared Lestrade. 'It was Carvel all along, and it was you, Mr Holmes, that put us on to him in the first place. There's probably some taint in the blood that runs in the family.'

'I wouldn't be so sure,' said Holmes. 'I would prefer to wait until we have more information on the latest victims before we leap to any conclusions.'

'Oh, come along, Mr Holmes!' Lestrade's exasperation was evident. 'The blighter sneaked out, got the drop on poor Coleman, did away with him, then sneaked off to do his dirty work. It's as plain as day.'

Holmes remained dubious. 'You're saying he was able to get out of the house without your man spotting him, sneak up on him from behind and strangle him?'

'That must be what happened,' Lestrade insisted. 'Coleman must have been distracted. Either that or he dozed off.'

'If Carvel was able to get out of the house without Coleman spotting him,' Holmes objected, 'why did he not simply make his escape? Why take the trouble to tackle an experienced police officer who would prove a far more challenging victim than the women he has targeted?'

'Because he likes it!' Lestrade slammed a fist down on his desk. 'He likes killing so much he wouldn't pass up the chance.'

Holmes turned to Perkins. 'You say officer Coleman was strangled?'

Perkins blanched at the memory. 'The marks round his

throat were obvious,' he replied. 'His tongue was swollen and his eyes bulged horribly.'

'But there were no other injuries, no knife wounds?'

'No, sir, none at all.'

'That doesn't make any difference,' growled Lestrade. 'It's women he hates, so it's only them he mutilates. But Coleman was strangled just like all the others.'

'The inspector does have a point,' Rayner agreed. 'And from what you've told me, Mr Holmes, there's quite a lot pointing to this man Carvel.' His eyes narrowed threateningly. 'If I had been shadowing him, things would have turned out very differently.'

'But what about Conrad Brown?' I asked. 'That was the name given to us by one of tonight's victims.'

'If she was taken from behind, she might not have got a good look at him,' said Lestrade. 'She might have been mistaken or just blurted out the name of somebody she thought had it in for her.'

'There is another possibility, sir,' Perkins interjected.

'Oh really?' Lestrade raised an eyebrow at his subordinate. 'And what might that be?'

'That there's two of them working together,' Perkins suggested, 'Carvel and this man Brown.'

'There, Mr Holmes,' said Lestrade, turning to my friend with some satisfaction, 'what do you say to that?'

Holmes sat down and pulled out his pipe. 'I should prefer to say nothing more for the present, not until all the facts are in.'

Gail rose from her chair with a weary sigh. 'Well, when you catch up with that bozo, give him a kick from me. I'm going to get some sleep.'

'I'll see you home,' I volunteered. After the shock of seeing her run off into the night with my revolver, my fears for Gail's safety had gained new impetus. If the killer was aware that she had pursued him, she might have marked herself out as a potential victim.

'You're on, doc.' Gail suppressed a shudder. 'After a night like this I wouldn't mind a bit of company.'

Holmes had filled his pipe and now lit it with a match. 'Yes, you go ahead, Watson. I'll remain here for the present while the inspector's men are tracing the victims' movements.'

'You're welcome to hang around, Mr Holmes,' said Lestrade magnanimously, 'but it's Carvel we're after – you mark my words.'

To my trained eye Gail's exhaustion resulted as much from excess of emotion as from lack of sleep. I could well imagine the dread, grief and anger that had harrowed her all night, exacerbated by her insistence on accompanying the body of Emma Wainwright all the way to the morgue. From there she had returned to Scotland Yard where she learned of the second body and the fate of PC Coleman.

The killer's taunting letter had drawn her into the centre of this horror and still we did not understand what had persuaded him to make her his intermediary. Had she some future role to play in his plans? Was there a connection somewhere that we were failing to see?

When we got out of the cab at Morley Manors, I had to catch her as she stumbled on the kerb. Once inside we climbed the stairs to her front door. I kept a firm grip on her arm to steady her the whole way.

Fumbling in her bag for her key, she said flatly, 'Doc, we've got to catch this bastard. If we can't stop one maniac with a knife, what chance do we have against one who's got a whole war machine to do his killing for him?'

'Don't worry,' I reassured her, 'I have never known Sherlock Holmes to fail. You may depend upon him absolutely.'

After she had twice missed fitting the key into the lock, I took it from her and let us inside. The parlour was plainly furnished with paintings of horses and photographs of aircraft on the wall. On the desk was a small typewriter with a half full ashtray and an empty whisky glass beside it.

'Shall I make you some coffee?' I offered.

'Just get me to the sofa,' she yawned. 'I'm all in.'

We sat down and I did not resist when she leaned against me for support and rested her head on my shoulder.

'You know, doc, we're supposed to have stories to tell our grandkids,' she murmured sleepily, 'about all the brave and clever things we've done. The only stories I've got to tell would scare the bejeezus out of them. I wish I could come up with just one happy ending to give them, just one. If only . . .'

Her eyes closed and her voice tailed off.

'When it comes to bravery,' I said, 'I'm sure you already have many tales you could tell them, and there will be many more to come.'

Whether my words provided any comfort, I could not tell, for she had fallen asleep. After a few minutes of listening to her quiet breathing, I gathered her up gently in my arms and carried her through to the bedroom. I laid her down carefully on top of the eiderdown and delicately removed her shoes.

I then slipped out, leaving the door slightly ajar. I settled myself in a tolerably comfortable chair, stretched out my legs and closed my eyes. When she awoke from whatever dreams might follow upon so terrible a night, I had decided she would not find herself alone.

I returned to Baker Street late on that dank, overcast afternoon. A fire roared in the grate, illuminating from behind the tall, lean figure of Sherlock Holmes as he wielded his violin with rapt concentration. I recognised Paganini's Caprice No. 4, the longest and most mournful of those twenty-four pieces which were reckoned among the most difficult in the whole history of music.

The deft bow work, the sweeps and flourishes, bespoke a ferocious mental intensity, while his haggard features told of a night and day without sleep when he had sustained himself by coffee and willpower alone. I hoped he had not resorted to something worse.

My eyes drifted to the drawer where I knew he kept the needle and vial that had once caused me so much anxiety on his behalf. Following my gaze, Holmes interrupted his playing to allow himself a thin smile.

'No, Watson, I was not tempted. I must keep my mind clear and my faculties undimmed now more than ever. I forswore that remedy many years ago and keep the instruments of my folly only as a reproach and a reminder of my all-too-human fallibility.'

So saying, he set down his violin and dropped into a chair before the fire. I sat down opposite him, noting how the flickering flames cast haunted shadows over his features, starkly accentuating the sharpness of his bones. In his eyes there glinted an almost inexpressible sorrow.

'Holmes,' I began, surprised at the hushed softness of my own voice, 'over the years you and I have witnessed many awful things, but never have I seen you affected to such an extreme as this. You've taken a blow directly to the heart, I fear.'

A faint smile flickered across Holmes's lips. 'Is that your

opinion as a medical man?'

'It is my opinion as a man – and as a friend.'

He fingered his pipe thoughtfully, but made no move to fill it. For a moment he remained silent, as though steeling himself for some onerous endeavour. I merely waited, and eventually he spoke.

'There is a tale to be told,' he began, 'which I have kept in the utmost secrecy for many years. I suppose now is the time for you to hear it, not only as my one irreplaceable friend but as my chronicler. I would not, however, have you repeat a word of it until long after my passing.'

'I shall respect your wishes, as always,' I vowed.

Holmes accepted the assurance with a brief nod, then drew a deep breath. 'I believe you have always suspected that there was more to my activities in the Great War than the few snippets and vague hints I dropped in your way.'

'Those did seem to me to be mere scraps of something greater,' I admitted. 'Whatever it was that held them all together was shrouded in an impenetrable obscurity.'

'And you were gentleman enough not to press me.' Holmes's tone was one of resolution as he hunched forward. 'Obscure no more, then. Here is the story I have for so long kept locked away in the deepest vault of my memory.'

26

A HIGHER JUSTICE

'By 1917 I had worked my way into the confidence of the German military under the identity of Patrick O'Rourke, an Irish industrial engineer whose hatred of England had prompted him to put his talents at the service of the Kaiser. This enabled me to pass vital information back to London concerning the German war plans, and finally led me to my ultimate goal, a castle in Bavaria which had become a centre for scientific research. Here I met a brilliant young woman named Hannah Goldman, a chemist, who had been assigned to a project developing a new form of poison gas, ten times more lethal that anything yet deployed in the war.

'In the person of O'Rourke I befriended her, initially as a source of information, yes, but something more developed. Her beauty, but even more than that her luminous intelligence and courageous spirit, opened up doorways in my soul I had never known to exist before. I learned that she was revolted at the work she was being compelled to do, a project whose outcome could only be death on an incalculable scale.

'I could not reveal my true identity, but made it clear to her that O'Rourke too had undergone a change of heart and would not see this inhuman weapon deployed against even his worst enemies. We secretly made common cause and formed a daring plan of sabotage. By our joint efforts we were able to destroy the stockpile of gas and the means of producing it in one massive fire that utterly consumed the castle.'

Holmes gazed deeply into the glowing coals of our own hearth, as though he beheld once again that hellish conflagration that had caused so much destruction and yet saved so many lives. With a voice that seemed to come from some distant place, he continued his tale.

'Before we could make our escape, however, we were captured by Colonel Viktor Zarden, the project's head of security and one of the most feared men in the whole Prussian empire. We were separated and I found myself subjected to a brutal interrogation. Without surrendering my true identity, I took the full responsibility for the sabotage upon myself, casting Hannah as an innocent dupe who had not been aware of my intentions.

'That facility of mine with bonds and locks, which you are well aware of, Watson, I had already developed by this time. I was able eventually to escape my cell and overcome the sentry who stood watch over that corridor. Donning his uniform as a disguise, I made a hurried search for Hannah, only to find her already dead from the tortures Zarden had inflicted upon her. To this day I am haunted by the thought that if I had made my escape sooner, if I could have reached her . . .'

Holmes's fingers clenched convulsively around the unlit pipe and he took a few moments to command himself before continuing.

'Zarden was entirely without remorse when he found me crouched over her body, asserting that while I was merely a spy, she was a traitor to her country and so merited much harsher treatment. Before I could lay hands on him, he ordered his guards to open fire on me. I fled before a hail of bullets and only escaped by leaping from a window into the freezing river far below.

'Now my priority had to be returning alive to England in order to deliver the crucial information in my possession. It was a long and arduous journey, and by the time I reached

London my health was quite shattered. Long months in hospital followed and then, when the war was over, I learned that Zarden had vanished like a ghost, leaving behind no clue or trail to be followed.'

Holmes rubbed his temple, as though to ease the pain that still lingered from that long period of recuperation. Gathering his thoughts once more, he resumed his tale.

'My duty to king and country done, I left the employ of our government, for it was necessary to my intentions that I operate as an independent agent with complete freedom of action. And so I created this unique career of consulting detective, which gave me scope to further develop those skills which you have so dramatically delineated in your records of our exploits. I established contacts all over the world, convinced that one day I would recognise some indicator of Zarden's reappearance, and so indeed it proved.

'He had travelled through many countries under a variety of names, in one place trading in state secrets, in another in drugs. Wherever he went, there was a blossoming of evil and death, so I resolved to track him down and put an end to him for once and for all.'

I glimpsed in my friend's eye that predatory gleam I had seen so often before when he was closing on a long-sought quarry. 'That then was the period you disappeared from sight,' I realised, 'and many assumed you were dead, slain by some vengeful enemy.'

'It was I who was the agent of vengeance, Watson, driven by the loss of the one creature who had cast a wondrous light over my whole existence. Eventually, in the back room of an opium den in Shanghai, I confronted the man whose destruction had been my hidden obsession for so many years. I had lured him on in the guise of a customer seeking to purchase arms from him. Instead of negotiating a lucrative deal, he found himself seated across a table from a man who held him at the point of a gun.'

Holmes paused and I held my breath as the tale approached its climax. After he moment he continued.

'When I revealed to him my true identity, he made a cold show of dignity and courage. He had been doing his duty, protecting the security of his nation, he maintained. If I had come here to murder him out of mere revenge, he challenged me, which of us was then the better man?

'But I had no intention of murdering him. No, Watson, I could not act solely out of vengeance, much as I despised him. I had decided to place his fate in the hands of a justice higher than any human court.

'I set the gun down at my elbow and took a small pill box from my pocket. Opening it, I laid it on the table between us. Inside were two identical pills and I explained to Zarden that while one of them was entirely harmless, the other contained a poisonous alkaloid that would kill within seconds.

'Cold beads of sweat broke out on his brow as I outlined my purpose. He had one chance to leave that place alive. He was to pick one of those pills and I would take whichever he left behind. We would then each swallow our pill simultaneously and let whatever providence guides the fates of men decide which of us was to live and which to die.

'At first he attempted to bluster, but when he looked into my eyes he understood the utter seriousness of my purpose, and that if he did not agree to play this macabre game with me I would take up my pistol and shoot him dead. This way at least, I told him, offered an even chance of survival.'

Holmes's tone was implacable, as if he were reliving that dread moment. It chilled me to the bone to think of my friend placing himself in equal danger of death as his hated enemy out of a sense of honour that would not permit him to take on the role of executioner. The firelight dimmed momentarily, as if to reflect this ominous turn of the story.

'Zarden attempted to maintain his composure,' said Holmes, 'with a scornful curl of the lip and a sneering guffaw, but the fear that shrivelled his spirit was only too evident. Gesturing at the pills, I told him to go ahead, that the choice was his.

'Slowly he moved a hand across the table and let it hover over the box. He licked his lips and narrowed his eyes to a squint, as if there were some way for him to discern which pill contained the poison and which was the key to life. There was a tremor in his fingers as he finally picked one up and raised it towards his mouth. I took the remaining pill and prepared to place it on my tongue. "Together then now," I said. "Life or death." "Life or death," Zarden repeated in a hoarse whisper. He inched the pill towards his mouth with a trembling hand, but at the last instant he dropped it and dived across the table, making a desperate play for the gun.

'I fended him off and snatched up the pistol. He hurled himself at my throat and we tumbled to the floor, locked in each other's arms. We rolled this way and that, his curses seething in my ear as we grappled for control of the gun. In the midst of our struggles it went off and shot him squarely through the heart. He died instantly.

'Panting for breath, I dragged myself up and stood over my fallen enemy. In the ignominy of his death he did not appear so very terrible. Not a monster, just a man, ultimately a weak man, who thrived on selfishness and cruelty until he was left with nowhere to run from the consequences of his crimes.'

Holmes looked up at me, fire reflected in his harrowed eyes. 'Hannah's death remains the most profound failure of my entire existence. Can you wonder that I have chosen never to speak of it – until now, when the deaths of these innocent women are like a resurfacing of my worst nightmares?'

I longed for some eloquent words of comfort, but all I could find to say was, 'I understand, Holmes, I understand.' In truth, at that moment I felt the burden of his sadness as heavily as my own long bereavement.

Holmes returned his gaze to the fire, as though Hannah Goldman's face was visible amid the flames. He drew a shuddering breath. 'She was that one, singular woman, Watson. There can never be another.'

I reached out to lay a sympathetic hand on his arm. 'Of course. For me also there can never be another.'

Holmes turned his head. 'You underestimate yourself, my old friend.' The faintest of smiles touched his thin lips. 'Your heart is far more capacious than mine. You will not end your days alone as I will.'

Abruptly he rose from his chair, shaking off the cloud of emotion which had enfolded him in the telling of his tale. 'Enough of the past,' he declared decisively. 'We have facts before us, enough perhaps to allow us to close in on our phantom and seize hold of him at last.'

'Yes, Holmes,' I said, following him to his desk. 'You have spent the day gathering information?'

'Indeed.' He picked up some pages of notes and ran a brisk eye over them. 'Emma Wainwright, the nurse whose life you fought to save, worked at St Mary's Hospital in Paddington. When she went off duty last night, one of her colleagues spotted her outside the front entrance in conversation with a man. In the darkness this colleague, a Nurse Winters, could make out nothing of his features, but stated that they appeared to be on cordial terms.'

'Then he was known to her, as you supposed was the

case with the previous victims.'

'Even so, Watson, even so.'

Holmes's sombre mood of only a few moments ago had given way to that intellectual excitement that always seized him when the details of a mystery were finally coming into sharp relief.

'And the other victim?'

'Miss Bronwyn Hughes, aged nineteen. That she arrived in London only last week we learned from her cousin Verna Evans, who has lived here for the past three years. She it was who suggested to Bronwyn that she join her here in the city to escape the unhappy life she endured in Swansea with a drunken father and shrewish mother. Bronwyn had never been to London before and the lure of the big city was strong. Without money to spend, however, she was forced to spend some tedious evenings at home in her cousin's flat. On Monday she could tolerate the boredom no more and set out on to the streets in search of a good time.'

'So she was killed the night before her body was found, just as you supposed, Holmes.'

'Yes. Dr King's examination has confirmed that and the fact that it was only after the body was brought to last night's location that the throat was cut and the usual organs removed. The killer then signed his name to this crime, which he was unable to do with the other due to Constable Mullen's interruption.'

'But Holmes, if this Welsh girl had only been in London for a week, she could not be one of those referred to by Mags Hopkin when she spoke of them all meeting with this faceless stranger some weeks previously.'

'Exactly so, Watson,' Holmes agreed on a note of triumph.

'But then why kill her?'

'For two very good reasons. Firstly, in order to maintain the appearance of a crazed imitation of the Ripper murders it was necessary that two bodies be found last night. Secondly, by choosing a victim who had no connection to him and the motive behind his crimes, he muddied the waters in hope of throwing us off the track.'

At that moment I heard Mrs Hudson admitting a visitor downstairs. That she had been led to expect this arrival was evidenced by the fact that she allowed the newcomer to ascend the staircase unaccompanied. A knock on our door was followed by the entry of an elderly man with a steely spade of a beard dressed in clerical garb.

'You, I take it, are Sherlock Holmes?' he addressed my friend.

'I am,' Holmes affirmed. 'And this is my friend and colleague Dr John Watson. Watson, may I introduce you to the Reverend Conrad Brown.'

27

MINISTERS OF GRACE

'Of St Luke's in Blackheath,' the clergyman added, removing his wide-brimmed black hat.

'Please come in,' said Holmes, ushering our visitor to a chair.

'The Reverend Conrad Brown,' I repeated in surprise. A chill ran down my spine at the notion that we might be in the presence of the very man we had been seeking all along.

'I received a message that you wished to see me, Mr Holmes,' said Brown, as we seated ourselves opposite him. 'I confess myself at a loss as to why I should receive a summons from so prominent an upholder of the law.'

'I hold no official position, reverend,' Holmes responded modestly, 'but I do what I can in the interests of justice.'

'So I am aware,' said the clergyman. 'Yet I fail to see what help I can be to you in that regard.'

'May I say, reverend, that your works of charity are as well known to the people of London as my own efforts in assisting the police. In fact, I might go so far as to say that your influence is immeasurably greater than my own.'

I simulated a cough to conceal my amusement at my friend's insincere humility.

The clergyman made an exaggerated show of appearing abashed. 'Please, Mr Holmes, my blushes.'

'You have established a number of hostels across the city for the care of women who have, let us put it discreetly, fallen on hard times,' said Holmes.

'That is correct, Mr Holmes. My father, the wealthy sugar merchant Tacitus Brown, devoted some measure of his fortune to helping the poor. When it became clear that my elder brother would inherit the family business, rather than accept a role subordinate to his I chose to enter the church. It was there that I found my own way of continuing my father's good works by founding my first Penitents' Refuge, as I chose to call it.'

'Very appropriate, I'm sure,' I commented stiffly.

'You rescue women from the streets,' Holmes summed up, 'and assist them in acquiring some respectable means of earning a living.'

Brown nodded primly. 'Exactly, Mr Holmes. The first step, of course, is to divest them of the garish trappings of their former existence. We provide them with suitably sober clothing, forbid makeup absolutely, and insist on cutting their hair to a modest length to remove any temptation to vanity.'

Holmes's eyes narrowed briefly, but he refrained from comment as the clergyman warmed to his subject. 'We then put them to work doing laundry and sewing garments for the poor. We have prayers and hymns three times a day and a simple diet of vegetables for the sake of their health.'

'And all this is financed by charitable contributions?' Holmes prompted.

'That, and the welcome support of certain philanthropists, most notably my friend and benefactor Sir Carlton Jessop under the auspices of the Committee for Public Decency.'

'There has been some criticism of the committee, I believe,' I interjected cautiously.

The Reverend Conrad Brown drew himself up. 'I am aware that there are those who have called us interfering busybodies.' He flicked some dust from his sleeve, as though by that gesture he disposed of such doubters. 'However, I prefer to believe that we are ministers of grace, bringing hope to the benighted.'

'Sir Carlton appears very active,' I noted, 'even to the extent of forcing a meeting with the Prime Minister.'

'We share a common purpose in seeking to cleanse our streets of vice,' Brown declared proudly. 'I'm sure you approve, Mr Holmes.'

'My business is with those who cruelly exploit their fellows,' Holmes responded brusquely, 'not with those who are driven to desperation by poverty. I would not condemn a starving man for stealing a loaf of bread, nor a woman for doing whatever she must to feed her children or escape a violent husband.' Seeing the clergyman was discomfited by these remarks, Holmes moderated his tone. 'Still, I am sure each of us in his own sphere believes he is doing what is right. And on this occasion we can cooperate.'

'Really?' Brown's eyebrows were hoisted quizzically. 'In what way?'

'You are no doubt aware of the recent series of murders which has claimed the lives of four women,' said Holmes.

The reverend tutted his distress and disapproval. 'It is dreadful, Mr Holmes, quite dreadful. One can only hope that as a consequence some women may reconsider the errors into which they have fallen.'

I could tell from the tightening of his jaw that my friend was biting back on a caustic retort. 'Be that as it may, reverend, given that in the course of your good works you come into contact with a great number of women, any one of whom might be at risk, I wonder if any of these names are familiar to you?'

From memory he slowly recited the names of the four victims. I watched the clergyman closely as Holmes named Emma Wainwright, alert for any sign of recognition, but there was no hint of one.

'I am sorry, Mr Holmes,' Brown stated placidly. 'Much as I would like to help you, none of those names means anything to me other than having seen them in the newspapers.'

'Perhaps you would be good enough to study these photographs,' said Holmes. He fetched a folder and from it extracted a series of pictures he had obtained of the victims. These he presented for our visitor's inspection.

The reverend popped a pair of spectacles on to his nose and peered closely at each of the four faces. He shook his head and removed his glasses. 'Once again, Mr Holmes, I see nothing familiar here. None of these women has ever crossed my path.'

Holmes returned the photographs to their folder and stood up. 'Well, reverend, I am very sorry to have taken up your time with so little result.'

'Not at all, Mr Holmes,' said the clergyman, rising and straightening his black clerical coat. 'I only regret that I could not be of assistance.'

We walked him to the door and he turned before leaving.

'I wish you the best of luck in your search, Mr Holmes. *Seek and ye shall find*, it says in Scripture. When you find this man,' he added, 'please remember that he is a lost soul and treat him as such.'

'I shall see to it that he receives the treatment he deserves,' Holmes promised.

Once our visitor was gone I uttered a disgusted exclamation and felt a measure of warmth return to the room. 'I suppose Scotland Yard unearthed this reverend for you.'

Holmes nodded. 'The only other Conrad Brown we were able to locate was a boy of ten, whom I feel it is safe to eliminate from our inquiries.'

'So, Holmes, do you believe that this is the man named by Emma Wainwright with her dying breath?'

Holmes picked up the bow of his violin and fingered it thoughtfully. 'He hardly strikes one as homicidal, but you will recall that Wilkes the optician appeared the mildest of men and yet he poisoned five people.'

'Whether or not the reverend is capable of murder,' I said, 'it would be a desperate woman indeed who accepted whatever cold refuge that mean-spirited Pharisee has to offer.'

Holmes started and pointed the bow directly at me. 'Refuge?' He echoed the word as though the sound of it opened a magic portal. 'Refuge – yes, that's it!'

Setting aside the bow, he darted to where his map of London was spread out on the dining table, marked with pins of red, blue and green. He ran a hand lightly over the streets, murmuring softly to himself.

'Holmes, what are these pins?' I asked, eager to know what was passing through his mind at that moment.

'They mark places associated with the three victims who knew the killer,' he explained, 'red for Mags Hopkin, blue for Clara Bentley and green for Emma Wainwright. And there is one spot, here in Holborn, where all three colours come into close proximity.'

With mounting excitement, he continued. 'Mags Hopkin was a frequent customer at the Wheat Sheaf public house – here – on the corner of Rossum Lane. The landlord, we know, was a friend of hers as well as a client, and a source of free drink. The Rialto cinema where Clara Bentley was an assistant manageress is in Theobald's Road , which as you can see is adjacent, while Nurse Wainwright's mother, whom she visited frequently, lives at the bottom of that very same road.'

He looked at me expectantly, but I did not yet perceive the root of his excitement.

'Even so, Holmes, that does not explain what brought three women of such disparate backgrounds together for their fateful encounter with this mysterious man Mags Hopkin spoke of.'

'Think, Watson!' my friend urged, his eyes blazing. 'There is one place where people of every walk of life are thrust together in the face of a common danger.'

With a lean forefinger he jabbed the map. Peering down, I recognised at once the symbol he was pointing to.

It was an air raid shelter.

28

ANGELS IN PERIL

At lunchtime the next day Wiggins was waiting for us on the doorstep of the Wheat Sheaf public bar, not far from the shelter Holmes had pointed out to me. Beckoning us inside, he pointed to a portly, middle-aged man standing by the public house. 'That's the chap I was telling you about, Mr Holmes.'

The man in question was wearing the uniform of an air raid warden. Wiggins approached him and laid a hand on his shoulder. 'Hello, Sid. Here's someone wanting a word with you.' Turning to us, he said, 'Mr Holmes, Dr Watson, this is Sidney Rumbold. The Peckham Road shelter is on his patch.'

'Sherlock Holmes!' Rumbold exclaimed wonderingly. 'Lord love us, who'd have believed it?' He chortled into his bushy moustache.

His amazement did not diminish as we found a table and sat ourselves down. 'Tommy, when you told me you were mates with the great Sherlock Holmes, I thought you were pulling my leg, so I did.'

'Mr Wiggins and I go back a long way,' said Holmes supportively, 'and more than once his assistance has been crucial to my work.'

Rumbold's eyes widened. 'Well, I never!' he declared. 'I can hardly believe I'm sitting here, sharing a pint with the great detective.'

He saluted us with his glass, demonstrating clearly that it was quite empty. Holmes took the none-too-subtle hint. 'Perhaps you'd care for a drink?'

'Why, that's very kind of you,' beamed Rumbold. 'Very gentlemanly, I must say.'

'I'll take care of that,' said Wiggins, pulling out his wallet. 'The usual, Sidney? Right. And you, Mr Holmes? Dr Watson?'

'I'll have a half of bitter, thank you,' I said, as Holmes politely declined.

While Wiggins was at the bar, Holmes got down to business. 'Mr Rumbold, you were on duty on the night in question – July the seventeenth?'

'That's correct, Mr Holmes, the night of the air raid.' He chuckled to himself once more. 'Well, I never – Sherlock Holmes. Who'd have thought it? Wait till I tell the missus about this.'

'Perhaps you could give us your account of what happened that night,' I prompted him before Holmes's patience could be further tested.

Rumbold screwed up his face in thoughtful recollection. 'I've a notion that those planes were a bunch that got separated from their wing, if that's what the Germans call it, and lost their way,' he theorised. 'They were headed for home and on the way decided to unload their cargo on London, so to speak.'

Holmes nodded encouragingly.

'Now, while they don't come much these days,' Rumbold continued, 'everybody remembers what it was like when they came over most every night, dropping death from the skies, if I may express it so dramatically. So soon as the sirens started up, it was panic stations, I can tell you. It's sort of a reflex left over from the Blitz when you had to leg it like billy-o to get to a shelter before the bombs came down. So there's the sirens screaming and me blowing on my whistle fit to burst my lungs, waving folk down the road to the shelter.'

'There were four women in particular we wish to hear about,' I prompted, trying to move him along to the matter that had brought us here.

At this point Wiggins rejoined us with the drinks and sat down. He had chosen to follow the example of his idol's abstemiousness. Rumbold took a long slurp of beer and wiped the foam from his moustache with the back of his hand. 'Ta very much, Tommy!' he exclaimed. 'Now, where was I? Oh yes, Mags was there for sure, Mags Hopkin. It's her that you're specially interested in, is that right?'

'Mags Hopkin and three other women,' said Holmes. 'And a man who was with them.'

'Right you are,' said Rumbold, pausing for another swallow of beer. 'There was a chap they were helping along the street and into the shelter. Mags told me he was dashing across the road in the dark, got clipped by a car, fell and bumped his noggin on the pavement. Kind of stunned he was. But Mags and them other ladies helped him to his feet and got him inside. There were four of them altogether, I recall that clearly.'

'Did you recognise any of the others?' I asked. I felt a certain excitement that we were finally approaching the heart of the mystery.

'Can't say as I did,' Rumbold replied. 'Don't think I'd seen any of them before. Bear in mind there was a couple of hundred crammed into that shelter and me responsible for the lot of them.'

Reaching into his pocket, Holmes took out the photographs of the three victims. 'Do you recognise any of these faces?' he inquired, spreading them out on the table

'That's Mags all right,' the air raid warden confirmed, tapping one picture. He shook his head dolefully. 'She was a good soul, you know, for all that she was on the game. Would do anything for anybody. A bloody shame what happened to her.'

'And the other two?' asked Holmes.

Rumbold shook his head. 'It could be them, but I wouldn't swear to it, not if I was in court with a hand on the Bible, so to speak.'

'And you are quite certain there were four of them?' I pressed him.

'I'll swear to that all right.' He raised his right hand solemnly. 'As God is my witness.'

'What can you tell us about the man?' asked Holmes.

'Nothing at all,' Rumbold answered. 'The way they were all fussing around him, I never even got a glimpse. They fetched him a cup of tea and got a cold cloth for his head. It looked like one of them might have been a nurse. He seemed to pull himself together after a bit. Proper angels they were, proper angels, and I'll not hear any different, not even about Mags.'

'Can you offer no description of the man at all?' I appealed.

'No,' said the warden, 'but if you can find any of those ladies, I'm sure they could tell you all about him. Not Mags, of course. Not now. Damned shame, it is.'

He consoled himself with more beer.

Holmes stood up. 'Thank you for your help, Mr Rumbold. If you recall anything else, anything at all, please contact me at once.'

'I'll do that, sir, you may be assured of that,' Rumbold promised.

'Wiggins, if you and our friend here could track down as many people as possible who were in the shelter that night,' Holmes instructed, 'perhaps one of them can identify the one woman we do not yet have a name for. Keep these photographs. They may be of help in jogging someone's memory.'

'We'll do our best, Mr Holmes,' said Wiggins. 'You can count on me.'

I swallowed the last of my drink and followed Holmes to the exit, leaving Wiggins to chat with his colleague. Behind us we heard a resurgent chuckle: 'Sherlock Holmes – would you believe it!'

Once we were out in the street I voiced my frustration. 'If only he could have given us something, some detail of the fourth woman, or this mysterious man who remains so gallingly faceless!'

'Yes. Unless we can find her first,' said Holmes, 'that fourth woman is in mortal danger.'

'It simply doesn't make sense,' I fumed. 'All they showed this man was kindness.'

'And yet,' said Holmes, 'it seems that very kindness is what has imperilled them.'

When we returned to Baker Street we found Inspector Lestrade enjoying a pot of Mrs Hudson's excellent Darjeeling. 'My word, but that woman brews a fine cup of tea.' He gave an enthusiastic smack of the lips. 'You two are lucky to have her looking after you. You should taste Mrs Lestrade's tea.' He made a sour face. 'It's like drinking watered-down tar. Not that I can ever tell her that, of course.'

Holmes and I pulled up chairs beside him. 'The excellence of Mrs Hudson's tea is indisputable,' my friend agreed, 'but I assume you are here to discuss something of more pressing import than refreshing beverages.'

'You're right, Mr Holmes,' said the inspector, swallowing the last drop and setting down his cup. 'Since Deeds and his friends started spreading the killer's assumed name all over town, the results have been what you would expect. We're already had a sackful of letters all signed Crimson Jack. All, that is, except one that claims to come from Adolf Hitler and another that's signed simply *God*.'

'I take it none of them is genuine?' I asked.

'Not unless our man has changed his style and the form of his signature,' Lestrade replied. 'As if that wasn't enough grief, we've got five or six blokes down at the station all confessing to being Crimson Jack. They're all shapes and sizes, so you can take your pick. One of them only has one leg but he says he'll be damned if we try to rule him out because of that.'

Holmes selected a pipe from his rack and began to fill it. 'It was only to be expected that the whole matter would be transformed into a public sport of the worst kind.'

'There's more,' Lestrade continued morosely. 'Some concerned citizens have formed what they call the London Vigilance League. They plan to patrol the streets, dishing out their own brand of justice as they see fit. I suspect that, as usual with that sort, their victims will be anybody that looks or sounds like a foreigner.'

'Surely, Lestrade, you cannot allow such unauthorised activities,' I said.

The inspector's face hardened. 'Don't you worry, doctor. I've already had their leaders in for a talking-to. I showed them the jail cells I've got waiting for each and every one of them if they so much as raise their voices out of turn.'

'One can hardly blame people for wishing to take matters into their own hands,' said Holmes, lighting his pipe and taking a puff. 'Not when the authorities appear to have made so little progress.'

'That's where you're wrong, Mr Holmes,' Lestrade

asserted with satisfaction. 'We are in fact following up a brand new lead even as we speak.'

Holmes removed the pipe from his mouth and stared intently at the inspector. 'You intrigue me, Lestrade. Do go on.'

29

THE STRANGER IN THE MIRROR

'Searching through the files, we've come up with a nasty piece of work named Conrad Breen,' Lestrade informed us with grim relish. 'There's a good chance he's the one behind these crimes.'

'Breen?' I puzzled at the name. 'I assure you, Lestrade, that the name spoken by Emma Wainwright was Conrad *Brown*. She even repeated it.'

Lestrade raised a placating hand. 'Now, now, doctor, nobody's saying you were mistaken. But you have to admit, it's possible the Wainwright woman misheard him or remembered it wrong. And believe me, this Breen fits the bill pretty snugly.'

'Please explain, Lestrade,' Holmes invited.

The inspector's brow darkened. 'He was just your typical vicious thug to begin with – the usual stuff: robbery, extortion, car theft. But then he got tangled up with some anarchist gang and their mad talk of smashing the whole of society went straight to his head. It's something we've seen more than once: a common thug gets a whiff of politics and next thing you know he's twice the villain he was before.'

'In what way exactly?' I asked.

'He was behind a string of bombings in the late thirties,' answered the inspector. 'Two people were killed and quite a few injured. A woman who spent the night with Breen fingered him for us as the bomber, but he escaped before we could lay hands on him. A few days later she turned up stabbed to death in an alleyway. Since then Breen's gone to ground, moving from place to place, always one step ahead of the law.'

'So you are no longer convinced that Dr Carvel is the killer?' said Holmes.

'I've not given up on him yet,' Lestrade adopted his most stubborn expression, 'but I admit we've nothing solid. It's more than likely that Breen's our man.'

'If he has eluded you for so long, what chance do you have of finding him before he strikes again?' I wondered.

'Your Mr Rayner has pulled a few strings to help us get a line on him,' said Lestrade. 'With any luck we'll soon have him cornered.'

'I hope you're right on both counts, Lestrade,' I said. 'That he is the killer and that you are close to catching him.'

'Don't you worry, doctor,' Lestrade exuded a bullish confidence, 'the net is closing on that character.'

Once Lestrade had left, I turned eagerly to my friend. 'So what do you think, Holmes? You pointed out that the word *anarchy* is concealed in Crimson Jack's little rhyme. Might that be this man Breen's signature?'

Holmes waved his pipe dismissively. 'That poem is a mere blind, intended to send us running off in a dozen different directions. The fact that it contains so many potential clues – art, chess, anarchy – tells us as much. No, if we are to follow the thread to the centre of the labyrinth and there confront the monster, reason must be our guide, and we must begin with the victims.'

Leaping to his feet, he began to pace the floor while his mind worked with the relentless precision of a machine.

'Here is this man – on the surface, we assume, a perfectly ordinary citizen – who, like everyone else, as soon as he hears the warning sirens hurries to the nearest air raid shelter. In his haste to cross the road he is struck by a car, the sort of accident that is all too common under the blackout. Four women, previously unknown to each other, converge on the victim, get him to his feet and take him with them into the shelter. Here they take devoted care of him while he recovers his wits.'

'I confess I see no motive for murder in any of this,' I sighed.

Holmes paused in his stride. 'Consider this, Watson: that he was, for some minutes at least, in a stunned and shaken condition. Let us imagine that during this period he let something slip that could later prove ruinous to him, but had no memory of having done so once he was in full possession of his faculties.'

I nodded slowly. 'Yes, I suppose that is entirely possible.'

Holmes took another turn around the room. 'Nothing comes of the incident until a few weeks later,' he speculated, 'when by sheer chance he once more encounters Mags Hopkin. Something she says alerts him to the fact that she, all unknowing, is in possession of some information which puts him at grave risk. So he charms her and takes the opportunity to question her closely on the subject of the other three women who tended him. Then he murders her and goes in search of the others, armed with whatever clues she has provided him with.'

'You already supposed,' I recalled, 'that he intercepted Clara Bentley and Emma Wainwright after work and led them to a dark place where he could murder them.'

'It was simple enough,' said Holmes. 'He merely approached them as though their meeting again was just a happy coincidence. *How lucky that I've run into you. I have not had the opportunity to properly thank you for your kind care and attention. Perhaps I could show you my appreciation by treating you to a late supper.*'

'But what danger could they pose to him so great that he would go to such extremes to silence them?' I wondered.

'Including the additional murders of Bronwyn Hughes and Constable Coleman, neither of whom knew him.'

'What danger indeed, Watson?' Holmes's tone was one of bitter resolution. 'Since I took up this investigation, two more women have died. I will not allow another to suffer the same fate. I will penetrate the mind of this killer and I will break him.'

He slumped down in his favourite chair, his face charged with an expression of deep inward concentration. 'I see a long night ahead of me, old fellow, and I expect to smoke several pipes.'

In the morning, when I rose for breakfast, I was greeted by an atmosphere heavy with the smell of tobacco and the sound of Holmes again assailing Paganini's most testing compositions. I had once heard him compare Paganini's revolutionary innovations on the violin to the scientific advances he himself had initiated in the field of criminal investigation, though whether this was intended as a compliment to himself or to Paganini was not entirely clear.

Without interrupting his playing, he acknowledged my appearance with the slightest inclination of the head. He showed all the signs of a sleepless night, his face pale and strained, his hair disordered and his breakfast untouched on the table.

'Any luck?' I inquired, picking up the morning paper.

'Luck – pah!' With a final flourish he completed the piece then tapped the bow impatiently against his thigh. 'I know it all fits together, so many pieces. There is just one final component needed to make sense of the whole. I can almost sense it hovering just out of my reach.'

He placed the violin beneath his chin again and raised the bow, turning to the mirror as he did so. Then he froze, staring fixedly at his own reflection as though upon the face of a stranger.

Slowly he lowered the instrument. 'Why, that's it!' he exclaimed. 'It was right in front of me all along. All we had to do was change the . . .'

He turned to face me, his whole body electrified by whatever insight had just flashed into his mind.

'Watson, it's so simple,' he began. It seemed he was about to reveal all, but he suddenly checked himself. I waited with bated breath for him to continue, but he appeared to be deliberating his course carefully.

Finally he spoke, fixing me with an urgent gaze. 'From now on, old friend, there is one thing – one vital thing – that you must bear in mind. It is this: we are searching for a madman, a lunatic who is driven by an insatiable hatred of women.'

I was taken aback by his intensity. 'But Holmes,' I protested, 'I thought you said . . .'

He cut me off with a chopping gesture of the bow. 'A madman, I say. Remember that above all!'

Setting aside the violin, he wheeled about and dashed to the small table where he kept the various wigs and items of makeup he used to disguise himself. Flinging open a drawer, he twisted open a jar and began rubbing an ointment into his face to darken his skin.

His behaviour was so unexpected, so utterly inexplicable, that for a moment I feared that, under the pressure of the case, he had suffered some form of mental derangement. Then I dismissed that passing thought. Sherlock Holmes was the most unshakably sane man I had ever met.

'Holmes, what do you want me to do?' I was quite bewildered.

'You carry on with your duties at the hospital,' he

instructed brusquely. 'Take Miss Preston to lunch, if you will.' He paused to cast me a reassuring glance. 'Don't worry, old friend, I'll call upon your assistance when the time comes, and a dangerous hour it will be.'

Within minutes, in the impenetrable disguise of a street vendor, he raced out of the door without a word of explanation.

Over the next few days he darted in and out of Baker Street under so many false identities, it was as if a cavalcade of colourful characters was passing through our lodgings. I occasionally caught him scribbling in his notebook and making marks on a map, both of which he then secured in a locked drawer of his desk. My attempts to strike up a conversation were met with abstracted grunts and disinterested inquiries about the weather.

I was relieved when one of these one-sided colloquies was interrupted by the ringing of the telephone. I picked it up to receive an urgent summons from Lestrade. When the inspector rang off, I turned to Holmes.

'Lestrade wants us to come to Scotland Yard at once. Rayner has learned that this anarchist Breen is holed up in a cottage near a place called Radley End, out beyond Walthamstow. He and Lestrade are leading a force of detectives to capture him and he urges us to join them.'

A wolfish smile passed across Holmes's lean features. 'Why, that is most timely, Watson! You must go at once, of course, and be sure to take your pistol.'

I stared at him, unable to believe my ears. 'Holmes, aren't you coming too?'

He shook his head decisively. 'If an explanation is required, you may tell them that the strain of the case has utterly exhausted me and that I have taken to my bed.'

I was dumbfounded by his attitude. 'But, Holmes, if this

is a breakthrough of such importance, then surely—'

'I have no time to argue,' he cut me off curtly. 'Fetch your gun and go. And for God's sake be careful!'

30

A MOST DANGEROUS MAN

When I arrived at Scotland Yard there was understandable surprise at Holmes's absence, but they were all so busy with preparations for the impending raid that no one bothered to question his rather inadequate excuse.

'I think we can appreciate the dreadful strain Mr Holmes has been under,' said Rayner, checking his ammunition. 'After all, he does have his reputation to worry about.'

'I assure you that reputation is the last thing on his mind,' I retorted sharply.

Rayner made an immediate show of contrition. 'Of course, doctor, of course. With any luck this ordeal will soon be over for all of us.'

'I hope to God that's true,' said Lestrade feelingly. 'There's one blessing at least – we'll have that scribbler Deeds out of our hair for a while.'

'Oh really?' I did my best not to sound overly pleased at the news. 'What's happened to him?'

'It seems that last night he confronted Sir Carlton Jessop with accusations that he'd been spotted sneaking into a house of ill repute in the East End.' Lestrade related the incident with obvious relish. 'Sir Carlton responded by using his cane to deliver a sound thrashing that's left Deeds in hospital with a concussion. The matter's now in the hands of the local constabulary.'

The expressions on the faces of my companions left me in no doubt that they felt as little sympathy as I did for either of the protagonists in this tale.

In addition to Lestrade and Rayner, there was young

Inspector Alec Macdonald, a tall, bony Scotsman whose deep-set eyes twinkled with a keen intelligence. The ever reliable Sergeant Froggat completed our number.

Macdonald was examining a small-scale map of an area of Essex countryside on which certain markings had been made in red ink. Turning to Rayner, he asked, 'You're quite sure Breen is hiding out in this cottage?'

'Oh, he's there all right, inspector, living under the name of Peter Longstaff. My information is completely reliable.'

I wondered how he could be so certain. 'And how did you come by this information?' I inquired.

'I uncovered the names of some of his former associates,' Rayner answered coolly. 'I then spent some time alone with each of them in a locked room and put my questions to them forcefully. I can be quite persuasive when the circumstances demand it.'

A disapproving scowl crossed Lestrade's face. I was aware that – in time of war in particular – agents of military intelligence were granted a freedom of action that lay well outside the bounds of normal police procedure. No matter how necessary such methods might be, however, I was no more reconciled to them than Lestrade.

'Well, from now on,' he stated gruffly, 'we all act like police officers – by the book. And that means following my orders.'

'Of course, inspector,' said Rayner, lighting a cigarette. 'It's your show.'

'I take it, sir, that means we're taking him alive,' Sergeant Froggat clarified.

'Aye, that's if he'll let us,' said Macdonald, fingering his pistol. 'He's a vicious bugger as I recall, and usually carries a sawn-off double-barrelled shotgun.'

At that moment Gail entered the office unannounced.

She placed a hand on her hip and surveyed the five of us with glib amusement. 'What's this? Is somebody throwing a party and nobody bothered to invite me?'

Stepping forward, Lestrade drew himself up in a stern show of authority. 'Miss Preston, may I ask what you're doing here?'

'I went to Baker Street but everybody was gone,' Gail explained, looking directly at me. 'Mrs Hudson told me you were headed to Scotland Yard so here I am.' She cast a glance around the room. 'Say, where's Sherlock Holmes? Not hiding under the desk, is he?'

'He's indisposed,' I answered, not wishing to say more.

'That's too bad,' said Gail, 'because I've got big news hot off the Preston presses.'

'We're rather busy right now,' Lestrade informed her tersely.

'Aye, we've no time to hang about,' added Macdonald.

'Oh, you'll want to hear this.' Gail arched a knowing eyebrow.

It was clear to me that she did have something of importance to report. 'All right, Gail, what's happened?'

'Yes, let's have it,' said Rayner. 'You're obviously bursting to tell us.'

'Well, I decided to pay a call on Parson Brown to see if I could figure out how he links into all this.' Gail leaned back against Lestrade's desk and crossed her ankles. 'I was going to pass myself off as a girl in a fix. I had a whole sob story worked out and I was going to lay it on real thick.'

'Honestly, Gail,' I reproved her, 'I think you like to act these parts just for the fun of it.'

'I guess I did pick up the acting bug at high school when we put on *The Merchant of Venice*.' She tilted her head and grinned at the recollection. 'You should have seen me as

Portia. I was pure dynamite.'

'That I can easily believe,' I said. 'But what about Conrad Brown?'

'Right. When I got there, all ready to cry my eyes out if need be, his housekeeper told me he was gone.'

'Gone?' Lestrade repeated incredulously. 'What do you mean, *gone*?'

'Seems he just packed a bag and took off, without a word of where he was going.' Gail gestured like a magician. 'Vanished into thin air like the Holy Ghost.'

'So that's another one!' groaned Lestrade. 'First the doctor disappears and now the vicar. If this keeps up I'll have to arrest myself because there won't be anybody else left.'

'I hope it won't come to that, George,' joked Macdonald with a wry smile. 'I'll send a man round to make inquiries about the vicar.'

'So what's going on here?' Gail asked, gazing round at us. 'I see you're all tooled up for action – a regular posse.'

'We're on our way to arrest a man named Breen,' I told her. 'He may well be the one we're looking for.'

'Great!' Gail pushed herself off the desk. 'Sign me up, sheriff. You got a spare shooting iron for a lady?'

'This is London, not Dodge City,' said Rayner. 'No gun for you, Calamity Jane.'

'It's no joking matter,' I informed her. 'This man Breen is both dangerous and desperate.'

'Seriously then,' said Gail, 'if this crook is the one that dragged me into this death game, then I want to know why.'

'Sorry, Gail, this caper is a boys only operation,' Rayner stated firmly.

'Oh no, you're not leaving me here to twiddle my thumbs,' said Gail, stepping in front of the door. She folded her arms and treated us all to a challenging glare. 'You'll have to slug me and hog-tie me first.'

I knew her well enough to be sure she was more than capable of following us if we tried to leave her behind. Not without misgivings, I said to Lestrade, 'It will be easier to let her come along. And if she should recognise Breen that might just give us an edge.'

'Very well, Miss Preston,' Lestrade acquiesced grudgingly, 'but only if you give me your word that you will stay back well out of danger.'

'Scout's honour, inspector,' Gail promised, throwing him a crisp salute.

Shortly after eleven we set out in two cars. The autumnal morning was bright and mild, and we were soon clear of the London suburbs. During the first stage of our journey I laid out for Gail all that we knew about Conrad Breen.

She listened intently, and when I had finished she shook her head. 'If this mad bomber ever crossed my path he must have been pretending to be somebody else.'

'You don't suppose, do you,' inquired Sergeant Froggat from the driver's seat, 'that Breen and that reverend might be one and the same person?'

'That seems highly unlikely,' I said.

'It doesn't sound any screwier to me than everything else that's going on,' said Gail. She reached into her bag for a cigarette.

Up ahead Lestrade and Rayner were in the lead car, with Macdonald driving. Eventually we turned off the main road on to a single-lane farm track. Pitted with potholes, it wound its way through an ill-tended patchwork of fields and hedgerows. Two miles on we came within sight of a ruined cow byre.

Here we pulled over and everyone piled out. We gathered round Rayner, who told us what lay ahead. 'Breen's cottage is in a hollow just beyond that stand of trees.'

'Right, we'll move out on foot from here,' Lestrade instructed us.

We set off, with Gail reluctantly bringing up the rear at my insistence. To our left lay a muddy meadow littered with rusty farm implements. Threading our way through the screen of larches Rayner had indicated, we arrived at the edge of a long abandoned vegetable garden choked with weeds and nettles.

Beyond lay the cottage itself, as dismal and neglected as its surroundings. The stonework was chipped and stained with mould and the windows were shoddily curtained with sackcloth. The paint had mostly peeled from the rickety door and the roof was missing a goodly portion of its tiles. However, a thin streamer of smoke issuing from the cracked chimney was a sure indicator of habitation.

'Well, somebody's at home,' said Lestrade. He took out his field glasses and scanned the scene. 'Are you sure it's our man?'

Rayner borrowed the glasses to observe for himself. He pointed to an old car that was just visible round the corner of the cottage. 'You see that wreck of a Morris Minor at the side there? It's registered to one Peter Longstaff, the name Breen has been operating under since February. That's him inside all right.'

'Right, Macdonald, you and Froggat circle round the back,' Lestrade ordered. 'Make sure he can't escape that way. I'll approach the front with Dr Watson and Commander Rayner.'

He turned to Gail with a stern glower. 'Miss Preston, I'll thank you to stay well back here out of sight, otherwise you'll be putting all of us at risk.'

'Don't worry, inspector, I'll be sure to keep my head down,' she assured him.

Macdonald and Froggat set off, following a wide, curved course that took them past ragged hedgerows and low, crumbling dykes. Once we were sure they were in position to cover the rear, Lestrade, Rayner and I cautiously advanced, keeping out of the line of sight of the front windows. There was no sign of movement from within, not even a twitch of the ragged curtains. If not for the smoke from the chimney and the car parked round the side, I would have assumed the place was entirely deserted.

When we reached the corner of the building, we gathered close and spoke in a hushed undertone.

'Inspector, if you'll take my advice,' Rayner offered, 'we should burst in and let him have it before he knows what's happening. No sense taking chances.'

'Rayner, I told you we're going to stick to proper police procedure,' Lestrade informed him with grave authority.

There was a brief flare of defiance in Rayner's face, then he conceded. 'As I said, inspector, it's your show.' Drawing his gun from its shoulder holster, he gave way to the policeman.

Ducking under the window, Lestrade drew his police revolver and positioned himself squarely in front of the door. At his signal, Rayner and I took up flanking positions on either side of him. Lestrade cleared his throat, then struck the door two resounding knocks with a heavy fist.

'Breen, this is the police!' he called out in ringing tones. 'Open up and come out quietly and it will go easier for you!'

He stood stiffly to attention and waited for a reply. A long moment of silence ensued. Then all at once Rayner yelled, 'Get down, inspector – now!'

As if warned by some sixth sense, he grabbed Lestrade

by the arm and yanked him to the ground. At that moment, with a shattering roar, a shotgun blast burst through the flimsy panelling of the door. I fell into a crouch as a second shot followed, sending a shower of splintered wood flying through the air.

With Lestrade flat out on the ground, Rayner fixed me with a steely glance.

'Now, doctor, before he can reload!'

Pistol in hand, I bounded to Rayner's side in front of the door. With one hefty kick he smashed it right off its hinges, revealing a dimly lit interior. He stepped inside and levelled his gun at a large figure vaguely outlined by the light of a broken window at the rear of the cottage.

'Stay back!' roared our quarry, hoisting a wooden box above his head.

Knowing his past history, I realised with a start that it must be packed with a volatile explosive.

Rayner spat out an obscenity and spun around, firing off three shots as he turned. He gave me a forceful shove, propelling both of us away from the doorway. We threw ourselves face down on the ground as, with a deafening boom, the cottage exploded in a massive fireball. I felt a gust of hot air sweeping over my back while fragments of brick and mortar rained down about us.

31

AN UNEXPECTED GUEST

For a moment all I could do was lie there. I felt as if I had been kicked in the ribs by a carthorse. Footsteps came running and an anxious hand pressed my cheek. Gail's voice came to me as though echoing down a long tunnel.

'John! John! Are you okay?'

With an effort I rolled over to find her kneeling beside me. Sitting up slowly, I gave her what I hoped was a reassuring nod and spat out some grit.

'I'm fine. At least I think I will be once my ears stop ringing.'

'I was watching from the trees,' said Gail with a shiver. 'What a stupid thing to do!'

Rayner had clambered to his feet and stood over us, brushing the dust from his suit. With a roguish grin he said, 'Well, that's about as close a call as I've ever had.'

Gail's grey eyes ignited in a sudden blaze of anger. 'Damn you! Why couldn't you two dopes just wait him out? Why did you have to go charging in like gang-busters?'

Rayner regarded her composedly. 'Really, Gail, I think that's a bit uncalled for.'

Gail drew a deep breath and lowered her eyes. 'Sorry. Nerves, I guess. Thanks, Phil. Really – thanks.'

Even through the lingering buzz in my ears, I could hear that she was thanking him for saving my life as well as his own by his quick reactions.

Rayner lapsed into a passable imitation of the American actor Humphrey Bogart. 'It's all part of the job, sweetheart, all part of the job.'

While Gail helped me to my feet, Lestrade stood with his hands on his hips staring disconsolately at the ruins of the cottage.

'Well, commander, I suppose you did what you had to do, but I don't mind telling you, I'd rather we had a prisoner. It'll take us long enough to dig the body out of all that rubble, let alone identify whatever's left of it.'

When I returned to Baker Street, Sherlock Holmes displayed a disappointing lack of interest in our deadly confrontation with Breen. To my profound annoyance, he was even less curious about the disappearance of Conrad Brown, even though it was quite clear to me that this could not be unconnected with the case. He stared absently out of the window through my whole recitation of the incident.

Finally I felt compelled to remonstrate. 'Really, Holmes, you perplex me. You refuse to pursue all sorts of highly important matters, any one of which might lead to the solution of these crimes. Instead you traipse in and out of here in a variety of costumes, from a postman to a costermonger. Why, if I didn't know better, I'd think you were in rehearsal for a variety show.'

This last sally brought a twinkle to his eye. 'An amusing speculation, Watson, but no. Really, old fellow, I'd have thought that after all these years you would have learned to trust me by now.'

While groping in my pocket for my pipe, I could not restrain a heated retort. 'I might if I had even the vaguest inkling of what you're about. Lestrade, Rayner and I were very nearly killed and the whole while you told everyone that you had to rest because you were under such a strain.'

Holmes had the grace to look chastened. 'It was a weak excuse, to be sure, but it was all I could come up with on the spur of the moment. I hope I didn't cause you any embarrassment.'

Having filled my pipe, I struck a match and took a moment to command my temper. 'I suppose we can take some consolation from the fact that we have three or four weeks before the killer strikes again. Ample time for you to apply yourself, if you so choose.'

Holmes rubbed his nose reflectively. 'I wouldn't be so certain of the time.'

'But if, as you supposed from the beginning, he is following the patterns set by Jack the Ripper, then the next attack will be on . . .' I paused to recall the dates of the original killings in 1888.

'November the eighth,' Holmes filled in. 'Quite so.' His manner suddenly assumed a fresh urgency. 'But nevertheless, I would be obliged if you would come to my aid whenever I summon you, whatever the date or time and wherever you may be. You will promise me that?'

His abrupt seriousness struck a chord of enduring loyalty within me. 'Holmes, when have I ever let you down?'

'Never, old fellow, never. And on no occasion has it ever been so vital that you answer my call at once.'

Mollified by his confidence in me, I gave him my solemn assurance. 'Of course, Holmes. You can count upon me absolutely.'

'And Miss Preston?' he inquired. 'Do you think she is someone we can count on?'

The question surprised me, but I answered it honestly. 'In my opinion she is utterly dependable.'

'Yes, yes,' said Holmes, tapping his chin pensively. 'She is a singular woman, Watson. You would do well to keep her in your sights once this is all over.'

I hoped the glow of the fire covered any flush in my face.

'Really, Holmes, you can't suppose that free-spirited lady and an old duffer like me . . .'

'Old, Watson?' Holmes indulged in a brief chuckle. 'I think not. Why, in these past few weeks you have appeared fitter than I have seen you in years.'

I was struggling for a rejoinder when, to my great relief, the door opened and Mrs Hudson entered, carrying a supper of cold ham, salad and fresh bread on a tray. I expected that Holmes and I would sit down together to enjoy a more convivial chat over our meal. Instead he grabbed his coat and hat, made a hasty apology to Mrs Hudson, and rushed out without a word of explanation.

'I'll keep some for you to have later!' our landlady called as the door closed behind him. She turned to me and tutted anxiously.

'Dr Watson, I'm sure I don't know what's got into him these days. Och, I know his isn't the usual sort of job and he's always kept odd hours, but I'm worried that he's going to run himself ragged.'

'Now, now, Mrs Hudson, don't you fret,' I told her consolingly. 'He has his methods. The best thing we can do while they run their course is to keep up our own spirits. I for one intend to sit down and enjoy this fine supper you've prepared.'

So matters stood until two days later when an urgent message reached me at the hospital on the Thursday evening.

'A phone call has come in from Mr Sherlock Holmes,' the porter informed me, reading the message from a sheet of notepaper. 'He says you are to come at once. He told me to underline that – *at once!*'

My pulse leapt. As quickly as I could, I delegated my remaining duties to one of my colleagues and hastened to

Baker Street by cab. Upon arriving, I rushed up the stairs in excited anticipation of finally seeing some light shed upon this business.

When I entered our rooms, however, I was brought to a startled halt. I could hardly believe my eyes, for there, seated at the table, taking tea with Sherlock Holmes, was Dr William Carvel. I fetched up short and stared at them. Carvel was somewhat dishevelled and his long, sober face had a haggard look about it. I scarcely knew what to say. I could not have been more astounded if I had come upon the entire royal family sitting chatting with Holmes.

Dr Carvel appeared equally surprised – and not terribly gratified – to see me.

'Why, it's that fellow Johnny,' he exclaimed with distaste, 'the companion of that scatterbrained female author.'

'I must apologise for that imposture, Dr Carvel,' said Holmes. 'This is my friend and associate Dr Watson.'

'Watson? Watson?' Carvel repeated testily. 'Then who was that outrageous woman?'

'We'll get to that presently, I assure you,' Holmes told him.

'Holmes, what on earth is going on?' I exclaimed, pointing at the unexpected guest. 'Is he under arrest?'

'Arrest?' Carvel was indignant. 'I should say not! I, sir, have been the victim of a heinous crime. Subdued while I slept with my own chloroform, then carried off unconscious to awake bound and blindfolded in some subterranean cell.'

I found myself utterly confounded by this unlooked-for turn of events. 'Who on earth would do such a thing?'

'My captor never allowed me to see his face when he made his infrequent visits,' Carvel said sourly. 'He only appeared to feed me some scant rations and check that I was still securely imprisoned.'

'But why, Holmes? Why?' I asked. A sudden inspiration struck me. 'Could it be that someone, believing Dr Carvel to be the killer, imprisoned him with the intention of forcing a confession from him?'

'There is an element of truth in that, Watson,' Holmes admitted, 'and Dr Carvel was indeed in serious danger. Fortunately I was able to free him from his confinement no more than an hour ago.'

Before I could press my friend to expand upon this, Carvel forestalled me. 'Grateful as I am for your assistance, Mr Holmes,' he interposed forcefully, 'I really must insist that we go directly to Scotland Yard and fill out a complaint against this mysterious kidnapper.'

Holmes made a placating gesture. 'Dr Carvel, it is of the utmost importance that you remain here for a while longer. Everything tonight depends upon the most exact timing.'

Carvel emitted a disgruntled growl and toyed with his teacup. After a moment's consideration he said grudgingly, 'Very well, Mr Holmes. I am aware of your reputation, so I suppose you must know what you're doing.'

'Thank you, doctor,' said Holmes, rising to his feet. 'Your cooperation is much appreciated. Mrs Hudson will take good care of you while Dr Watson and I are gone.'

'Holmes, where are we going?' I inquired.

Holmes was already donning his hat and coat. 'Arm yourself and I will explain on the way.'

I made haste to fetch my pistol and joined him downstairs in the vestibule.

'The car assigned to us by the police is parked outside,' he said. 'In the absence of WPC Summers, I wonder if you would be so good as to take the wheel.'

32

TERROR BY NIGHT

As we emerged into the street, I said, 'I take it we're going after the kidnapper of Dr Carvel.'

'That we are,' Holmes confirmed.

'And Crimson Jack?'

'One and the same. The trap is closing on him and on others too.'

'Others?' For an instant Charlie Deeds's theory of a conspiracy flashed through my mind, but I resolutely dismissed it. 'Are you telling me this murderer has accomplices?'

'In a manner of speaking. All will soon be clear, I promise you.'

Holmes handed me a set of keys and led the way to the black saloon parked a short distance down the street. I unlocked the doors and we climbed in. 'It would be of some help, Holmes, if you would tell me where we're going,' I said, starting up the engine.

'Of course, old chap. We're bound for Vauxhall, Apartment 3B, Wardour Court on Fentiman Road to be precise.' He added, 'Please make the best time possible.'

I was familiar with the neighbourhood from my medical practice. It was a quarter past nine and I estimated it would take us twenty minutes to reach our destination.

Releasing the handbrake, I guided the saloon along the blacked-out street. Without taking my eyes from the white-painted kerb markings, I said, 'Perhaps you could tell me why we are going there and in such haste.'

'It is the home of Dorothy Marx,' said Holmes, 'the

fourth of the Angels and the last of the intended victims of Crimson Jack.'

'But this does not fit the pattern at all,' I objected. 'Jack the Ripper's final murder took place in November and we are still in early October.'

'The eighth of November to be precise,' said Holmes, 'but I have pointed out before now that our man diverges from the exact pattern of the Ripper when it suits his own very different purposes.'

'Yes,' I acknowledged, 'operating outside Whitechapel, not restricting his victims to a particular class of woman.'

'Consider also the neatness of our present murderer's killing and mutilations,' said Holmes. 'A delay of more than a month before his final strike would be much too dangerous. Up until now Dorothy Marx may not have realised that three of the recently murdered women were those she met during the air raid of July the seventeenth, but with the investigation being widely covered in the press, she might eventually see photographs of the victims and make a connection with the injured man they had so kindly helped.'

I could see the soundness of Holmes's reasoning. 'So he has now abandoned his duplication of the Ripper killings.'

'Not at all,' said Holmes. 'Our killer has gone to far too much trouble to persuade the public at large, and even Scotland Yard, that these murders are being committed by a madman obsessed with making himself the new Ripper. That is the mask behind which he hides his true purpose.'

'But if he diverges too far from the pattern of 1888,' I protested, 'that mask will slip, surely.'

'Correct, Watson. But bear in mind, the last murder of the Ripper reign was committed on the night of November the eighth. Tonight is the night of October the eighth, close enough for the press to view it as another Ripper murder.

We may be sure that our perpetrator intends to cement that association by performing a more extreme mutilation and in one other way.'

I was appalled. 'What way is that?'

'Jack the Ripper's last victim was slaughtered in her own home. That is why we are on our way to apartment 3B, Wardour Court.'

'Thank heavens, Holmes that you were able to trace this woman in time,' I exclaimed. 'But how did you track her down?'

'I had Wiggins and his friend, the garrulous Mr Rumbold, seek out all the locals who were in the shelter on that fateful night. Through their efforts I learned that the fourth of those women we have termed the Angels had been speaking that night of her fiancé, a soldier named Anthony, who was listed as missing in action in North Africa.

'Armed with this clue,' he continued, 'I contacted the War Office and discovered that they have been receiving regular requests from a young receptionist named Dorothy Marx regarding her missing fiancé, a certain Lance Corporal Anthony Fowler serving with the Eighth Army in Egypt. It is to her apartment that we are speeding now.'

I was horrified at the thought that the murderer might even now be on his way to claim the unsuspecting victim's life. 'Holmes, you don't mean to tell me that you've left that young woman out as bait for the killer?'

'Only until tonight when the danger was imminent,' Holmes assured me. 'In the meantime I was able to observe him stalking her, timing her movements in such a way that I was left in no doubt that he planned to strike at ten o'clock tonight, the time she invariably retires. I have naturally taken appropriate precautions.'

Confident as I was of Holmes's abilities, I could not

repress a qualm of disquiet. 'Precautions of what sort?' I asked.

'Two days ago, while you were busy at St Thomas's, I met Miss Preston and told her about Dorothy Marx. I instructed her to manufacture a chance meeting with that young woman, to befriend her and to gain her trust. I think you will concur that she is admirably suited to such a role.'

'Admirably,' I agreed woodenly. In my mind, however, was a growing apprehension that Holmes had underestimated the risks involved in linking Gail with the Marx girl.

Unaware of my thoughts, Holmes continued, 'Tonight she was to get Miss Marx away to a place of safety, leaving an empty apartment for our man to stumble into. When he arrives, thereby exposing his guilt, we will be there to seize him.'

I braked as the traffic light ahead of us turned red. I stared at my friend. 'This killer,' I said, 'you can identify him?'

Holmes nodded. 'The vital clue was in his name.'

'His name?' I repeated blankly. 'You mean Conrad Brown?'

'Think for a moment, Watson. If you spell Conrad with a K instead of a C and spell Brown B-R-A-U-N, what do you have?'

'Konrad Braun . . .' I gasped. 'Why, that's a German name!'

Holmes smacked his knee in a gesture of triumph. 'Precisely. Our cunning adversary is no deluded madman – he is a highly trained German spy. And all along he has been operating right under our noses.'

As my mind reeled at the shocking implication, the light changed and we lurched forward. Pressing down on the accelerator, I was seized by a fresh sense of urgency.

'Holmes,' I told my friend grimly, 'as ever, your

understanding of women has its limits. That apartment will not be empty.'

As the import of my words struck home, Holmes slammed a hand down on the dashboard. 'You're right, Watson. I may have miscalculated Miss Preston's independence of spirit.'

Even as he spoke, the air was suddenly filled with the banshee wail of air raid sirens. From all directions searchlights stabbed into the sky, glancing off barrage balloons and lancing through wisps of cloud.

'A raid tonight of all nights?' Holmes exclaimed through gritted teeth. 'Can it be just a coincidence?'

The imminence of an attack only added further impetus to my desperate haste. I pressed down hard on the accelerator, taking dangerous risks as we raced through the lightless streets of Pimlico. Ahead of us we could see dark figures – men, women and children – hurrying to the safety of the air raid shelters.

As we swung round a sharp corner into Grosvenor Road, a family of five darted out of the darkness directly into our path. Even as I slammed my foot down on the brake, Holmes grabbed the wheel and twisted it savagely to the right. We missed the startled family by a whisker, jumped the kerb and ploughed into a pillar box with a savage crunching of metal.

Flung forward by the impact, I bashed into the steering wheel and cracked my head on the dashboard. I was consumed in a haze of pain as the rising scream of the sirens filled my ears. I emerged from the shock of impact with agonising slowness, drawn out by the voice of Sherlock Holmes.

'Watson old man, are you all right?'

'Yes,' I grunted groggily. 'Just a bump on the head. And you?'

'Only a few bruises.'

My door was jammed because of the buckled metal, but I threw my weight against it with forceful determination. It creaked open and I climbed out, reeling dizzily for a moment before recovering my faculties. I saw my friend emerge unsteadily from his side of the vehicle then pull himself together by an effort of will.

'There's no time to lose, Holmes,' I gasped. 'Which way?'

'That way, across Vauxhall Bridge,' said Holmes, jabbing a decisive finger.

I shook off the last of the fug from my brain as we bolted up the street, brushing past a constable who was hurrying to the scene of the accident. We rushed now as fast as our legs would carry us, aided by the fact that the sirens had cleared the streets of any other pedestrians. A blackout warden shouted at us to take cover as we passed but made no move to impede us.

Holmes's description of our adversary left me in no doubt as to his identity or the terrible danger Gail was in. Fear for her safety burned like acid in the pit of my stomach as I ran the most desperate race of my life.

The man who called himself Crimson Jack slowly ascended the stairwell, closing in on his final target with the silent concentration of a jungle cat. He was dressed entirely in black, which rendered him practically invisible on the lightless streets, and even here he was hardly distinguishable from a passing shadow.

Outside, air raid sirens maintained their warning wail, but this was no distraction from his plan. Now that the raids were so infrequent, in an area like this which had never been seriously targeted people tended to ignore the occasional howl of the sirens as they would a distant rumble of thunder.

Arriving at the door of his victim's flat, he forced the lock with practised ease, making almost no sound as he did so. The sleeping woman inside would receive no warning of her fate until she felt the cord tightening around her throat, and then it would be too late.

He had reconnoitred the interior of the apartment on a previous visit while the girl was at work, and he knew his way around even in the dark. The bedroom door was slightly ajar and with a touch of his hand he gently pushed it wide. Padding stealthily to the bed, he stood over the huddled shape beneath the covers.

For an instant he experienced a triumphant exhilaration as he reached for the garrotte in his pocket, then all at once he knew something was wrong. He could hear the ticking of the bedside clock, but there was not the slightest whisper of breath from the misshapen figure in the bed. A tingle of danger electrified his nerves as he whipped the blankets aside to reveal, not a human body, but a heap of pillows.

Behind him someone switched on a lamp. Spinning about, he raised a hand against the glare and squinted at the figure rising from a chair with a pistol in her hand.

'Hi there, Phil,' said Gail Preston. 'Bet you didn't expect to find me here.'

33

JUDGEMENT IN CRIMSON

Rayner lowered his arm to stare hard at Gail Preston. He pursed his lips. 'Hello, Gail. I see you got yourself a gun after all,' he noted drily. 'American military issue, isn't it?'

'I've got a pal in the forces who likes to do me favours,' said Gail, shrugging one shoulder. 'I told him I needed it to scare off an ugly creep who's been following me around. Speaking of guns, I want you to take yours out by the left hand, thumb and forefinger only, like you see them do in the movies. Make it real slow.'

Rayner complied, reaching slowly under his jacket into his shoulder holster. He drew out the pistol and held it dangling before him from the two fingers pinched around the bottom of the handle.

'That's right,' Gail approved, 'keep it nice and easy. Now toss it over here, but don't make me jump or I'm liable to shoot.'

Rayner crouched slightly and cast the gun away so that it slid across the floor, halting just short of her feet. When he straightened up he glanced inquisitively about the room. 'Don't tell me you're here all by yourself.'

Gail kept her revolver pointed unwaveringly at his midriff. 'The rest of the gang will be here soon enough. It's up to you whether they take you away in cuffs or a bag.'

Rayner smiled casually. 'Be honest with me – were you really expecting it to be me?'

'Sherlock Holmes told me most of it. The rest I figured out by myself. It occurred to me that if you found this place empty, you'd guess that the jig was up and lam out before anybody could grab you. So I decided to make sure you stick around.'

Rayner's hand drifted cautiously towards the inside of his jacket.

'Oh, I wouldn't do that!' Gail warned.

'I'm just reaching for a cigarette,' Rayner explained innocently. 'Under the circumstances I need something to relax me. See?' He opened his jacket with ostentatious care to display the packet protruding from an inside pocket. Carefully he flipped it open and drew out a cigarette.

'My lighter is here,' he said, patting the left hand pocket.

Gail extended her gun arm and shook her head. Without looking away, she reached into her bag, pulled out a box of matches and flung them at him. 'Use these.'

Rayner caught the matches with one hand while slipping the cigarette into his mouth with the other. He lit it, then threw the matches back. Gail let them fall to the floor without attempting to catch them, her eyes never moving from her prisoner.

Rayner sucked on the smoke. 'I don't suppose there's any way you'd consider letting me go?'

Gail gave a bitter laugh. 'After what you've pulled? I'm planning on booking a ticket to watch you swing.'

'Well, I guess we'll never have that drink now.' Rayner titled his head towards the bed. 'Mind if I sit down?'

'Suit yourself,' said Gail. 'We won't be waiting long.'

Rayner took a step backwards. A split instant before Gail read his intention, he snatched up the bedside clock and hurled it at her with murderous force. The expertly thrown missile struck her shoulder hard enough to jerk her round as she fired. Her shot went wild, smacking a bullet into the wall.

Before she could fire again Rayner was on her, knocking the gun from her grasp.

I bounded up the stairs to Dorothy Marx's apartment with Holmes, who normally took the lead, straining to keep up with my frenzied pace. As I leapt over the top step, there was the bark of a gun from up ahead. I bashed through the door of 3B and pelted down the hall to the bedroom, homing in on the sounds of a struggle.

The blood was pounding in my head as I erupted into the room to see Gail backed against the wall, kicking and clawing at Rayner who loomed over her with a long-bladed knife. I threw myself at him before he could react. Seizing his arm in both hands, I twisted his wrist until the bone snapped and the knife fell from his grasp.

He lunged to retrieve it, but I held on to him and we toppled to the floor. As Rayner stretched out for his lost weapon, I slammed a heavy fist into his face. In an even fight I had no doubt that he would have bested me, but the sheer surprise and ferocity of my attack had already overwhelmed him. I landed three more furious blows before the touch of Holmes's hand on my shoulder restrained me.

'That's enough, Watson. I think you've more than made your point.'

As I got up, puffing from the exertion, I turned to see Gail scoop a gun up from the floor. I recognised it as Rayner's own. She pointed it at him as he rose, wiping a streak of blood from the side of his mouth with the back of his left hand. Any movement of his right hand visibly pained him due to the injury I had inflicted.

The red mist of rage was only now clearing from my eyes as I took a step towards Gail. 'Gail . . . are you all right?'

She tossed back her hair and I saw a red weal on her cheek where she had been struck. She gave a crooked smile. 'Relax, doc – I'll pull through.'

Sherlock Holmes kicked the knife beyond Rayner's reach

and picked up a military pistol that was lying on the carpet. I drew my own gun and all three of us kept him covered. The prisoner gazed at us with the sheepish air of a guest who has embarrassed himself at a party rather than snarling like the predatory beast I now knew him to be.

'Well, it's a shame we seem to have fallen out,' he sighed in mock regret. 'We made such a good team.'

Holmes regarded him with cold disdain. 'You were never more than a viper lurking in our midst, Rayner – or should I say Herr Braun?'

'It's been many years since anybody called me that,' Rayner responded. He pulled out a handkerchief to dab the blood from his nose.

Gail eyed him with venom in her gaze. 'To think that the golden boy of British Intelligence turned out to be a murderous Nazi spy.'

'The real Philip Rayner was disposed of years ago by German agents while serving abroad,' said Holmes. 'This man bore a close enough resemblance to him for it to take only a modest touch of plastic surgery to accomplish the substitution.'

Rayner forced a smile through a grimace of pain. 'Surely you have to give me some credit for the quality of my performance.'

'There will be no applause for you,' I told him, 'only the end of a rope.'

'I hardly think Mr Mycroft Holmes is going to waste a valuable resource like myself in an empty act of revenge,' said Rayner with galling insouciance. 'I have many valuable secrets to trade on.'

'Fewer than you think,' Holmes informed him. 'Even as we speak your associates are being arrested all over London.'

When Rayner stared at him in blank puzzlement, Holmes

gave an explanation that afforded him obvious satisfaction.

'You did not, I take it, notice the beggar who followed you when you visited your friend the diamond merchant. Nor the bearded bookseller who observed you from the street outside that restaurant where you ordered more than a simple supper. Yes, I have been following you from place to place all week, and now your entire organisation is being rounded up.'

Rayner's assured demeanour finally began to crack, but he managed to rally and straighten his shoulders. 'No, Holmes, you don't know everything.'

'Oh really?' Holmes raised an eyebrow. 'Did I neglect to mention that while you were leading that diversionary raid against the anarchist Breen, I took the opportunity to break into your apartment and locate your secret drawer? So many interesting documents, code books and photographs you have collected there. And, of course, the Aurora Speedline No. 3 portable typewriter.'

'My apartment?' Rayner could scarcely conceal his astonishment. 'But I would have noticed if anyone had been poking around there.'

'You forget, Herr Braun, that I have been trained in the same arts of stealth and deceit as you. You have been so absorbed in your chosen role as the hunter, you were oblivious of the fact that you had become the prey.'

Rayner steeled himself to brazen out this further defeat. 'Yes, of course, Holmes, you too have lived among your enemies under a false name.' With calculated effrontery he added, 'Why, when you behold me, it must be like staring at yourself in a mirror.'

'Only if it is one of those fairground mirrors,' I corrected him, 'which grotesquely distorts whatever it reflects.'

I was aware that Gail had remained conspicuously silent

during this exchange, but she was clearly following every word, while keeping her eyes fixed firmly upon Rayner.

From outside we could hear anti-aircraft guns rattling out their blazing streams of bullets, and then came the loud concussion of a bomb detonating on its target somewhere in the distance. The noise of destruction seemed to restore Rayner's arrogant self-assurance.

'I can be of immeasurable use to your government,' he asserted. 'If they keep me alive I can pass on to Berlin whatever false information Mr Mycroft Holmes wishes to feed them. Such misleading intelligence would be of tremendous strategic importance.'

Holmes's eyes narrowed. 'You would do that?'

'Why not?' said Rayner with growing confidence. 'Also there are a great many things under way in Germany of which you are ignorant. The development of weapons so powerful they will reduce this city to dust. What would your brother give for the location of the underground laboratories and secret factories where they are being constructed?'

I could contain my disgust at his conduct no longer. 'Have you so little sense of honour that you will even betray your own country in order to preserve your existence?'

'I am a pragmatist, doctor.' Rayner gave a careless shrug. 'This game is lost and I admit defeat. But there is still a new game to play, one in which I can still achieve a certain measure of victory. No, there will be no hangman's noose for me, I can assure you of that.'

The first shot hit him square in the chest. There was only an instant for his startled eyes to register the shock before the second bullet hit and he fell down dead.

Gail watched him slump to the floor then lowered the gun with a shudder. She was gripping it so tightly that her knuckles stood out pale and sharp.

'You heard him,' she said in a low, husky voice. 'After what he did to those women, he was going to bargain his way out of a death sentence. That wouldn't be justice, would it?'

There was no hint of triumph in her voice, only a great weariness and a heavy sense of grief, not for Rayner, but for his victims. I stared at her in silent wonder. She had faced him alone and unafraid, fought him courageously, and finally put an end to his evil life, while Sherlock Holmes and I merely stood by and listened to him gloat over his own cleverness.

Holmes took a step towards her. He gently eased her fingers apart and removed the gun from her grasp. 'No, Miss Preston, that would not be justice at all.'

From the street below came the screech of cars pulling up, the slamming of doors, and a familiar voice bellowing orders.

'There is no sense in your making yourself a target for vengeance by our enemies,' Holmes told Gail. 'I am already in their sights, so it will make no difference to my welfare if I tell Lestrade that it was I who shot Rayner when he attempted to escape.'

'Sure, whatever you say, Sherlock.' She gave a wan smile. 'You're the genius after all.'

'Thank you, Holmes,' I said, slipping my pistol back in my pocket.

As Lestrade and his men came pounding up the stairway towards us, I took Gail in my arms at last.

'I still have that bottle at my place, Johnny,' she said softly in my ear. 'What do you say we go back there and celebrate being alive?'

34

BALM IN GILEAD

When I returned to Baker Street in the morning I found Holmes enjoying a late breakfast provided by Mrs Hudson. As I entered the room, that good lady was setting a dish of freshly baked muffins down in front of him.

'Thank you, Mrs Hudson,' said Holmes, taking a deep sniff. 'The smell of your baking alone is enough to rejuvenate the spirit.'

As he spoke, he sliced through his first muffin, buttered it with a single sweep of the knife, and took an enthusiastic bite.

'Oh, Mr Holmes,' beamed Mrs Hudson, 'it does my heart good to see you've got your appetite back. For a while there I was afraid you were going to waste away.'

Holmes washed down the muffin with a swallow of tea. 'No fear of that, Mrs Hudson, not so long as you keep providing me with these excellent muffins. Ah, Watson, please join me.'

'Dr Watson, can I fetch you some kippers or maybe a plate of kedgeree?' offered our landlady.

'Nothing for me, thank you, Mrs Hudson.'

As I sat down she departed in a rosy glow of good-hearted contentment.

'Miss Preston is well, I take it?' asked Holmes, looking up from his breakfast.

'Quite well,' I assured him. 'Holmes, there are one or two points on which you might enlighten me, if that wouldn't be too much trouble.'

'I shall take that as a rebuke,' my friend responded affably, 'politely phrased, but a rebuke none the less. I admit you have just cause to be vexed with me, but if you will allow me to explain, I believe you will appreciate my reasons for withholding from you so large a measure of the truth.'

'I should be delighted to hear those reasons. Take all the time you need.' I folded my arms in a pointed demonstration of patient forbearance. 'I understand, of course, that it was in that moment before the mirror that you had your insight into the name Conrad Brown, that it could be spelled in the German way. But it could not have been immediately obvious that the German spy in question was Philip Rayner.'

'Miss Preston was the key to that identification,' said Holmes. 'You will have noticed her keen intuitive insight where people are concerned.'

'I am aware of that.' I recalled some of the insightful remarks she had passed in relation to myself, which I had no intention of sharing with the great detective.

'She told you that Rayner reminded her of a gentleman named Bill Miller whom she knew in North Dakota. You repeated as much to me.'

I was, as ever, impressed by my friend's ability to call to mind even the most trivial points of information. 'Yes, but at the time I did not imagine it had any bearing on the case.'

'It had a great deal of bearing. You see, North Dakota has one of the largest German populations of any state in the union. In fact the state capital, Bismarck, is named after the famous Prussian chancellor. Now, during the Great War many German-Americans found it expedient to anglicise their names to avoid the suspicion and hostility of their fellow citizens, so that, for example, Johannes Schmidt became John Smith. It is no great leap, therefore, to suppose that William Miller was born Wilhelm Mueller.'

'You're saying that Gail's antipathy towards Rayner

sprang from an unconscious realisation that he was actually a German?'

'Precisely. Only after he had been assigned to the case did we learn that he had a previous acquaintance with the lady. This provided the answer to a question which has dogged us from the start: why did the murderer draw Miss Preston into his scheme by sending his letter to her rather than directly to Scotland Yard?'

'Are you suggesting there was some twisted romantic motive?'

'No, no, Watson. Like everything Rayner did, it was a coolly calculated move. He made it known to Mycroft that he was acquainted with Miss Preston and on that basis suggested himself as the obvious candidate to keep tabs on her – as well as on me. If he had not involved her, Mycroft might well have chosen someone else to be his agent in this affair.'

'So it was a means of inserting himself directly into the investigation. I see. That means he must have anticipated that the government would intervene rather than give you a free rein.'

'Their interference was predictable, and, understanding this, Rayner used it to his advantage. Now let me lay out the whole story in the proper order and everything, including the reasons for my silence, will be made clear.'

Almost absent-mindedly I reached for a muffin and buttered it while Holmes spoke.

'When our spy arrived in England, bearing with him the enviable reputation of the real Rayner, any slight differences would simply be attributed to the natural changes wrought in a man by many years in a foreign clime. Remember also that Rayner's parents and sister died aboard the *Lusitania*. No close family remained with memories of his childhood that might have tripped up an imposter.'

'It seems almost incredible that he was one of the enemy when you consider his role in breaking up Vosperian's espionage network.'

'I hope it is not immodest of me to recall that it was I who uncovered Vosperian's organisation. Rayner put on a show of heroism in order to further ingratiate himself with his superiors, but what he actually did was assassinate Vosperian to keep him from being captured and interrogated. He was now held in such high regard that he was in line to take up duty as the Prime Minister's personal bodyguard.'

I almost choked at so horrid a prospect. 'Why, with Churchill's life in his hands, the damage he might have done is almost incalculable.'

'And yet, he discovered all those opportunities were at risk when he encountered Mags Hopkin for the second time and learned that, dazed from his accident, he had let slip his true name, his German name. At once he began to form a plan to dispose of the four women who could expose him, one that would divert any suspicion of a rational motive for their murders. He had already adopted one false identity as Philip Rayner, so nothing was more natural than to create another – Crimson Jack, a homicidal lunatic obsessed with imitating the crimes of Jack the Ripper.'

I reflexively set aside the butter knife as I recalled those brutal killings. 'The cold-bloodedness of it is chilling, and yet I suppose it is quite brilliant in its way.'

'The fact of Mags Hopkin's occupation, and the imminence of the date that marked the beginning of the Ripper's reign of terror in 1888, must have suggested the whole scheme to him. Like the original Ripper, he wrote a taunting letter to the police, peppering it with meaningless clues that would drive Scotland Yard into a maze of dead ends. His final master stroke was to make himself part of the investigation, which would allow him to make sure that no one was able to catch a glimpse of the truth.'

'But, Holmes, on the night of Emma Wainwright's murder, wasn't he busy trailing Sardinas?'

'No, he merely provided himself with an alibi by seeming to give one to Sardinas. He even wrote up a report which would not be followed up, since it removed Sardinas from the list of suspects. No one would bother to check and find that Sardinas' actual movements that night bore no resemblance to those reported by Rayner.'

'So he murdered Emma Wainwright, narrowly evading discovery, then laid out the body of Bronwyn Hughes, whom he had murdered the night before. I see that, Holmes, but why on earth did he strangle Constable Coleman and kidnap Dr Carvel?'

'Because if the murders remained unsolved, the investigation would go on, and there was a risk that it would eventually end up on his doorstep. It was I, at that time all unsuspecting, who sent him to steal the Ripper diary from the doctor's safe. Knowing Carvel was under suspicion, he openly approached poor Coleman, who did not suspect that this man he had met already at Scotland Yard was seeking the chance to catch him off guard. With the watcher out of the way, Rayner abducted Dr Carvel and kept him imprisoned in the deepest cellar of a derelict building.'

'With the intent of pinning the murders on him, a blood relative of the Ripper,' I realised, 'and so closing the case.'

Holmes nodded slowly. 'Within a few days of the final murder, Dr Carvel's drowned body would have washed up somewhere, just like his uncle's. A note would be left behind, typed on the same machine as Crimson Jack's letter – a suicide's confession.'

'Unaware that you were following him, Rayner led you right to where the doctor was being held.'

'Yes, but I could not free him until the last possible instant, otherwise Rayner might be alerted.'

'But what about the Reverend Conrad Brown, Holmes? What in heaven's name has become of him?'

'He is safe and well, I assure you. With the abduction of Dr Carvel, it occurred to me that the murderer might have some dark purpose in mind for the reverend also. Moreover, there was the danger that if word should get out that the murderer's name was Conrad Brown, then our unsympathetic clergyman might become the victim of vigilante justice. I therefore judged it prudent to arrange with his bishop that he take sanctuary within the Abbey of St Dunstan's, where the monks' life of silence would guarantee his anonymity.'

I could not help but be impressed by my friend's resourcefulness, but one aspect of the affair niggled at me still. 'I do have to say, Holmes, I am more than a little disappointed that you did not choose to trust me with what you were up to.'

'Your forthright honesty is one of your outstanding qualities, my dear old friend, but in this case your inability to dissemble would not have served us.' Holmes laid his hands flat on the table as a gesture of sincerity. 'I needed time to follow Rayner and uncover the whole network he had inherited from Vosperian. If you had crossed paths with him while in full possession of the truth, you would have been unable to conceal your disgust and that would have been all the warning he required.'

The explanation was made with such a warm show of friendship that I could not bear a grudge. 'Well, Holmes, faced with the most devious mind we have ever encountered, you have triumphed. You have destroyed an enemy spy ring, rescued Dr Carvel and saved that young woman Dorothy Marx.'

'There is even better news on that front,' said Holmes with a broad smile. 'Miss Marx's missing fiancé, Lance Corporal Anthony Fowler, has been found alive and well. It seems as though, in spite of all the evils of war and murder, a merciful Providence has decided that they both should be spared to find a happier future together.'

So it was that Sherlock Holmes stripped away a false face of madness to expose the relentless logic of a purely evil intent. To think of a whole nation in the iron grip of men such as these was almost more than the mind could bear, for they appeared capable of justifying any horror in the terms of their own cruelly arrogant philosophy, no matter how inhuman the consequences. But as Holmes had defeated them in this small but deadly battle, I believed we would defeat them in the larger struggle also.

For myself, my life was altered in ways I could not have foreseen. When a man approaches his fifties and has behind him a history of military service, medical practice, and an almost incredible series of investigative adventures, he might think his best years are past and there only remains a quiet path towards that final rest. He might think that and be quite wrong. All the foregoing might be a mere prelude to what is yet to come and his greatest adventure may only now be opening up before him. I dared to hope that it might be so.

And if there was hope in the future for me, there was hope for all of us. Perhaps one day, when the world emerged from this dread conflict, there might await us yet that wonder the poet so longed for, a cure for all our ills and the mending of our sorrows.

There's a cold wind coming . . . such a wind as never blew on England yet. It will be cold and bitter, Watson, and a good many of us may wither before its blast. But it's God's own wind none the less, and a cleaner, better, stronger land will lie in the sunshine when the storm has cleared.

SHERLOCK HOLMES, IN
His Final Bow
BY SIR ARTHUR CONAN DOYLE

AUTHOR'S NOTE

The films which served as the inspiration for this novel have been favourites of my entire family for many years. They are famous all over the world, and yet, as far as I am aware, it has never occurred to anyone to base a novel on this version of Sherlock Holmes. I felt that in doing so I could remain faithful to Sir Arthur Conan Doyle's immortal characters, while at the same time viewing Holmes and Watson in a new light. I was encouraged by the approving words Denis Conan Doyle wrote to the producers of *Sherlock Holmes and the Voice of Terror* in 1942:

> *Gentlemen:*
> *My sincere congratulations. This is incomparably the best Sherlock Holmes film ever made. Mr Basil Rathbone is extremely good as Sherlock Holmes and Mr Nigel Bruce is perfect as Dr Watson.*
> *The modern setting was a daring experiment which has succeeded admirably. Truly, genius has no age.*
> *Yours sincerely,*
> *Denis P. S. Conan Doyle*

Those who have seen the films will be aware that Dr Watson was sometimes made a figure of fun for the sake of comic relief. I have not followed that course in the novel, though Watson remains suitably baffled by Holmes's brilliance.

Many thanks must go, as ever, to my wife Debby, who is my in-house (and most demanding) editor. Her contribution to this novel is beyond measure. Kirsty Nicol provided invaluable research, while her daughter Elspeth contributed the initial cover design. Dr Toby Lipman acted as my own personal Watson in matters both medical and musical. Thanks also to all those at Birlinn/Polygon who have been so supportive of this project.

On a historical note, Henry Carvel, whom Holmes names as Jack the Ripper, is a fictional character, but many details of his life are based on those of one of the real suspects in the Whitechapel murders, Montague Druitt. This does not mean that I have any personal favourite among the ever-increasing number of Ripper candidates.

The character of Gail Preston was inspired in part by Helen Hiett, the American NBC reporter who broadcast from Europe in the early years of the war and recorded her experiences in her memoir *No Matter Where*.

For more on my novels and other projects, please go to my website at www.harris-authors.com.

R.J.H.